UNEXPECTED PRESENCE

E. Rox felt as if a door to his mind had been suddenly pulled open to allow a draft of icy cold to sweep in, followed by a strange, rough heat and a pushing and shoving about of his mind. It was as if he were being *invaded*!

"Sorry, pal..."

He *heard* those words. "I've gone quite mad..." E. Rox whispered.

"No, you're not mad," the inner voice said. "You've got company."

E. Rox had an impression of a strange creature—intense, dark blue eyes, a face partly fur-covered, not dangerous, even friendly. Coarse, yet refined in some ways. A very strong, rough-hewn personality.

"Let me introduce myself," the inner voice said. "My name is Harry Borg."

By Ward Hawkins
Published by Ballantine Books:

BLAZE OF WRATH

RED FLAME BURNING

SWORD OF FIRE

TORCH OF FEAR

a novel by
Ward Hawkins

Torch Of
Fear

A Del Rey Book

BALLANTINE BOOKS • NEW YORK

A Del Rey Book
Published by Ballantine Books

Library of Congress Catalog Card Number: 86-91658

ISBN 0-345-33612-7

Manufactured in the United States of America

First Edition: May 1987

Cover Art by Ralph McQuarrie

CHAPTER 1

When the pursuit had begun two days ago, there had been a certain exhilaration in the running. As a child, Harry Borg had often fantasized running at this speed—it had to be something close to thirty miles an hour—running effortlessly for long periods of time, tirelessly with the wind of his passing strong in his face, running gracefully, with his legs long and limber, bounding over any obstacle, almost flying.

But this was no childhood fantasy. This was real And they were running for their lives. After two days of it, the exercise had become torture—lung-burning, heart-pounding, muscle-screaming torture.

It was true that the gravity of the planet Orca was a fifth less than the gravity of the planet Earth; and it was true, also, that if he, Harry Borg, had been able to run on his own two feet, he would have been able to exceed anything possible for him on Earth. But there had to be a limit to how long even an Orcan could run on Orca, and now, running as one with an Orcan—an Orcan he had come to know as E. Rox—Harry Borg knew they had about reached theirs.

Using the eyes of his host, Harry Borg had watched

as their feet pounded down—on and on, left, right, left, right, sending up puffs of dust with each thudding impact—dodging and veering through the rocks on a long slope that led toward a towering cliff of red stone still several miles distant.

A deep gully easily fifty feet across came underfoot. A surge of effort took them—Harry Borg and E. Rox— up, leaping, and they soared over the gully, landing on the far side, feet crunching into the hot sand. They stumbled, regained balance, and drove on, even though their strength was about gone.

Looking back along the way they had come, still through the eyes of his host, Harry Borg saw the Ancans again. They were coming after him and his host across the floor of the desert, five black specks, perhaps a mile distant, as relentless as bloodhounds, as unerring. The letas the Ancans rode were tireless trackers. They followed the trail Harry Borg and his host had left as if drawn by a long string.

They had been gaining, closing the distance through the afternoon. Now, though the huge, red Orcan sun was only an hour above the horizon, it was all too obvious that the Ancans would catch up to them while there was still daylight left.

"We'd better find a hole," Harry Borg said. "At least a wall we can put our back against."

"I agree," E. Rox said. "But where?"

"At the cliff."

"Yes."

The footing became more uncertain. They often stumbled, almost falling, but they lunged on, fighting their way upward. Near the foot of the cliff the running became very difficult. Rocks, large and small, fallen from the cliff, barred their way, gave underfoot, and brought them to their knees twice before they finally found a redoubt of sorts against the foot of the cliff.

Breath scorched their throat; their chest heaved.

They were in a slight depression. Two giant rocks guarded either flank, and beyond those the ground sloped steeply away. The back of Harry Borg and his host was protected. Before them, the ground sloped less steeply, but the scree they had just crossed would slow the approach of the Ancans.

Harry Borg and E. Rox watched them come.

"I counted five a minute ago," Harry said.

"They are four now. One must have fallen."

E. Rox was tall, even for an Orcan, perhaps ten feet tall, and when he erected the antennae that grew from his forehead above his eyes—a pair of two-foot-long frondlike appendages that lay combed neatly over his head and down his back when not in use—he seemed very tall indeed. Harry had become enchanted with the antennae. When they were up, listening and sniffing, all senses were amplified many times over. In not having antennae, Harry had become convinced, humans had been severely deprived.

He was beginning to feel more like himself again, even though he was now sharing the exhaustion of his host. He was beginning to feel more clear-minded, more his human self again. His own body, his human body, was lost somewhere in space. God only knew where. And God only knew when, if ever, he would be reunited with his own body again. Now, he was still suffering periods of semiconsciousness, periods of feeling hopelessly lost. Thankfully, they were becoming fewer and less severe with each passing hour.

It had been during one of his worst periods of confusion that E. Rox had decided to take his patrol out on the desert in search of Ancas engaged in illegal activities.

Harry knew now that had he been in full possession of his faculties, he would have found some way to have prevented the mission. E. Rox was a citizen soldier, badly trained and not at all qualified to lead a scouting expedition. The truth of that had been proved late in the afternoon of their first day.

They had been puttering along in their carrier, not really looking hard or expecting to find anything. E. Rox, certain because of Harry's presence in his body that he was going mad, had been more interested in concealing his supposed insanity from his four troopers than in looking for trouble. And Harry, suffering from foggy periods, feeling dazed and lost, had been mostly out of it. Then, suddenly, rounding a bend in the narrow valley between the high walls of red stone, they had found themselves staring at an enormous—and illegal—Ancan colony.

"Alla toxia!" E. Rox had cursed, awed.

The antennae of all the patrol had been suddenly standing up like the long ears of the jackrabbits Harry had known back home. Their saucer-size eyes, as blue as Dutch china, were even larger and rounder and bluer than usual, staring, frightened. Even though still only half-aware, Harry had smelled the rich, stinging odor that E. Rox's antennae had brought in—the scent of Ancans, Harry was to learn later—and through the antennae he had heard the high, keening whine of the letas as they caught the scent of the Orcans.

"What is it?" Harry had asked.

"An illegal colony!" E. Rox had whispered, still dazed.

The Ancan colony had been a huge honeycomb of dwellings built at the far end of a cul-de-sac, fixed to the cliffs and hanging like myriad balconies. Below them, letas had scurried about, excited by the sudden arrival of

E. Rox and his troopers, their antennae waving, their many legs raising a dust cloud.

"Take us out!" E. Rox had suddenly ordered the driver.

Harry had experienced the same blinding panic the discovery of the Ancan colony had caused in E. Rox, but he had had to admire the way E. Rox had concealed that panic from his troopers. The command E. Rox had given had been as cool and precise as the voice of a schoolmaster ordering a student to some simple task.

"Yes, mas!" the driver had responded.

The driver had spun the carrier, applying sudden power. The blowers had set up a billowing cloud of desert sand as the craft had lifted . . . and it had been at that moment that they had suffered a direct hit. A streak of light, a burst of brilliance, and a great concussion had lifted E. Rox and Harry Borg and had flung them—as one, to be sure—like a loosely tied bundle of sticks into a thicket of desert shrubs. There had been searing pain for a few moments, and then, when vision had cleared, they had watched the quick and merciless killing of the troopers and the final, rather senseless destruction of the carrier.

"Get out of here!" Harry had said.

"Oxie, yes!" E. Rox had answered.

In a moment they had been racing away, shafts of deadly blue ray kicking up desert sand all around them. Fumbling at an empty holster, Harry had realized with E. Rox that they had lost their weapon in the explosion, that they were defenseless, unable to do anything but run away on foot.

And they had run away on foot at an incredible speed.

Panic—blind, senseless panic—had been the only force that had driven E. Rox during the first half hour of their escape, and Harry had shared it since he was one with the Orcan, yet he had been sensible enough to have been utterly astonished at the speed with which the Orcan could run. The long and slender legs of his Orcan host had proved to be speed machines. They had carried E. Rox and Harry over the desert floor with great, long, leaping strides at a rate of two strides a second. Then three strides a second! An absolutely incredible feat as far as Harry was concerned, and one accomplished with no apparent effort or overstrain.

"How long can you keep this up?"

"I don't know."

"An hour?"

"More than that."

"Till dark?"

"I hope so."

The panic in E. Rox had subsided gradually. In a little while it had become no more than plain fear. Harry had begun to understand the reasons for that fear: There would be pursuit, and when they were caught, they would be killed. There had been a thought, half formed in E. Rox's mind, of a head—their head, the one they were sharing on E. Rox's shoulders—mounted on a spear and paraded down a street lined with Ancans... but it had been too frightening to be allowed to take a clear shape.

"Where we going now?" Harry had asked E. Rox.

"Back to Atoxia... if we can get there."

Atoxia was the ancient city, long abandoned and in ruins, that had been the outpost E. Rox and his troops had manned before leaving on the patrol.

"Can we call for help?" Harry had asked.

"How?" E. Rox's question had been almost sarcastic.

Their communication device had been lost, Harry had realized, with the carrier, the troopers, and their sidearm. Then Harry had felt the sudden anguish E. Rox had felt at the reminder that his troopers had been killed.

His troopers had died, and he had lived!

How was that going to sound to S. Hoxie? S. Hoxie, E. Rox's superior officer, was going to think that he, E. Rox, had turned cowardly and had fled, leaving his troopers to die without him.

"Baloney!" Harry had scoffed.

"What does that mean?"

"It means no way!" Harry had told him. "Your men died in that first strike. You—we—were thrown clear. We were *lucky*, man!"

"*I* know that," E. Rox had said. "But will they?"

"Screw them."

"Whatever *that* means."

"*Watch it!*" Harry had yelled suddenly.

A scattering of huge rocks had suddenly appeared in their path. E. Rox, blinded by his anguish and despair, had seemed about to smash into them, and at the speed they had been traveling, they would have ended up with broken bones.

"I see them."

E. Rox had guided his long, flashing legs among the rocks with a skill that would have made O.J. Simpson or Eric Dickerson green with envy, Harry was sure, weaving, slanting, leaping high, driving on without losing speed. In a moment, they had been safely through, out on the flat desert floor again.

"All right!" Harry's admiration had been happily sincere.

"I assume that is a compliment," E. Rox said morosely.

"You know it!"

And they had gone on . . . and on . . . and on . . . across the sands.

"Y' think we can outrun those Ancans?" Harry had asked.

"Ancans, yes. But not the letas."

"Letas? What's a leta?"

"You saw them. Large creatures with many legs."

"Those overgrown termites? The Ancans *ride* them?"

"Yes."

"Why not use land vehicles? Aircraft?"

"It would not be a fair hunt."

"Fair hunt? What kind of crap is that?"

Harry had been a while getting the straight of it. As they had run on through the desert heat, kicking up sand, avoiding obstacles, leaping ravines, leaving behind a trail of dust, E. Rox had tried to explain: The Ancans knew that E. Rox was without a weapon. One Orcan, running on foot, became a quarry, not an enemy. Hunting was the Ancans' favorite sport, and the swift-running Orcans their favorite game. Traditionally, the Ancans had always hunted any Orcans they were able to find out on the desert alone from the backs of letas and had taken the Orcans with spears rather than the more lethal modern weapons. It was logical to expect that they would again use the ancient method.

Harry had been outraged. "They're going to hunt us down like *animals*?"

"Almost certainly," E. Rox had said.

"They got a goddamn nerve! And they got a surprise coming!"

"Surprise?"

"We're no ordinary Orcan now. There's two of us in this one body now. You and me. One Orcan and one human being. And you can take it as gospel, my friend, this human being is one tough son of a bitch!"

"What does that mean?"

"Means if they try to spear us, they're gonna get their heads shoved up where the sun don't shine."

The words may not have made much sense to E. Rox, but the meaning had been abundantly clear.

"I like your confidence."

The tone of E. Rox's response had made plain that he didn't like it at all. And it had been at that point that Harry had realized that he was sharing the body of a person who was something of a defeatist, a negative thinker.

"You give up too easy," he had said.

"I face facts!"

"The hell with facts! Sometimes you gotta lie a little. Y' gotta tell yourself you're a hero! It don't really matter shucks if you're a hero or if you're not. Say it hard enough and you'll begin to believe you are."

"Whoosh..." E. Rox had said despairingly.

And they had kept on running through the rest of that day. Running toward the mountains, toward the distant ruins of the ancient city of Atoxia and hoped-for safety.

They had found temporary refuge when darkness had fallen that first night, and for an hour or so, when daylight had come again, there had been reason to hope that the Ancans might not have come in pursuit after all. But those moments had been short-lived. From a rise, looking back over a vast stretch of desert quivering with heat waves, they had seen the distant black specks of the letas following their trail.

And now...

They had been run to ground at the foot of this cliff. Safety lay above and beyond the cliff, still a distance of two Earth-miles away—about three gleggs in Orcan terms. There were more Orcan troops there, and more weapons, but to attempt to skirt the cliff now would mean they would be caught in the open. And from the impression Harry Borg was receiving from E. Rox, caught in the open meant getting speared like a couple of caras.

Whatever caras were.

They had to face the Ancans here, and the Ancans were coming on rapidly. There were four of them. A fifth had fallen out of the chase or had lagged far behind. The letas negotiated the scree without difficulty, their many legs acting much like the treads of tanks, almost flowing over the broken rocks. The riders reined up at a distance of about one hundred meters.

One Ancan dismounted and strode forward.

He was a big sucker. Harry thought he was at least eight feet tall. His build was almost identical to the human build—arms, legs, torso, head in the same positions and in about the same proportions. But what he looked like more than anything was an enormous human who was about half lion. He was covered with yellow fur, and there was a huge mane of yellow hair growing around his head and shoulders. His face had a lion's muzzle. Right down to the black nose. He had large, glowing red eyes. His mouth was wide, and the teeth that showed when he curled back his lips could only be called fangs. He did that now—curled back his lips and showed those fangs. Then he ruffed up his mane. It was a display meant to cause fear in any potential victim that happened to be cornered against a cliff.

And it sure did. E. Rox had begun to tremble.

"Cut it out!" Harry told him. "There's only four of 'em!"

"Only four! And look at those spears!"

The spears were easily three meters long, the outermost meter of each forged into a long blade, sharp and gleaming. In addition, the Ancans carried curved knives belted at their waists. They wore uniforms, boots, shorts, and vests of some shining metallic fabric. The vest of the Ancans who had come forward bore a large crimson insignia, a coiled, fire-spitting serpent of some kind, twisted about a spear.

"Sana . . ." E. Rox breathed, terrified, unbelieving.

"What's a sana, for chrissake?"

"It is! It must be!"

"Come on! What's a sana?"

"Sana, himself!"

"So?"

"He's the son of Tanta!"

"And I'm a son of a bitch," Harry said impatiently. "But I still don't know what a son of a sana is! Is a tanta supposed to be something important?"

"Tanta is their Krill!"

"I get it. Like a king, right?"

"And Sana is Tanta's son. The heir to the throne!"

"Gotta say we go first class," Harry conceded. "We don't fool around when we pick our enemies. Strictly top of the line."

Now, the remaining three Ancans came forward to range up beside their leader, Sana, the son of Tanta, the heir to the throne—or whatever the hell he was. Harry didn't much care. The Anca was one mean-tempered cat, that was clear. And he was a mean-tempered cat full of bad intentions.

Sana tipped his head back, opened his mouth, skinning back his teeth, and let go with a great, booming roar that echoed off the cliffs and rolled out across the desert like the Last Summons, like righteous thunder. Another one of those moves meant to scare the wits out of potential victims.

It scared more than that out of E. Rox.

"For God's sake!" Harry said. "You wet us!"

"Couldn't help it . . ."

"Crap! What a mess!"

"Oh, rixx," E. Rox moaned.

"Orcan!" Sana bellowed. "Come out and die!"

So there they were, back against the cliff, with four of those big, hairy, lion-looking suckers with swords and spears and great ugly teeth right out there in front of them, daring them to come out and die.

And didn't it beat all to hell, Harry marveled, the trouble a man could get himself into when all he had set out to do was to help somebody?

CHAPTER 2

This trouble had started in Guss's rec room.

How long ago had that been?

Well, how long ago was hard to say—to within twenty years or so. Because, the way Los Ross had explained it, to travel a distance that was measured in light-years meant that time, as well as distance, had to be tinkered with if a man was going to reach any planet outside the solar system while he was still alive to enjoy getting there. And in sending Harry to Orca, Los Ross had tinkered with time more than somewhat.

But it seemed as if it had taken only a day or two.

He and Guss had been playing lissippi around midnight in Guss's recreation room. This playing lissippi was something they'd taken up to pass the time while waiting for the Jassan gonsiliss to okay what the president of Jassa had already agreed to pay Harry for doing the country a big favor. Like the United States Congress, the Jassan gonsiliss could hardly ever agree on anything, and deciding to pay Harry the bundle they owed him was going to take a while.

"Would you believe six years?" Guss had asked.

"It's nuthin' to kid about!"

"Six years is not kidding," Guss had told him. "It's a real possibility."

"Keerist!" Harry had said dismally.

Guss was a celebrity. He was probably the best sissal-player around. Harry had called him "the Elvis Presley of Jassa," though his skill was creating symphonic fragrances, not popular music. He was a good-looking character, too, by Jassan standards. By human standards, he looked rather like a human wearing a perfectly fitted lizard suit of gray, faintly scaled skin. He had large, golden eyes with vertically slitted pupils and a forked tongue which he kept flicking—with elegance, of course—out past delicate nostrils. His hands had eight fingers, and his feet, clad usually in soft boots, had eight toes. He always dressed in expensively tailored clothes—mid-thigh shorts, silk shirt, embroidered vest.

"Your move," he reminded Harry, chiding gently.

"I know, I know, already!"

The implant in Harry's head was translating Guss's telepathy into vernacular familiar to Harry, finding words and expressions suited to the need and mood of the moment. Guss had no implant. Since he lacked a voice, telepathy was his normal way of communicating, and Harry's thought-words got through to him loud and clear.

Harry made a move and looked smug.

Guss cocked his head and looked surprised.

Lissippi was a game much like chess, except that it was played in three dimensions with pieces that were moved electronically about in a cube. Guss almost always won. But it was not, Harry kept saying, because Guss was smarter than he was. Or because Guss could visualize in three dimensions better than he could. It was just that Guss had been playing lissippi since he was a little squirt, barely out of the pollywog phase, and the game was like second nature to him.

"Besides, you're just bull-futz lucky."

"Horsefeathers!"

"Horsefeathers" was probably not what Guss had said. It was probably something profane in the Jassan lexicon, but "horsefeathers" was the way the implant in Harry's head had translated it.

"You humans are really too primitive for three-dimensional games."

"Primitive, your butt!"

Harry Borg was a robust six-four, two hundred and forty pounds of "red-blooded American, and damn proud of it," he liked to say. He had dark blue eyes set in a rugged face that could be warm and smiling or dark and ferocious as the need required. He wore a short-cut, reddish-brown beard. The beard and the heavy gold band clamped tightly in the lobe of his left ear gave him a look that was faintly piratical.

And he didn't look a day over forty.

His age was a little hard to believe, seeing that he had flown Lockheed P-38s over Germany during World War II, which would put him in his late sixties now, if the years were counted right. But a Jassan surgeon named Sassan had wiped those years away with a special kind of magic. By using implants and surgical techniques Harry could only guess about, he had transformed Harry from an aging alcoholic with one foot in the grave to a youthful, cheerful bruiser half his rightful age. Got him off the booze, too. Gave him a whole new outlook on life. Now, even though he was a college graduate with a master's degree in aerospace engineering, he looked like a very healthy roughneck. And he enjoyed playing the roughneck. The salty-talking character seemed to fit better a man who looked meaner and more dangerous than an NFL nose tackle.

Actually, he was a big fake. Except when the goal line, or his life, or the life of someone he cared about was on the line, he was a pussycat. His wife, Lori, would tell you that.

Now, Guss said, "You humans were still in trees when lissippi was old to us." And to keep Harry simmering, he added, "Hanging by your tails."

"We never had tails," Harry said. "Never ate bananas."

He made his countermove then. A quick decisive jab at the control button under his hand moved one of his pieces one square down and two over. The move put Guss's principal piece in inescapable jeopardy.

"Cliss!" Harry said.

Guss looked shocked, staring at the board, unable to believe that Harry could do this to him. Harry was rubbing his chin and squirming like a little kid. He wasn't able to beat Guss often enough to matter, and it was worth a month's pay when he did.

"Check it out, turkey," he said. "You're dead!"

He was right, and Guss knew it. But Guss took a long time, pretending to check out every possible move. "All right," he said finally. "Even a primitive can get lucky once in a while."

"Lucky, hell!" Harry protested. "I kicked your butt!"

"Ahhh! I wasn't really trying."

Guss wanted Harry to enjoy his rare moment of triumph to the fullest, and he knew that the best way to make that happen was to act like a sore loser. So he acted like a sore loser. He drew the gray inner lid across his large, golden eyes, folded his eight-fingered hands, and pretended to withdraw into a pout.

Harry enjoyed the moment immensely. "Suffer!" he chortled. "Bleed!"

He treated himself to another glass of vassle, the mildly euphoric, nonaddicting Jassan drink he'd learned to like better than booze.

"Human smarts—that's what it takes," he said. "The only thing dumber than a dumb human being is a smart Jassan—you know that!"

"Wiss!" Guss answered. "Pure, unadulterated wiss!"

At that point, a telepathic chime sounded.

"That's it!" Harry said. "Gotta be!"

He meant that it had to be the call they had been waiting for—the one from the president's office saying that the gonsiliss had okayed Harry's payment—and that now Harry, his wife, Lori, his infant son, Charlie, his stepdaughter, Tippi, and the young men of his cadre, Chad, Homer, Sam, Eddie, and Arnie, were free to go home to Earth.

But it was not the call he'd hoped for.

The call was from Los Ross, a member of the Jassan Science Foundation, a very good friend of both Harry's and Guss's who had served with them through some very dangerous times. And with almost his first words he made it clear to them that he was scared half to death.

"Will you come at once?"

His telepathic voice almost squeaky with anxiety, he asked them to come to his laboratory. His laboratory was clandestine and very illegal, and he wanted them to come *there*? At this hour? Did he know what time it was? It was almost midnight!

"I know!" Los Ross said. "And if you hurry, there may still be time!"

"Time for what?"

"To save me," Los Ross said. "And all I've been doing."

"We'll come," Harry said. "Right, Guss?"

"If you say so."

"You get the cassal. I'll tell Lori I'm leavin'."

"Hear that, Los?" Guss asked. "Iron Balls says we're coming."

"Good! And please hurry!"

While Guss went out to bring the flight-craft around, Harry made a quick trip to the darkened sleeping quarters to tell Lori he was going out. His lovely wife lay curled beneath soft covers. His joy, his treasure, his love—she smelled warm.

"Back in an hour," he said.

She didn't open her eyes. "Mmmmmph?"

"Los Ross called. Somethin's buggin' 'im."

"Mmmmph?"

"Guss's goin' with me."

"Mmmmmph . . ." She burrowed deeper into the covers.

Harry stopped at the crib where Charlie, his infant son, lay wide awake, kicking and gurgling. The child had his mother's gray eyes: always wide and alert, always laughing. Harry poked the child in the tummy with a loving finger. He got a happy grin, a kick, and a gurgle.

"Way to go," Harry told him.

Guss had his cassal, a Triss-nass, hovering on the paved entryway. Harry got in and buckled up. Guss applied the power, and they lifted into the sky and zipped away.

Los Ross's laboratory, the *illegal* laboratory that the government was not supposed to know about, was in a very ancient stone building that would have scared the daylights out of Dr. Frankenstein. The little scientist had no business operating an illegal laboratory, but the way things were in Jassa—and the way they had been for the last several centuries—a scientist who wanted to carry on any independent research had to go underground and do it clandestinely or go to prison.

Very often he did both.

"It is because of the classon," Los Ross had explained to Harry.

"What's a classon?"

It seemed the classon was the end product of a process very similar to nuclear reaction, though many times more powerful, that had almost resulted in the extinction of all the creatures alive on the planet of Essa.

"That's bad," Harry agreed.

"They blamed us, the scientific community."

"For using it?"

"No, for discovering the principle. *They* used it."

"And blamed you."

"Yes."

"Figures," Harry said. "We've got a bunch of jack-asses on Earth who'd do the same thing. Goes with being a 'they.' A politician, usually."

Since that near catastrophe, Los Ross continued, the scientists had been restricted by law to minor tinkering. New recipes for old concoctions—that sort of thing. Nothing big. Nothing new.

"It's been very frustrating."

"I should think so," Harry agreed. "Like passing a law telling a bird he can do everything but fly."

"Just so."

Because of the restrictions, Los Ross had set up the private laboratory in the pile of ancient masonry on a stony mountainside. Where he could "fly" if he wanted to—if he didn't get caught.

When Harry and Guss got there it was raining hard, a wind-driven rain, complete with rumbling thunder and flashes of lightning and streams of rainwater that sluiced like a waterfall off the old slate roof. Harry, who had been there on several previous occasions, was willing to swear that the terrible weather was as much a part of the place as the stones themselves. A storm seemed to be always howling around, cannonading, streaking light, pouring down rain. Gave the place a spooky feeling.

The place was so spooky, in fact, that when somebody opened the big old iron-bound door, you expected to see he had a bolt in his neck.

"Fright castle," Harry said as they ran for the portal.

Los Ross let them in immediately. There was no bolt in his neck. He looked scared, not scary. There was also a look of nervous apology in the little Jassan's large yellow eyes as they peered anxiously at Harry over steel-rimmed spectacles that perched aslant, as always, on his nose. Los Ross's feeling toward Harry Borg was one of almost reverence. The big human was so powerful! So capable!

"What's happening?" Harry asked.

"It will take some explaining," Los Ross said.

He guided Harry and Guss through several empty stone-walled rooms where dust lay thick and cobwebs streamed. Then he took them down a narrow corridor to a blank wall where a mental signal unlocked a combination, and a section of the wall became a heavy door that swung open to admit them into a brilliantly lighted laboratory.

"Well, all right!" Harry said.

There was nothing ancient here. Every time he had come here—was it three times now?—Harry had found new apparatus of ever more complex design. Huge televisionlike screens were set into one wall like staring eyes, eyes that were wild, filled with insane, constantly changing, wildly fluctuating lines. Another wall held an array of glowing lights—red, blue, green, purple—

blinking on and off. Still another wall held a bank of meters with pointers flipping with extreme sensitivity or standing frozen, pointing resolutely at one calibration alone. A fourth wall held a chair surrounded on three sides by shining metallic walls. It was a comfortably cushioned chair, but was it a throne or an executioner's device?

Harry couldn't decide which.

"Why are you frightened?" Guss asked Los Ross.

"The ESSE," Los Ross said. "They've found out about me—about what I've been doing!"

"Riss!" Guss swore. The ESSE were the Jassan secret police.

"What's so bad about what you're doing?" Harry asked.

"I've opened the library of the Ancients—the one *you* brought out of Tassar when you saved the Lassa Crystal—"

"That suitcase was a *library*?"

"Indeed, it was—is!" Los Ross said. "A library infinitely compressed."

"And you've been reading it?"

"How could I not?" Los Ross's telepathic voice was plaintive. "The great discoveries of the ages—all there! So much of it has been forgotten." He wrung his eight-fingered hands together. "I couldn't let all that information, all those discoveries, die. It was my responsibility to the entire race of essans to restore that information!"

"That sounds like you," Guss said helplessly. "You can get yourself in prison—you can even be *executed*!— and you've got to be a hero!"

"I'm not a hero!" Los Ross protested. "I'm a responsible scientist, discharging my duty to my profession."

"Whatever," Harry said. "The bottom line is you've got your ass caught, right?"

The little scientist gulped. "Right."

"They're coming after you? The ESSE?"

Los Ross gulped again, his golden eyes huge. "Yes."

"So where are they?" Harry asked.

"They're coming tonight. I've been told."

Guss jumped, suddenly frightened. "Tonight?"

"At any moment," Los Ross said. "Before morning without fail. You see, I have friends in high places..." His huge yellow eyes ranged about his laboratory; he seemed on the verge of tears. "All this will be destroyed!"

"And the library?"

"Confiscated... incinerated..."

"Book burners!" Harry swore, properly outraged.

Los Ross looked up at Harry. The anger in Harry's manner had given him hope. "You can prevent it," he said tentatively.

"*Me*?" Harry said. "*I* can prevent it?"

"Yes."

"Prevent it... how? Knock heads? Kick ass?"

"No. No, not that!" Los Ross's glasses were about to fall off his nose. He straightened them and put a restraining, pleading hand on Harry's arm. "It wouldn't help. There are too many of them. They are too powerful."

"So? What then?"

"Let me show you something."

Los Ross guided Harry to the bank of televisionlike screens and focused Harry's attention on one particular screen. Guss followed to look over Harry's shoulder, and they both saw an irregular-shaped object with no particular identity.

"What's this?" Harry asked.

"In your language—a virus."

"Really? I didn't know you could see a virus."

"That one has been electronically magnified. Many, many diameters."

"All right. What about it?"

"That virus causes lethal disease in humans," Los Ross said. "Like all viruses, it has a tough, protein outer shell that prevents the human immune system from destroying it before it can implant its lethal genes in the human cells. Once implanted, the viral genes multiply, break out, spread, and eventually cause death."

"Polio," Harry said. "AIDS, influenza, pneumonia, the common cold . . ." His expression was sharp, cold.

"What are they—those things you said?" Los Ross asked.

"Viral diseases," Harry answered. "Cripplers. Killers."

"You know about them! Good!"

"So? What's all this mean?"

Apologetically, almost fearfully, Los Ross said, "I set up this experiment—this demonstration—just for you, Harry. The need is so great."

"All right, Los." Harry's expression darkened; his look was penetrating. "Get on with it."

"Watch!" Los Ross said.

The little scientist pushed his glasses up and put his yellow eyes to eyepieces, and while staring at something, he moved the dials with slender, delicate fingers. Harry, watching the image on the screen, saw the virus attacked, its shell pierced and broken. In a moment, the virus was destroyed.

"What in the hell did that?" he asked.

"The defense system of the mammal produced a protein—"

"Interferon," Harry said.

"Yes," Los Ross said excitedly. "With the help of a

new protein, the interferon was able to isolate and attack the virus—and destroy it!"

"What new protein?" Harry asked. "Human scientists have been trying to develop a new protein for years. It would be a cure for cancer, for AIDS, for all virus-caused diseases. But actually finding it could still be many years away. Millions of people are still going to die—"

"*You* can find it!"

"Me?" Harry had brought his dark blue eyes to bear on Los Ross, fierce, probing . . . even demanding.

Los Ross was actually sweating now. "There is a plant, Harry. A . . . what you would call an herb. An extract can be made from that herb that will supply the protein—Harry!" Los Ross had seen disbelief in Harry's eyes. "There *is*!"

It was not disbelief that Los Ross had seen in Harry's eyes. Skepticism, yes. But not disbelief. For Harry said then, "The Soviets in our world have found a plant, eleuteroccus—a brother to ginseng, a member of the family Araliaceae—they hope will do the same thing . . . to some small extent, at any rate."

"Yes! Yes!" Los Ross's excitement had grown. "But an extract of *this* plant—it is called Ursis—has *proved* its ability. It's in the records of the Ancients! They saved the bassoes from extinction using it!"

Bassoes, a mammalian species native to this planet, Essa, were as near a duplication of Homo sapiens as a species could be—they could, in fact, interbreed with humans. If what Los Ross was saying was true, if there was a protein that would enable the interferon of the human body to selectively attack a virus—any major virus—it would be worth any effort, any risk, any sacrifice to obtain it.

"Where is this plant?"

"A great distance away," Los Ross said fearfully, staring up at Harry.

"How great?"

"Too great..." Los Ross was beginning to cry. "You won't go..."

"Aw, for Christ's sake!" Harry said. He turned to Guss. "What do I have to do? How do I make him speak up?"

"Los..." Guss was gentle, coaxing. "You've got to tell him. Let him decide if it's too far." Then, on second thought, he became not so gentle. Rather more alarmed, in fact, than gentle. "How far is it?"

"Light-years," Los Ross said faintly.

"Shoot!" Harry said in sudden disgust. "What's all the blathering about if it's light-years? How the hell could I go light-years?"

"I—I could send you," Los Ross said timidly, faintly.

"*What*?" Harry yelled.

Los Ross fainted.

Guss managed to catch Los Ross before he fell to the floor. He scolded Harry. "Now, look what you've done!"

"Sorry," Harry said.

They both knew that yelling caused Los Ross to faint. Every time. Working together, they loosened Los Ross's collar and began fanning him. The gray inner lid had closed over Los Ross's eyes, and his forked tongue hung from the side of his mouth.

"Light-years," Harry said. "You hear that?"

"I heard."

"He was going to send me somewhere *light-years* away?"

"He said he *could* send you."

"But, my God, Guss—*light*-years?"

"That's what he said."

"Do you know how far a light-year is, Guss?"

"Yes. The distance light travels in a year's time."

"At one hundred and eighty thousand miles a second, Guss. A *second*, Guss! How many seconds in a year? Thirty-one million five hundred and thirty-six thousand —that's how many! And twenty times that's—holy smoke! He wants to send me *that* far, Guss?"

Guss blinked his large yellow eyes. "Well, if it were for a good cause—"

"Cut it out!"

"I...knew you wouldn't go..." Los Ross said. He had regained consciousness.

"I should hope not!" Harry said.

"Even for a good cause?"

"No way!"

"To free your species from all viral diseases?"

"Hey! Come on! What're you saying?"

"I'm saying if you did agree to go, there is a very good chance you would be able to free your species of all viral diseases. But...twenty light-years—I know that's too much to ask. Even if there is no great risk involved."

Harry glared at Guss. "Y' see what he's doing?"

"No. What is he doing?"

"Trying to make me look like a coward!" Harry said. "Like I'm a schnook if I don't go! Like I don't care how many of my kind virus kills." Harry began walking up and down, waving his hands. "He didn't even mention little kids. Babies. He didn't even say if I didn't go, millions of little *babies* will die." He came back to stand over Los Ross, to glare. "How about it? You were going to hit me with the little babies next, weren't you? The old tearjerker routine?"

"As a matter of truth—"

"I knew it!" Harry yelled.

And Los Ross fainted again.

"You can't yell at him, Harry!"

"Keerist!" Harry exclaimed.

They began fanning Los Ross again.

Neither Harry nor Guss had lost track of the fact that time was of the essence—that, if they were to believe Los Ross, the ESSE were due to break in at any moment. Nor were they unaware of the fact that if the ESSE *did* break in and found *them* there, *they* would be imprisoned, along with Los Ross. Or executed.

When Los Ross had recovered again, Harry began very carefully to nail down some crucial particulars.

"Where is this place you said you could send me?"

"A planet. A planet named Orca."

"Twenty light-years away?"

"Yes."

"And you could send me there?"

"Yes."

"You're absolutely dead sure?"

"There would be some risk. Very slight, but some." Los Ross was nervously apologetic. "The process was used extensively by the Ancients millennia ago, according to their records. And if I had more time—a few weeks—I could perfect the process to the point where I could guarantee safe passage both ways. At this point, I've only sent laboratory animals. A quiss and a lariss—"

"I'm in no hurry," Harry said. "I can wait."

"There isn't time!" Los Ross said.

"The ESSE," Guss reminded Harry. "Any moment now!"

"They'll break in and destroy all this equipment," Los Ross said. "The opportunity will be lost forever!"

"Crap!" Harry said.

He suffered a sudden urge to yell again, but he controlled it. Carefully, he said, "What if you send me to Orca and the ESSE break in and destroy the equipment?

Where does that leave me? Somewhere in outer space, right?"

"Now you see," Los Ross said pleadingly.

"See what?"

"Why it is so important that you go. Not only will you save all those little babies—"

"You said it! Little babies!"

Los Ross didn't faint. He plunged on. "Not only will you save those little babies from death by viral disease, you will save the library of the Ancients from being lost forever." He pleaded. "Harry, you saved the library once. Don't you want to save it again? Think how important it is! To your species as well as ours!"

"What is he saying?" Harry asked Guss. "If I go, the library will be saved? How will me going save the library?"

"If I send you—you, the famous human being—the ESSE wouldn't *dare* destroy the library. Or this apparatus."

"They wouldn't?"

"Of course not! We wouldn't be able to get you back!"

"He's right, Harry!" Guss said. "You're that famous, that important. No government agency would put you in jeopardy—that is absolutely certain."

"You think."

"I know!"

Harry stared first at one, then the other. He was willing to accept the fact of his own importance, but about the rest he was not so sure. "By sending me into outer space, you can save all this?" He waved his hands at the equipment lining the room. "That the idea?"

"That's it!"

"What about the protein? The plant? The virus killer? All that a bunch of hogwash? Or is there any truth in it?"

"It's true! It's true! If you go, and return with seeds of the Ursis plant, you can be the means of saving millions of your kind from dying! Even little—"

"I know—babies!"

Harry walked away. He stood facing a bank of screens, not seeing them, just staring, thinking. When he turned back, his eyes had narrowed.

"I've got this feeling I'm being suckered," he said.

"I don't understand...suckered?"

"Baited into doing something I shouldn't do."

Los Ross looked nervously at Guss. Guss lifted his hands, shrugging helplessly. Los Ross turned back to Harry.

"Please explain."

Harry was not unkind.

"Your first priority all along," he said, "was to save the library. Now, wasn't it? Be honest with me."

"Yes, it was," Los Ross admitted weakly.

"I don't blame you," Harry said. "Once, a long time ago, we humans burned a library in a city called Alexandria, and the loss we suffered from that stupidity you wouldn't believe."

"Knowledge is *so* important," Los Ross whispered.

"I agree," Harry said. "But you didn't think saving knowledge would be a strong enough reason to persuade me to risk my ass in your space transporter—or whatever the hell you call it—so you decided to sweeten the pot with this talk about a virus killer. Right?"

"I thought the virus killer might help persuade you, yes."

"What about it? *Is* there such a thing?"

"There is! There is!"

"And if I'm gone, the ESSE would keep their hands off this equipment to keep me safe—you're sure about that?"

"Very sure!" Los Ross was eager now. "And if you

go, and come back safely, the value of the library will be so clearly demonstrated, I know it would be safe forever!"

"To do all this," Harry said, "all I've got to do is—"

"Sit in that chair over there," Los Ross said quickly.

Los Ross was pointing at the chair in the alcove with the shiny metallic walls. And now, looking at it, Harry was reminded more than ever of the chair humans used to execute condemned murderers.

"That's all there is to it?" he asked, trying not to sound sarcastic.

"That's all. And it's painless."

"Painless?" Harry's voice climbed. "I'm supposed to fly twenty light-years, and that's painless? You're outa your head! I'd never get there alive. And I'd never get back. Twenty light-years, man! At the speed of light, even! That's forever!"

"It would only seem a few days at most."

Los Ross went on to explain about time and space and how they would be altered and warped. Harry would not be gone for the length of time it took light to travel all those millions of miles, he said. He said it would only seem like a little while. But when Harry got there, he said, the Orcans would be living in a time period that was twenty years or so in the future of the time it was now, here, where Harry was. But they wouldn't know it. And neither would Harry. It would seem only a day or so later to Harry when he got there. So what difference would it make? Or, to put it another way, the time Harry was leaving behind would be twenty years in the past compared to what the time would be when he got to Orca—

Harry turned him off. "Einstein I'm not!" he said.

"I'll take your word. But I've got to think about it. I've got to talk it over with Lori. And some other people."

"There is no time!"

Both Los Ross and Guss had become very alert. They were listening, hearing telepathic sounds too faint for Harry's implant to register. Genuine alarm had come into their eyes.

"They're here!" Los Ross said, despairing.

"Here? Who's here?" Harry asked, as if he didn't know.

"The ESSE," Guss said. "They're at the door now, breaking it down."

Harry could hear the banging.

"It's go now," Los Ross said, "or not go at all.'"

"Crap!" Harry said.

"You could sit in the chair," Guss said. "Try it for size."

Harry looked at the chair, uncertain.

And somehow, then, he was moving toward the chair. Los Ross was on one side of him, Guss on the other. Neither touched Harry, but they guided him, gently urging. Now Harry could hear the distant banging and crashing growing louder as the inner wall was broken open.

"It's a very comfortable chair..." Los Ross was patting the cushions persuasively. "Really, it is. Try it and you'll see..."

"Here," Guss said. "Let me help you."

"Stop it, will yuh?" Harry said. "Let me think."

Somehow, he lost his balance—was it a nudge from Guss?—and then he found himself sitting down in the chair. It was surprisingly comfortable. The cushions seemed to wrap around him. Guss, he found on looking

up, was standing close before him, too close to permit
Harry to rise without shoving him away.

"Oh, for God's sake!"

Harry knew he could brush Guss aside with a single
sweep of his arm. But he didn't do it. And he didn't quite
know why. He was being conned—*that* he knew. He was
being conned into doing something no sensible man
would even consider doing for a moment.

"This is crazy!"

"Harry!" Guss said. "You would want to go if you had
time."

"Time for what?"

"To think," Guss said.

He was blocking Harry's view. Harry leaned to see
past Guss and saw Los Ross at a control board. The little
scientist was making adjustments with his flowing, eight-
fingered hands, closing switches, turning dials. Lights
had come on and had begun blinking.

". . . think how important going is," Guss was saying.
"All those lives, Harry! Only *you* can save them. You
want to save the lives of those little children, don't you,
Harry?"

"Yeah, sure. But, holy hell, man—"

There was another loud crash, this one very close.

"They're in the corridor, Harry!" Guss said.

Harry was sweating. He looked at Los Ross and
found the little scientist looking at him, a desperate plea
in his large, golden eyes. His hand was poised over a
large red button.

"Please, Harry!"

Harry took another moment. This was insane! This
was stupid! This was the wildest kind of folly! Good God
almighty! The equipment hadn't even been tested! A
dozen things could go wrong!

"Now or never!" Guss said wildly.

Harry heard the ESSE very clearly now. In another moment, they were going to break in...and then it would all be lost forever—the library of the Ancients, the chance to bring home a protein that would defeat AIDS. Even the common cold. But in the end it was most probably the vision of a throng of children that leaped into his mind. Children with huge eyes, staring at him, pleading.

He had always been a sucker for the eyes of children.

"All right!" he said hoarsely. Sweat was glistening on Harry's forehead. His neck cords were stiff; his lips were drawn back off his teeth in a snarl. "Hit the damn button!"

"Wiss!" Los Ross squeaked.

He slammed his eight-fingered hand down hard.

Guss, watching with his golden eyes the size of saucers, frightened out of his wits, saw Harry suddenly stiffen in that comfortable chair, saw the walls of the cubicle gleam with an eye-burning brilliance. Then he saw Harry enveloped in a purple radiance. There was a moment when Harry strained, eyes bulging, neck corded, teeth gleaming, sitting in a shroud of purple light, his big hands gripping the arms of the chair.

Then, *snap*!

He vanished.

"You did it!" Guss said. "You did it!"

"Yes..." Los Ross sounded dazed. He was staring at the empty chair, his mouth open, his tongue hanging out like a ribbon, the split ends limp. His expression was one of shocked amazement. "Oh, liss," he whispered. "It worked!"

"Worked?" Guss said. "Worked? What do you mean, worked?"

"It sent him," Los Ross said. "It *really* sent him!"

"You didn't *know* it would?"

Apologetically, Los Ross said, "With these things, one can never be absolutely certain—"

"You shriss!" Guss yelled. "What am I going to tell his wife?"

Los Ross couldn't answer.

He had fainted again—just as the last door gave before the charging ESSE.

CHAPTER 3

Lori Borg awakened slowly.

It was morning, and the sound of birds was insistently cheerful outside her bedroom window. Like the mockingbirds on Earth, they seemed to be bursting with enthusiasm and good feelings. It was kind of pretty, she thought. But so early in the morning? Even birds should not be so cheerful before a first cup of coffee.

"Harry?" She groped across the bed and found an empty pillow. Then she spoke loudly enough to be heard in another room. "You up already?"

He didn't answer.

Well, she thought. He's out running with Guss. They had gone absolutely gorilla about running. Ten kilometers before breakfast. Before coffee. Before *anything*! Bad enough they should be hung up on some goofy planet where everybody looked like lizards, but that Harry had to spend half his time running over hill and dale like some gazelle or something...

And that reminded her.

She got out of bed and started doing aerobics, humming her own musical accompaniment.

"Tippi!" she called.

"Yeah, Mom?" Her young daughter came to poke her head into the bedroom.

"See about Charlie, will you, hon?"

Tippi was thirteen. She had close-cropped brown curls, large brown eyes, and a charming grin. "Sheez!" she said. "See about Charlie, she says. What d' you think we've been doing since breakfast? We've had our bath, even!"

"I didn't know it was so late."

"Halfway to noon!"

"Fibber."

"Eight o'clock, anyway."

"So, okay. I overslept." She changed from hopping straddles to running in place. "Where's Harry? You seen 'im?"

"Gone running with Guss, I guess."

"I guess."

Tippi went away, leaving the image of her bright gamine's face in her mother's mental eye to be relished. A cheerful soul, Tippi. Wise beyond her thirteen years, a joy, a treasure. Still slim and gawky with youth, but with the promise of a beautiful woman plain to see. Lori considered her own figure as she bounced it up and down. Ample? Yes, certainly. Ample was probably the kindest thing she could think to say about it. But she was being unkind to herself. It had only been six months since the birth of Charlie, and there was some flab left over, but in all truth she was in pretty good physical shape.

She began squatting.

Lori Borg, though not fat, was a lot of woman by any standard. And strong. She wore her hair in thick, yellow braids. She had gray eyes. She had finely arched brows that needed no artificial drawing, strong cheekbones, and a wide mouth that smiled easily. Like her daughter, she had a sunny nature, and that, Harry Borg had said, was the source of her charm.

He also said she could be goddamn cranky when there was need for it, but you could take it to the bank she wouldn't stay cranky for more than ten minutes. She was that kind of woman.

There should be millions like her, he said.

Sissi came to stand in the doorway.

Sissi was their hostess while they were staying here at Guss's rather luxurious country estate. She was not Guss's legal mate. Not yet. But she was *going* to be. His *legal* mate, that is. And very soon. *He* said so, and she *hoped* so. It was just that some things took longer than other things, and when a young female was trying to catch a famous sissal-player who was notoriously frightened of long-term contracts, she was up against a thing that could take a very long time. But Sissi was a patient and determined young female.

Guss could run, she liked to say, but he couldn't hide.

Lori didn't know where she had learned to say it.

Watching Lori doing her aerobic exercises, Sissi was again impressed by the ungainliness of it. Humans were funny. They had no appreciation of gracefulness. At least, not as much appreciation as an essan female. If one was an essan female, one was graceful—it was as simple as that. The human, Lori, *could* be graceful. Oh, very! But squatting?

An essan lady would *never* squat.

Lori smiled invitingly at Sissi. Equipped as they all had been with telepathy-receptors, she could communicate with all essans. "Come join me," she said.

"By no means!" Sissi pretended more alarm than she felt.

"Okay, get flabby," Lori said. She hopped up and then squatted again. "So, what's happening?"

"I was wondering if you knew where Guss and Harry were."

"Running?"

"I don't think so." Sissi looked about the room, trying to appear unconcerned. And failing. "Guss didn't come home last night."

"He didn't?"

"Did Harry?" Sissi asked.

"Why, yes. I thought—" Lori stopped the squatting to stand erect, frowning. "Well, now you mention it, I don't really know. I remember him— Oh. He came in to say he was going somewhere with Guss—that's right. And I took it for granted he came to bed later. Hmmm. But I guess he didn't." She smiled weakly. "Dr. Sassan gives me something to help me sleep, you know."

"I know."

"Maybe they didn't come back."

"It seems not."

Sissi was a very attractive essan. She was of the reptilian family, of course, but she was made very much like a human—arms, legs, head, all in the same places and in about the same proportions. She had the same large, golden eyes that Guss and Los Ross had, the same vertical pupils that were sometimes hair-thin slits and sometimes round, dark apertures, sensitive and appealing. Her skin was bluish-tinged gray, imperceptibly scaled. Lori had come to love her deeply as a friend, knowing that a very warm and caring person lived within that very different body. Sissi's tongue flicked, the forked tips curling, and she asked a very feminine question: "I wonder where those guys were all night?"

"Good question," Lori said. "Give me a minute to shower and dress and we'll go find us some answers."

The answers were slow in coming.

They went the communications route first—everything from yelling telepathic queries like: "Ha-*rrry*? Where the hell are you?" to "Has anybody here seen Harry Borg? Big turkey, gold earring?"

"And Guss?" Sissi would add.

With no result.

Then they got into Sissi's cassal to fly a ground search of the estate and adjoining lands. Since the planet Essa, where Harry and Lori and the others were living at the moment, was a mirror image of the planet Earth, the land had a familiar central California look: Big Sur, Carmel—that area. Rugged and beautiful. They were not far from Larissa, the city by the bay, which was not all that different from San Francisco, except that the architectural style of Larissa was ancient-fantastic with a strong dash of Disney rather than American-goofy.

They followed the trail they knew Harry and Guss used for jogging, searching for possible points of ambush. Harry and Guss had a million friends, true enough, but they had a lot of mortal enemies, too.

There were the Peacekeepers, for instance.

These were the idiots who would do anything to prevent war. And that included murdering anyone they considered might be a threat to peace. Harry, a no-nonsense, don't-mess-with-me kind of guy, was certainly such a threat. Fights of one kind or another seemed to follow him around, itching to happen.

And then there were the meat-packers.

Bassoe-meat meat-packers, that is.

Harry had put the packers of bassoe-meat out of business. Bassoes, the Homo sapiens species of the planet Essa, had been a principal source of food for the essans since the dawn of time. They ate bassoes the way humans ate cattle. Harry had made a deal with the President of Jassa—he would save the country from an invasion if they would stop eating bassoes. He had saved the country, and they had stopped eating bassoes. Almost. Lori was willing to bet there were a million out-of-work bassoe-meat-packers who would like to put Harry out of business. Or, better yet, put him on a spit and barbecue him over a slow fire, basting him well.

They found no dead Harry and no dead Guss along the trail.

Not even any dead Peacekeepers or bassoe-butchers.

Getting on to midday, they stopped in at the Cliss Complex, where Harry's cadre were living. Chad Harrison, lean, tall, deeply tanned, with white hair and the coldest gray eyes this side of God—that was the way Lori thought of them—was the nominal head of the cadre. He was only twenty-two years old, but that didn't matter, because the others were the same age or younger.

The others, in alphabetical order, were: Sam Barnstable, huge and powerful; Homer Benson, the wide-shouldered, big-handed lad from the farm country; Eddie Cole, the smiling, slick-moving black from south central L.A.; Arnie Garrett, a brown-eyed, curly-haired middleweight who would fight a tree if he had to. All these young men had been kidnapped in the recent past by the Jassans and brought to Jassa, the country they were now living in, for a purpose too demeaning to even talk about: They'd been used as seed bulls, without their knowledge and certainly without their permission, to revitalize the diminishing race of bassoes.

Harry had bargained for their freedom, and they had helped him save Jassa from being overpowered by another race of essans, the Ussirs; and they were waiting now, here on the planet Essa, in the country of Jassa, with Harry for whatever he might want them to do next.

In addition to the young men of Earth, there was another very important member of Harry's group living here at the Cliss Complex. Her name was Illia, and she was Chad's wife.

Illia was a bassoe. And she was beautiful. She had enormous brown eyes like all bassoes, and, like all bassoes, she was covered with soft, gray fur, so fine, so wonderful to touch. Chad had saved her from the meat-packers; and after her mind had been restored, she had proved to be most intelligent. Smarter than a lot of Earth-people, Tippi said. Tippi and Illia could spend hours together, heads close, talking and giggling.

"Harry not been here," Illia told Lori and Sissi when she found them at her door. "But come in. I call Chad. He will say what to do."

Chad came when called, and he summoned the others —Homer, Sam, Arnie, and Eddie. When they all had been told Harry and Guss had gone missing, they became deeply concerned.

"There's a lot of suckers'd like to see Old Iron Balls dead," Arnie said.

"A lot more wouldn't, you turkey!" Eddie said quickly. He was concerned for Lori. "Mr. Borg and Guss just wandered off, is all."

"Not likely," Sissi said.

"Harry wouldn't leave me to worry," Lori said. "He'd be in touch by this time. If there was any way he could do it."

"So would Guss," Sissi said firmly.

"Listen up," Chad said quietly.

He explained that Harry had sworn him to secrecy, because the life of Los Ross, the little scientist they all knew and cared about, might well be the price of word getting out; but now that it seemed that Harry's life, as well as Guss's life, might be in danger, the time had come to lay it all out. He laid it out for them then: the secret of Los Ross's illegal laboratory.

"That's it!" Lori said. "I'll give you anything!"

"Y' mean, they went there and got themselves *busted*?" Eddie asked.

"It's possible," Chad said.

"Probably," Sissi said.

"Oh, my God!" Lori said. "A secret laboratory? The police would throw away the key if they caught Harry and Guss fooling around with something like that!"

"Even execute them!" Sissi added.

Homer's voice was quiet. "You know where that lab is, Chad?"

"I know."

"That's where we'll start looking."

"I'll call!" Lori said. "I'll call President Moss, himself! They can't do that to Harry!"

"I can go there . . . ask around . . ." Sissi said.

"Homer and I will go—" Chad said.

"Not without me!" Lori said.

"Mrs. Borg—"

"That's an order, Chad," Lori said. "I'm not Old Iron Balls, but when he's not around, I'm in charge, and I'm the Iron Queen."

There was no use arguing with her. When the Iron Queen set her mind to something, that was the way it was going to be, and you could bet your last dollar on it.

"And I'm going," Sissi said.

Two of a kind. Bad-ass stubborn, the both of them.

Chad knew when to surrender. "Let's go," he said.

Lori, Sissi, Chad, and Homer went in Chad's cassal. They flew north, high and fast, and in less than an hour they were over the top of the old stone fright-castle Los Ross was using as a laboratory. There were dark clouds. There was rain. And there were police craft all over the place. Three of the craft were close by the craft they recognized as the one belonging to Guss. Lori's reaction was one of anger.

"There you go!" she said. "Old Headlong Harry has walked into another one!"

"And the joint got raided," Homer said.

"Take me down," Lori ordered.

"It might be dangerous—"

"Who cares, dangerous? I've got some hell to raise!"

Chad took them down, and grim-faced government militia escorted them straight into the old castle. They went through the dank outer part, through the beaten-down doors and walls, and into the brightly lighted laboratory.

"Whoo, boy!" Sissi said. "Would you look at this!"

"Where's Harry?" Lori asked. "See 'im anywhere?"

Harry Borg was nowhere in sight.

But Guss and Los Ross were there. No sweat finding *them*. They were backed up against a bank of glowing monitors, both wearing manacles and leg chains. They had been bruised up some, but they were essentially un-harmed. And the laboratory was essentially intact. Several high-ranking police officials, looking almost as harried as the two prisoners, met the newcomers with furious accusatory eyes. The highest-ranking officer, a portly individual wearing the most medals on his uniform who said his name was First Koss Riss Oss, seemed on the verge of apoplexy.

"Arrest these creatures! Chain them!"

Several of lesser rank started forward to obey.

Chad drew a gun from someplace and put it under the Koss's chin. "No chains," he said.

"No chains!" Riss Oss ordered.

The lesser rank backed away to a safe distance. Lori put her face close to the face of the portly First Koss. "What have you done with my Harry?" she demanded.

The gun Chad was holding under the First Koss's chin was causing the official considerable distress. His eyes were bulging. His telepathic voice was a shrill squeak.

"Ask *him!*"

He waved a frantic hand toward Los Ross. Lori looked at Los Ross closely for the first time and found him to be a frightened little wreck. Her concern was immediate and loud.

"Los! What have they done to you?"

The poor, skinny little scientist was in terrible shape. The pupils of his large, golden eyes were round with anguish. His long, forked tongue hung limply from the side of his mouth. He could hardly talk. "I—I haven't been hurt, Mrs. Borg . . ."

Lori fussed over him, straightening his glasses, buttoning his smock correctly. Then she turned to storm at the police. "Take these damned handcuffs off him! D' you know who he is? And Guss! Do you know who *he* is? Good heavens! You can't treat these people like this!"

All this storming was done telepathically, to be sure, but it lost none of its thunder and lightning because of that. First Koss Riss Oss was thoroughly upset by it. He tried to bluster.

"I know who they are. And they are under arrest!"

"By whose orders?"

"The orders of District Ess Miss!"

"All right. He's the one I want to talk to. Get him here!"

"Certainly not!" The officer seemed to gather strength. "His Excellency has been informed. He is considering the developments. When he has reached a decision he will notify me, and I will obey his orders. And his first order, I am sure, will be to execute these law-breakers, and *that* I will do with great pleasure."

"Like hell you will!" Lori said.

"This is none of your affair!"

"It *is* my affair! My husband's missing!"

Riss Oss pointed a shaking eight-fingered hand at Los Ross. "Ask him where your husband is. Go on! Ask him!"

Lori turned to Los Ross. "Los?"

The anguish of the little scientist had grown. "Please, Mrs. Borg..."

"You know where Harry is?"

"Yes..."

"Well? Where is he?"

"I—I sent him away..."

"Away? Away, where?"

"To Orca..." The telepathic words were faint.

"Orca? Where in the world is Orca?"

Los Ross looked at Guss for help. The only help he got was a helpless shrug. Los Ross turned back to Lori, gulped, and tried twice before he could get his mind to form the words.

"It's a planet," he said finally.

"A planet?"

"In orbit around a sun called Urus."

"Where is *that*?"

"In the constellation Cebus. Twenty light-years—"

"*Twenty light-years?*"

"Yes."

"Are you some kind of crazy? Twenty *light-years*?"

"It won't seem that far, Mrs. Borg. I promise you—"

"You sent my Harry twenty *light-years* someplace?"

"Mrs. Borg. Really, I—"

"I don't believe this!" Lori's wheels were spinning. "Orca . . . Urus . . . twenty *light*-years?"

She looked at Guss. Guss shrugged helplessly. She looked at the official, Riss Oss. He nodded. Now she looked back at the anguished little scientist. He was scared.

"You sent my Harry *where*?"

She shouldn't have yelled. Los Ross fainted again.

CHAPTER 4

Like vapor through a hole . . .

Streaming out swiftly. Becoming thin and transparent. Becoming long, long, long. Going away. Far. Far. Far. Turning. Reaching. Into the distance. Dwindling. Growing big again. Enormously big. Encompassing everything. Streaming out again. Thin. Thin. Thin. A brilliant flash. A tiny glow. Still.

Unmoving.

Suddenly, a lance of keen force, piercing.

On. On. On. On.

Humming. Growing shrill. Whining . . .

These were sensations.

Harry Borg felt them, sensed them, heard them.

He did not know how long each went on. Or how far each carried him. Each had no substance. Was each only imagined? Each nothing? Each only a shredded dream? Fragments of reality? Randomly chosen? Passing. Or were they real? And, in passing, too swift to know with certainty? Too brief to hold?

How long?

Time was an inchworm, stretching almost to infinity, then doubling up to a singularity, then stretching out again with unimagined elasticity across distances beyond measuring. Dizzy. Whirling. And suddenly laid flat, long and thin, clear as glass.

How far?

From here to there. The longest of all reaches. Into the beyond, and when beyond was attained, and put behind, a new faraway. A new goal. Beckoning. Ever elusive. Infinitely distant.

Nothing mattered long.

He traveled without pain. Nothing enclosed him. He had vanished. He was everywhere. He was vast, nonexistent. He was transparent. He was an infinitesimal speck turned inside out. He was everything. He was nothing. Convoluted. Endlessly roiling.

Still and clear again.

Glittering specks of light.

Streaks.

Stop.

Moving again, drifting slowly. Hovering. And then a growing awareness came to him. A sense of arrival. Hazy and unformed. Becoming certainty. He was here! Here...here...here...Where was here? What was here? Gradual understanding told him it was an old, old place. Long unused. Abandoned. Left out. Cold.

He lay in something.

He was, and he was not.

There was no substance to him! He was himself, and yet he was not himself. He was nothing! He was nothing in which to be Harry Borg. But he was Harry Borg. Alarm filled him with clanging bells. What had become of his big and powerful self?

His body?

Where had it gone?

Arms and legs and strong muscles?

Jaws? Teeth? Hands and fingers?

He had none.

He was emptiness.

He was nothing.

Though here he was.

Floating.

Cold.

Greatly alone . . .

Perhaps he lived a day of this. Wondering. Perhaps only an instant of this. Time had no real meaning, no shape at all. There were spaces of lost awareness. There were spaces of stinging clarity.

"I am dead," he said.

There was no sound to his voice.

"But I must be alive to speak."

He could hear.

And what he heard was squeaking, thin and shrill.

He could see.

And what he saw was a quiss.

The last quiss he had seen had been in a cage in Los Ross's laboratory, small, faintly reptilian, cute. Now it ran across the floor, skidding, squeaking, and pounced on something.

Harry saw that the floor was the floor of a vault.

He was in a vault.

The vault was a chamber, a place that enclosed him. Apparatus held him gently suspended, glowing. Glistening rods, pulsing lights, streaming rays of warm radiance. The walls and the ceiling were of some gleaming substance. Metal. Reflecting light.

He found he could rise and move away, as if walking in a body without substance. Yet a body that was of his usual size. Six-four, two hundred and forty pounds— that body. Bull-strong. Bearded. Dark blue eyes. And a thinking mind. He *was* Harry Borg!

And yet he was not.

He could feel nothing. Whatever he reached to touch became as nothing, giving no resistance at all, allowing unhindered passage.

Right on through.

He heard the quiss squeaking again. Looking, he found it against a distant wall, sitting up, holding something in its paws, eating it while looking in Harry's direction. The quiss was eating an insect. Harry saw the small, transparent insect wings fall to the floor. He saw the body of the insect disappear down the throat of the quiss, then saw the quiss run on again, searching further.

Understanding came suddenly to Harry.

Los Ross had sent the quiss, just as he had sent Harry, across twenty light-years. The quiss had arrived, just as Harry had arrived. But with a difference. The quiss could catch and eat insects. The quiss left tracks in the dust of the floor. The quiss, therefore, had a body. It had substance. It existed in all dimensions.

It *was*!

While he, Harry Borg, was *not*!

He, Harry Borg, had no body!

A slow-shaping but truly enormous outrage began building in Harry Borg. The quiss had traveled all those millions of miles of space unharmed. It had arrived, complete with its normal appetite—and its physical ability to satisfy that appetite—while he, Harry Borg, had arrived with one very serious deficiency.

He had arrived.

But his body had *not* arrived.

"Los Ross, you blasted idiot!" he roared. "You goofed!"

There followed, then, a stream of profanity. Dreadfully obscene profanity. Marvelously expressive. A mixture of the worst of his own language and the language of the Jassans. The kind reserved for only the most dire circumstances, the most aggravating pain. Intense blue in color. The kind that layered the atmosphere breathed by gentler folk, the kind that stung the nostrils and made the eyes of reverent people water.

"Los, what in blazes have you done to me?"

"I am sorry . . . I am sorry . . . I am sorry . . ."

Harry Borg had had no hope that his complaint, however forceful, however profane, would reach the little scientist. It was utterly impossible. Twenty light-years? No way! Of course not! How could it? It couldn't.

Twenty light-years! Forget it!

"Harry, I *am* sorry . . ." The telepathic voice was coming from a speaker contraption. Dim. Very dim. Faint. Wavery. Scratchy. It couldn't be Los Ross talking all that distance. And yet—

"Los? Los, is that you?"

"Yes, Harry . . ." Los Ross's voice was distant. Very distant. And very scratchy.

"You can hear me?"

"Faintly, Harry. Could you speak louder?"

"Louder?" Harry's outrage grew. "I'm yelling, for chrissake!"

And indeed he was. Rather, he was going through the motions. He was yelling physically as well as telepathically. But since he had no body, no vocal chords, and no brain—in the physical sense of having a brain—it was hard to understand, let alone believe, how he could be communicating at all. Let alone roaring.

But it was also utterly impossible for him to have traveled a distance of twenty light-years through space in any sensible length of time. But if he could travel across that distance, in the short time it had taken, he could communicate across that distance. Couldn't he? Whether he could or not, he was doing it, and that took care of that.

And very satisfying it was, too.

Like the truth that a tree falling in a distant forest makes no sound, wrath vented in a vacuum serves no purpose. Now that he had the Jassan equivalent of eardrums to receive what he had to deliver, to feel the impact of his fury, he delivered it in great detail. And it must have been effective, for the next voice he heard, distant, thin, and wavery, belonged to Guss.

"Harry . . . you made him faint again."

"Oh, hell!"

There was a long silence.

Then, thin, afraid, "Harry . . . Harry? Are you there?"

It was Los Ross, the little scientist who had sent him here, recovered and speaking again. Now Harry spoke carefully, with his fury bottled and corked.

"Los, whatever in the hell did you do to me?"

"You . . . *You* . . . you got there all right?"

"Yeah. I got here, all right. But Los, listen!"

"Yes, Harry?"

"There's something missing, Los," Harry said very carefully.

There was a pause.

"Your body, Harry? Is . . . is that missing?"

"You better believe your goddamn ass my body's missing—" He was yelling again. He choked off the message.

"Harry . . ." The voice was very, very faint. "I'm sorry, Harry . . ."

"So you're sorry. So what happened to my body?"

"I'm checking, Harry. I'll get right back to you . . ."

That distant, thin, scratchy voice faded out.

Harry swore again.

This was ridiculous.

He was standing in some kind of a vault, with shiny metallic walls, with some kind of tubes glowing, yelling, cussing, talking to some little scientist twenty light-years away, with a quiss over there in the corner eating another bug. He, Harry Borg, had gone out of his skull. No doubt about it. Bonkers. He was rowing with one oar.

"Los!" he roared. "Where the hell are you?"

Guss's voice again. "He's checking, Harry."

"Checking what?"

"Checking where your body went...a problem of some kind."

"Problem? What problem? I got here, and my body didn't."

"That's the problem."

Guss's voice was very distant, thin.

Harry fumed.

Then, after long minutes: "Harry? Are you there?"

"I'm here, Los."

"I can find your body. I know I can."

"So find it, already! Find it now!"

"It will take a little time, Harry. But I'll find it. I'll send it."

"When?"

"When what?"

"When are you going to send my goddamn body?"

"As soon as I can, Harry."

"How soon will that be? In ten minutes? An hour? A day? A week? A month?"

"Soon. Very soon."

Communication ended.

Los Ross's telepathic voice, as thin and as scratchy as it had been, dwindled to nothing. And it wouldn't come back. No matter how hard Harry Borg tried, he couldn't get either Los Ross or Guss back on the line again. And he tried, and tried, and tried...

He cursed, threatened, coaxed, pleaded.

Nothing worked.

He gave up finally.

A fine kettle of fish was what it was. He had gone one place, and his body, like airline luggage, had gone to another. Here *he* was, and there his body was. Somewhere else. Somewhere else in the universe. And, in case anybody wanted to know, it was one helluva big place, the universe.

Keerist!

He didn't know how long he roamed around that vault, with its tubes glowing, with the quiss scampering, leaving those damned footprints in the dust to mock him. *It* had a body. *It* had gotten through all right! Sure! A blasted Jassan excuse for a guinea pig could get through, no sweat. But a man? Not on your life!

Like that.

Raging, ranting, kicking lockers, punching out drinking fountains, ripping up uniforms. All wasted effort, of course. Wasted time and energy, because no good came of it at all.

It just pooped him out something fierce.

Finally, then, there was a time of feeling sorry for himself.

Poor goddamn Harry Borg, lost in outer space. Something that shouldn't happen to his worst enemy, it had to happen to him! Murphy's Law? Forget it. This was Borg's Law. With Borg's Law, everything went double.

And he got tired of that, too.

Feeling sorry—how much of that can a man stand?

He went outside the vault. No problem. Just go up to the wall and walk right on through. But what he found outside was no bargain. Nighttime. A million stars in the sky. Cold. Gradually, he began to understand that he was in the ruins of an ancient city.

He set out, walking, wandering.

So this was Orca!

Maybe once it had been something. Now it was nothing, just crumbling, decayed ruin. Streets hardly discernible. Buildings collapsed, weathered, destroyed. He drifted through the collapsed buildings, wandering, searching.

It got very cold.

And very lonely.

And he began to feel run-down, tired.

So very, very damned tired.

When he finally came to a camp—a military camp of some sort, though he couldn't identify the strange-looking soldiers as being any kind of creatures or soldiers he had ever seen before—he didn't much care what kind of a camp it was. Or who they, the soldiers, were. All he wanted was someplace to lie down. Someplace warm, for Christ's sake! Where he would feel protected. Going around without a body was like walking through town on a winter's day dressed only in underwear. He needed a refuge. A haven. A lee shore . . .

And he found one beside one of the soldiers.

Lying down beside the soldier, he found that the soldier was ten feet tall. *Ten feet tall?* Godfrey mighty! What kind of an army was this? Then he thought, the hell with it. Ten feet, twenty feet—he could care less! Never mind how tall the bugger was. He was warm. He was friendly.

He didn't move as Harry stretched out beside him.

Or was it *inside* him?

It was.

Inside him . . .

CHAPTER 5

E. Rox knew the moment he awakened that he had gone mad. Somehow during the night he had suffered a cataclysmic episode of some kind, a mental disordering far beyond anything he had ever heard about, or read about, or seen depicted on vid-screens. As he lay in those first shivering, sweating moments after awakening, his mind had raced through the history of the Family Rox, searching for ancestors who may have suffered mental disorders. He had found none. None at all. The Rox family had never had a recorded case of mental disorder.

He was the first!

Images of his father, his grandfather, his great-grandfather came back to him. He had known them all. Healthy, vigorous, mentally alert Orcans, they were, like himself, four ricos tall and physically powerful, if slender. Their faces were dominated by expressive, rather large, intelligent eyes of lican blue. They had been, each in his turn, the Uro of the Department of Interstudies at the Enclave of Sirix, a post that demanded clearheadedness, incisive thinking, mental stability. Stability above all else! And he, E. Rox, had been designated to succeed his father when O. Rox chose to step down, possibly within the next rill, or even sooner.

True, none of his immediate forebears had been required to serve in the military, as he had. The Anca problem had not become a serious matter until the present deca. The population of the Ancas had now become so enormous so suddenly, and their demands for equal representation had become so violent, that now constant military action was needed to suppress their rioting and terrorism. All physically able males—and he, E. Rox, a three-stripe distance runner, was certainly physically able—were required to serve six ossos a reco in a combat unit.

There had been no question that he would do his share. Even though the military life was, for him, a cruel and unusual duty—he was an academician, a sensitive, creative person, by birth as well as inclination, and not a combat warrior personality. The rugged life, the long hours of patrol, the responsibilities, the ability to fight a ruthless enemy, to kill without mercy—these things did put an unusual strain on his sensibilities, and he had expected to suffer because of it. Sleeplessness. Perhaps a loss of appetite. A diminishing of his reproductive abilities—though, thankfully, he had noticed none. Any of these difficulties might reasonably have occurred.

But a total mental collapse?

Never! Never in his most awful periods of depression had he ever fantasized a crack-up of this severity happening to him. And yet it had. It had come on more or less gradually sometime after midnight.

There had been a period, he remembered now, of most disturbing dreams. No, not dreams. Nightmares! How could that sudden coldness he had felt invading him be described otherwise?

It had been as if a door to his mind had been suddenly

pulled open to allow a draft of icy cold to sweep in, all-pervading, penetrating.

The eerie, dank cold of a frozen burial ground, terrifying as well as shivering. The cold had been followed by a strange, rough heat and a crowding, a pushing and shoving about of his mind. It had been as if he were being *invaded*! Invaded by a grunting, complaining someone, wanting room, wanting a share of his space in life. No, *insisting* on a share of his space, professing some great need.

"Sorry, pal . . ."

He had *heard* those words.

Yes, he had! He had heard them clearly, as if he had spoken them to himself, though never in his wildest imaginings would he have *used* those words. He didn't even know what they meant, except that they, in a rough way, conveyed some sort of an apology.

"Cold out there. Gotta get some rest . . ."

"Who are you?" he had whispered, afraid.

"A friend . . . passin' by. Explain later. Let's get some sleep for God's sake. I'm bushed. Been a hard day . . ."

Incredibly, then, he had felt the sensation of a part of him going to sleep. A *part* of him. Not all. Just a part. A part of him going to sleep. A visiting part? A new part? A guest part? *A guest part?* If that were not madness—a total, catastrophic mental collapse—then what could it possibly be?

Insanity.

He had lain awake for what seemed hours, made stiff with the realization that he had suffered that most awful of all fates, insanity, afraid to move lest some new calamity come crashing down on him. He had lain awake while that madness, that "friend . . . passin' by" had slept deeply somewhere in what had been his mind. Then he had fallen asleep out of exhaustion, without willing it or even wanting it.

Now he had awakened again.

His troopers were still asleep. It was still not daylight. The queeqs had only just begun to chirp. The odors of the gradually warming ruins of Atoxia, the ancient city they were using for their advanced outpost, filtered dry and dusty into his antennae. Usually, he would have enjoyed these moments—they were the best of the day, the usual unpleasant duties still comfortably distant—but now he could only lie, stiff and trembling, wondering if that dreadful hallucination would recur.

Invaded by another personality?

Rot. Absolute rot!

It was a momentary weakness. Something he had eaten—or had not eaten. A brief episode of senselessness. The vapors. Occasionally, in the past, he had suffered moments of vertigo, of brief disorientation brought on, usually, by an overindulgence in crox. Something of that nature. Or, quite possibly—this was the most probable of all—in this instance he had only imagined something, or someone, had invaded him.

Imagination can play queer tricks.

Thank Osmos, it was all over now.

"Good morning. It *is* morning, isn't it?"

Rizzitti! There it was again!

It was not vertigo, then! It was not weird tricks. It *was* insanity.

"I've gone quite mad," E. Rox whispered.

"No, you're not mad," the inner voice said. "You've got company."

"Company?" His voice was querulous, afraid.

"Yeah. Give me a minute . . ."

"A minute?"

"To get things straight. This's all new to me, too, you know."

Silence followed.

The inner voice disappeared.

But the presence was still in his mind, E. Rox knew. Very strongly there. He found he had an impression of a strange creature—intense, dark blue eyes, a face partly fur-covered—not dangerous, even friendly. Coarse. Yet refined in some ways. A very strong, rough-hewn personality—that described it best.

"Let me introduce myself," the inner voice said. "My name is Harry Borg. I'm a human being from the planet Earth. I should say, 'from the planet Earth by way of Earth's sister planet, Essa.'"

"I don't believe this!"

Hysteria was beginning to rise.

"Steady, lad," the inner voice said. It was a deep voice, calming. "You're going to be all right. There's nothing wrong with you. You're not insane. You've just had an attack of unexpected company, is all."

"Unexpected company?"

"A guest. A visitor from outer space."

"Rizzitti..." Hysteria was on the rise again.

"Easy, lad! Easy!" The tone was of careful scolding. "I won't stay a minute longer than I have to, believe me. I know I'm an imposition. But I'm really no worse than a bad cold."

The voice was so reasonable...the personality so real!

"I don't understand...any of this."

"Can't say I blame you. Try to relax."

E. Rox lifted his head to look at his troopers. They were all still asleep. Thank Ixxi for small favors! Perhaps in a moment this attack of madness would go away. He lay back and tried to compose himself. And while he was lying thus, eyes closed, antennae folded, fingers entwined, the deep, calm voice quietly began to explain what had happened.

He, E. Rox, had become a dual personality—that was what had happened. Because of a small contretemps, the body of an Earthman from the planet Essa, a sister planet of a planet called Earth, had gone astray. The Earthman had arrived here as scheduled. Rather, his *personality* had arrived. His body had not arrived.

Was that clear?

"No, it is not."

"Hang in, son. We'll get it straight."

Without going into the scientific details, none of which the visitor himself understood very well, he said, the visitor went on to say that he meant E. Rox absolutely no harm. He had only come, he said, for the best of reasons—to help his race. He had come in search of a plant from which an extract could be made that would help his race defeat viruses that caused lethal disease. Once he had found the plant and had taken seeds or a whole specimen that could be transported back to Earth, he would leave quietly, never to return.

"Are you following all this?"

"No, I am not."

"Can't say I blame you. It's hard to believe. Now that I'm telling you about it, I can hardly believe it myself."

"It is *not* true."

"It's true, all right."

"No."

"I'm here, right?"

"You're not here. I'm suffering an attack of madness."

"You're wrong, sport. You're as sane as anybody. You're just a dual personality now. I'll admit that takes a bit of getting used to. Here we are, talking to each other, and I didn't even know I knew your language. How about that?"

"What?"

"Knowin' your language, talkin' to you. Beats all what science can do nowadays. Those eggheads get any smarter, I don't know what will become of us. I surely don't."

"Go away," E. Rox said.

"Aw, come on, now!"

"Go!"

"I can't!"

"Whatever you are, whoever you are, please go away. Now!"

"Sorry..."

Harry Borg—if that was what it was, or who it was, the second self, the other half of what was being described as a dual personality—went on to explain that he couldn't, or wouldn't, go out and wander around on this strange planet without a body. Like it or not—and he certainly didn't like it very well, either—he had to stay until Los Ross, whoever that was, found his body, wherever that was, and shipped it here. When would that be? Soon. That was what Los Ross had said. Soon. And if he—what was his name again? E. Rox. "A pleasure to meet you, Mr. Rox. Not Mr. Rox. E. Rox. All right, E. Rox. It's still a pleasure."—if he had ever had anything go missing in the mail, he'd know that "soon" was at best an indefinite term.

"An hour, a day, a month—you pick it."

"Oh, crixx!"

"That's what I say." The voice tried to be consoling. "Tell you what, though. I'll be as little trouble as I can be while I'm here. I guess I'll have to use your conveniences and like that, but I'll try to be neat around the place. And stay out of the way? Okay?"

"What . . . what is the meaning of 'okay'?"

"Do you agree? That's what it means. A slang expression—"

"I do *not* agree."

"Sorry about that."

It was a tired apology. And with it Harry Borg withdrew.

Then a new voice spoke. "Sir? Sir? Are you awake, sir?"

It was the voice of Rux S. Ris, his second in command. Despite his youth, Rux S. Ris was a very capable rux. If it was true that the military was run by the ruxes, that the success or failure of a superior officer depended exactly upon his rux, then Rux S. Ris was E. Rox's guarantee of success. He was brave. He was intelligent. He was loyal. He was understanding. But there are limits. One did not enter into conversation with a subordinate that went something like this:

"Rux."

"Sir!"

"I have just made a startling discovery."

"Yes, sir! A startling discovery!"

"It concerns my mind."

"Your mind, sir!"

"I have discovered that my mind has failed me."

"Your mind has failed you, sir!"

"You may ask in what way my mind has failed me, Rux."

"In what way has your mind failed you, sir?"

"I have gone mad, Rux. Utterly mad."

"Mad, sir?" A wide-eyed, very unmilitarylike stare, then. "You mean uxxy, sir? Like yisso?"

There are limits to the control of even the best-trained soldier.

"Yes, like yisso. My mind has collapsed. I think I am two people—"

No! A thousand times no!

He could *not* confide in Rux.

He could not confide in anyone!

He had to conceal his madness somehow; he had to go about his duties as if nothing at all had happened— the cool, clearheaded, unflissable officer whose first thoughts were for his assignment, whose second thoughts were for the safety and comfort of his command, and whose third thoughts—only his third, very last thoughts—were for his own physical and, yes, mental condition . . .

E. Rox swallowed hard, almost gulping.

It wouldn't do for a rux to see his commanding officer suddenly in tears, weeping in self-pity! He spoke crisply. "Prepare the squad, Rux. Full field gear."

"Full field gear, sir!"

"Three days' rations."

"Three days' rations, sir!"

"We are going on an extended reconnaissance. South and east. I don't believe that area has been surveyed as well as it might be. There could be clandestine Anca activity out there, Rux. Illegal camps, terrorist assemblies, smuggling—things of that nature."

"Of that nature, sir!"

"Nature?" E. Rox's inner voice—the voice of Harry Borg—asked sleepily, yawning. "What nature?"

"Nothing. It doesn't concern you!"

"It doesn't, sir?" Rux S. Ris asked, his young face startled.

"Not you!" E. Rox said. "I mean—I was thinking out loud, Rux." Panic-stricken, E. Rox tried to hide that panic from his subordinate officer behind a front of impatient anger. "See to your duties!"

"Sir!"

The young subordinate, properly chastised, turned away immediately to get the other ranks of the small command cracking. There were eight altogether in this small outpost set up in the ancient ruins of what had once been the great city of Atoxia. They had vid communication with headquarters, they had land transport. They had sidearms, rifles, and one small ray-cannon. But they were not combat troops. They were a search-and-report unit. Their assignment was to keep approximately one hundred and sixty cletes of barren desert under surveillance. An impossible task, really, given their number and transport. They were to report any illegal activity by the Ancans to headquarters. It was an assignment that had not in the past been taken very seriously. But in recent times—since the Ancans had increased so enormously in numbers and since their demands for equal representation in government had become so insistent, even militant—the assignment was being given more importance. Now the traditional neutral buffer, Rota Desert, was being watched on regular schedule for possible Ancan infringement. Every six dicos or so, a unit such as the one E. Rox commanded was sent to various distant outposts and told to keep watch and report back. A dismal assignment, certainly, especially coming as it did when the weather in the desert was at its very worst, hot and dry and windy, and the weather at home was at its most salubrious, warm and moist and still.

But one did what one could to serve one's country.

Particularly if one would be shot if one did not.

"What's goin' on?" Harry Borg asked.

Harry had come into the forepart of E. Rox's consciousness and was watching—through his host's eyes, to be sure—as his host watched the members of the reconnaissance group loading the land transport with equipment and supplies.

Harry Borg didn't feel very well.

He felt lousy, as a matter of fact. Very tired, only half-awake, achy, feverish. A touch of the flu? Not hardly, since he had no body of his own. He still hadn't recovered from his trip, he supposed.

Jet lag? Yes. Something like that.

Twenty light-years, for God's sake! There was bound to be jet lag after a twenty-light-year trip . . .

"We goin' someplace?" he asked.

"Stop it! Go away!" His host's mental voice was tight, jittering, almost hysterical. "This doesn't concern you!"

His host, Harry realized, was afraid his men would find out that he was entertaining a visitor from outer space—that he had gone bananas, to put it more exactly. His host still would not believe that Harry was who he was or that he had come from where he had said he had. What he believed was that he was suffering from a sudden attack of some kind of schizophrenic madness.

Imagining he was two people.

That he was nuts.

So, okay. Harry couldn't blame an officer for wanting to keep that kind of information from his men. How could you have any discipline if your men thought you belonged in a rubber room? "I'll stay outa the way," he said.

"I would appreciate that!" his host said tightly.

Later, when things settled down a bit, Harry thought he would try to work things out with his host. His host was a nice guy, really. And once he understood—once he *accepted* the situation for what it was—he would be easy to get along with. Meanwhile, Harry *was* still suffering from jet lag. Or flu. Or whatever. And he needed his rest . . .

He watched, in a detached way, as the group finished their preparations. Being a military man himself—he'd been a bird colonel when he had retired from the Air Force—he knew about such things. These citizens of Orca—citizens? Creatures? Inhabitants? You couldn't very well call them men, could you? Why not? All right. Men. It seemed as if these men of Orca were pretty fair soldiers. Tall, though. My God, they were tall! The shortest of them would go ten feet. At least. And thin? One of these characters would have to stand twice in the same place to make a decent shadow. A single stripe would be enough if you wanted to make one a pinstripe suit. And they were rickety-looking, like they'd fall apart in a brisk wind.

Maybe not. The way they were heaving those crates around said they were probably strong enough to do ordinary work. They were not bad-looking, either. Weird, compared to humans, but in their own way they were more than just passable. They had these great antennae, like three-foot-tall jackrabbit ears, which could flip up and down as easy as they could raise their arms, and brought in scents and sounds like the nose of a Labrador retriever. Harry was discovering how great antennae were, because he was sharing the scents and sounds that were being brought in by his host's antennae.

All right! Everybody should have antennae.

And he liked very much, he decided, the eyes of these people. Their eyes were a dutch-china blue, as round as saucers, huge and friendly. And they had these little ski-jump noses and small, smiling mouths.

No ears!

With antennae, they needed ears?

Of course not.

Harry found himself getting very sleepy as he watched the Orcan soldiers going about their preparations for the reconnaissance mission. Sleepy and tired. And he lost interest. Rest was what he needed. Later, when he had his strength, he would take an active part, but now all he wanted to do was to cut a few z's.

He withdrew and went to sleep.

CHAPTER 6

It wasn't going to be much longer, Harry Borg decided, before something bad was going to happen. That big sucker, the one with the fang teeth, the lion's mane, and the mighty roars, the one E. Rox had called Sana, son of Tanta, was going to get tired of strutting up and down, pounding his chest, and shaking his spear.

All that was was just showing off, anyway. He was trying to build his ego and impress his buddies.

And he was trying to scare the wallop out of E. Rox.

He was doing that, all right.

"What're you going to do?" Harry asked.

"There's nothing I *can* do!" E. Rox moaned.

"Y' mean you're just going to stand here, shivering and shakin' until that big gorilla comes up here and whacks our head off? It's my head, too, you know."

"There's *four* of them!"

"I can count."

"And they've got those spears!"

"Yeah."

"And swords!"

"So they have."

"We . . . *I* don't have *anything*!"

69

"Gives them a bit of an edge, I'll agree with you there."

"You miserable Orcan!" Sana bellowed. "Come out and die!"

The Ancan was playing with E. Rox like a cat playing with a mouse, enjoying himself, never for a moment doubting the outcome. That made two of them, Harry was discovering, who never doubted the outcome: Sana and E. Rox.

"I'll be go to hell," Harry said.

"What does that mean?"

"Means I'm surprised."

"At what?"

"You. You've quit! You've just plain thrown in the towel."

"Riddles!" E. Rox moaned. "At the moment of dying."

Harry had heard of such reactions—this total surrender, this willingness to accept death without fighting to the last drop of blood, without kicking and clawing and doing whatever the hell you could until the lights went out. But he had never experienced it.

"We haven't got a lot of time," he said.

That was true.

The huge, red Orcan sun was low over the horizon; the shadows racing across the red desert floor, thrown by the bleak rocks, were growing very long. The air had a sharp chill in it that was not caused by fear alone.

"Tell you what," he said. "It's time I took over."

"Took over?" E. Rox's voice held a quaver.

"Yeah. You give me control."

"Control?"

"Will you for chrissakes quit playing echo?" Harry was losing patience. "I want control of this bundle of sticks you call a body. Let me take over. You climb in this here back seat. All right?"

"Anything you say. What difference?"

"I'll show you what difference! Move over!"

And somehow that was managed. E. Rox moved over and allowed Harry Borg to move to the forefront, to dominate—to take control.

"It will not serve. We are going to die."

"I'm a hard bastard to kill," Harry said.

"Enough!" Sana roared. His lion's mane was flared up around his head and shoulders, and his huge yellow eyes were blazing. Apparently, he had had enough of fooling around. He wanted action now. He wanted blood. And his three companions were in a like frame of mind. Two of them lowered their spears so the long, gleaming blades were pointed directly at E. Rox.

"What do they expect you to do now?" Harry asked his host.

"Expect me to do?"

"Under normal conditions," Harry said, trying to be patient. "Without me around, what would an average Orcan do now?"

"Go out . . ." E. Rox whimpered from somewhere far in back. "Go out there and kneel before him . . ."

"So he could whack your head off?"

"That is all we can do."

"Okay. That's what we're *gonna* do."

"We are?"

"Yep."

"Good-bye, Rani."

"Rani? Who's Rani?"

"My loved one . . . my mate . . ."

"Now, that's *touching*. It really is."

"What are you *doing*?"

"Spittin' on my hands," Harry said.

"How disgusting!"

Disgusting or not, Harry spat on his hands, rubbed them together, hit his nose with his thumb, then walked out of the sheltering rocks toward the waiting Ancans. He held his palms up in a gesture of peace, surrender, and obeisance.

Sana roared approval.

Harry had time to wish for his own body. He could trust his own body. With his own body, he could take these jokers apart in nothing flat. With this long and tall collection of arms and legs, he didn't know what he could do. But he knew that whatever he could do, before he was finished with these Ancans they would know they had been up against the baddest bastard this side of a junkyard dog.

He knelt on the ground.

Sana, grinning, his lips curled back from his fang teeth, strode toward him. His three buddies followed, one on one side, two on the other. Four of them—careless, confident, enjoying.

"Filth!" Sana said. "*You* would rule *me*?"

Harry didn't answer.

"Never!" Sana said. "Your time has ended. Soon you and all your kind will be my slaves!"

And he went into a windy lecture, for the benefit of his buddies, about how it was going to be when his father took over *all* of Orca, and when later, he, Sana, took over in his father's place . . . pricking E. Rox and Harry Borg contemptuously with the point of his spear from time to time, but never quite getting into the right position.

"What the hell?" Harry said.

"What do you mean?" E. Rox said.

Their words were thoughts and did not carry.

"This slaves bit—I thought all they wanted was equal representation in government."

"That is what they say. But any fool knows they lie."

"They want it *all*?"

"They would make us slaves...and finally murder us."

"Shucks!" Harry said. "Who can you trust anymore?"

And at that moment, Sana got in the right position.

Harry Borg, in the body of E. Rox, came up with a suddenness and a force unheard of—even unimagined—in the history of the interrace relationship between Ancan and Orcan.

"Sucker!"

Harry caught Sana's spear just at the base of the blade, jerked it forward hard. At the same moment, he raised up and whipped a hard kick into Sana's midriff. The blow, helped a good bit by the planet Orca's low gravity, sent Sana ass over teakettle back among the rocks. Turning without a moment's pause in the flow of motion, reversing the spear, he drove the blade through the chest of one Anca, then another.

"Heeeeee!" the third shrieked in sudden terror. He was fumbling clumsily, unable to decide whether to use his spear, draw his sword, or run for his life, when Harry ended his indecision by kicking his legs out from under him. Then Harry pinned him to the ground with a spear thrust through his chest.

Harry left the spear there—left the Ancan pinned and clawing at the shaft that held him, squawking his life away—and took the sword from the Ancan's sheath. Standing erect, he faced the last of the Ancans, the charging Sana, the son of Tanta, or whatever the hell he was called.

Ruler of all Orca.

"Got news for you, pal," Harry said. "You ain't gonna

rule no goddamn body. Not in this world...or any other."

Braggin'. That's what that was. Pure and simple.

In all truth, he wasn't all that sure what he could do with this rickety Orcan body he was sharing now that the other side knew he was willing to make a fight of it. The advantage of surprise was gone. Now he had an eight-foot lion-type, who looked as strong as a couple of horses, charging at him, whistling that head cutter of a sword around like he meant business.

Harry met the swinging blade with a swinging blade.

Both blades shattered. And the way it felt, it liked to have shattered E. Rox's arm into the bargain. Hurt like hell, anyway. But the hurt was nothing like the hurt that came next.

Hand to hand, now, he had the son of Tanta at his throat.

He was maybe a foot taller than Sana. He had maybe a foot on him where reach was concerned. But Sana had fangs, and in a close fight, fangs could make a serious difference.

"Crat-eater!"

Harry didn't know what that meant, but, coming from E. Rox, it seemed to work like a kick in the gut on Sana. E. Rox, Harry realized now, was taking more than a spectator's part in the fight. Somehow the Orcan's fear had been forgotten. He had taken heart. Harry thought he might even be taking a fierce pleasure in the battle.

"Row—ahhhhh!" Sana bellowed.

Some kind of a battle cry, Harry supposed.

They went at each other, then, like two bobcats in a burlap bag, hammering, pounding, scratching, clawing, and biting. They were close to even when Harry finally caught a blow on the side of the head, a real bell ringer that knocked him kicking fifty feet across the rock-strewn slope. The sky wheeled, and his head rang like a can full of gongs. He was sorry E. Rox had no battle cry to roar about then, because he sure could have used one.

He was flattened.

But in that moment of final desperation, he managed to come up with something even better. It was the product of hard-earned knowledge of dirty fighting he had gained in what his father had called a misspent youth. What he had learned was that anything, any goddamn thing at all, was fair in a fight to the finish.

He came up with rock the size of a baseball in his fist. And he hauled back and threw it.

Jim Palmer couldn't have thrown a better strike. Ninety-eight miles an hour on anybody's radar gun.

The rock caught Sana square in the face. Fangs flew, and blood sprayed. And Sana was *gone*! The Ancan landed on his shoulders, out colder than a well digger's ass. Harry did not stop there. Lesson Two in that book of hard knocks said if you laid somebody out and then turned your back on him, the chances were better than even he'd get up and stop your clock when you weren't looking.

None of that for Harry.

He went straight to get himself a spear and spiked Sana, son of Tanta, to the ground, just as he'd done to the others. Only with this Ancan character, this first cousin to a man-eating lion, he made double-damned sure. After he had shoved the blade through the sucker's chest, he went on shoving until the blade was a foot deep in the rocky soil.

"There!" he grunted. "Blow that out your ear!"

Then he wobbled around, hunting for a place to sit down.

It was quiet then . . .

Hurting quiet.

Harry Borg was surprised to learn that the body of E. Rox was as capable of aches and pains as any human body had ever been. Man alive! You name it and he had it. Face busted up and swelling. Arms hanging limp. Legs too weak to hold him up. Back about broken, the way it felt, in three or four places. Even one of his antennae had a kink in it, and the pain from that kink couldn't have been worse coming from a broken nose. Harry didn't know if they were going to live through it or not.

The sky had gone dark during the fight. Now the stars were coming out, and the first of Orca's four moons had already risen. Harry looked up. There were a million-billion stars up there, just like home.

But no Milky Way. No Big Dipper. No Polaris.

Home was a long, long, long trip away. This was *Orca*!

"There's something I ought to tell you," he said.

"What would that be?" E. Rox's voice, while in the same body and in the same mind, had seemed distant. Perhaps it was the pain. Or the exhaustion.

"This body of yours is all right."

"Kind of you to say so," E. Rox responded with weary sarcasm.

"I mean it," Harry said seriously. He lifted one of E. Rox's arms, groaned, and let it drop. "When I started that fight, I was sure the first solid whack would break us in half. But it didn't happen. We took a lot of beating. Sure, we're hurting. We're hurting to beat hell. But we're still in one piece."

"I am as surprised as you are."

"You may be frail-lookin', son. But you're whippy."

"Is that a compliment?"

"Meant to be."

"Thank you."

Harry stretched against another pain.

"Could you have done it?" E. Rox asked tentatively.

"What do you mean?"

"Could you have done as well . . . with your body?"

Harry thought about that.

He thought about his body. Could he have done as well with it? Yes, probably a helluva lot better. There was less gravity here on Orca, and that alone would double his strength and agility. In his body, here on Orca, he would be formidable.

But he thought he would lie a little.

"I doubt it," he said. "You're very good."

E. Rox was comforted. "Thank you again."

"We've got to get moving," Harry said then. Creaking and groaning, he forced himself—and E. Rox, of course —to stand erect. "What about those damned letas?"

"What about them?"

"Will they attack?"

Four of the creatures the Ancans had ridden had not gone away. They were keeping a distance, scuttling back and forth like dodging shadows in the moonlight, antennae waving, making clicking noises. Huge, antlike creatures, black, many-legged. Harry thought they could be a dangerous problem.

"They are not usually aggressive," E. Rox said.

"Okay. But let's get the hell outa here."

"If that means leave, I agree."

"You know the way. You want to take over?"

"I think I should."

"Come on in," Harry said. "You're in charge."

In what was probably the briefest of moments, Harry Borg moved into the background and E. Rox came forward to once more become the commanding personality. And when he was in control, he seemed to need a mo-

ment longer to gather up the reins, to assess all the possibilities, to assume all the responsibilities.

"Yes," he said. "We must try to hurry."

With E. Rox in control, they began making their way
along the foot of the cliff, clambering over scree, searching for a path that would lead them to the top. Atoxia
was up there, and, hopefully, so still was the outpost
manned by two of E. Rox's command. If they could hang
together long enough to reach that outpost, a vid-call
would summon help.

After they had traversed a mile of difficult terrain,
they found a road that promised to take them to the plateau above. Needing a moment's rest before beginning
the ascent, they collapsed to sit on a rock, breath burning in their throat, head hanging, arms almost too weak
to lift.

And now something that had lain submerged in the
pain and the trauma that had followed the murderous
fight worked its way to the forefront of E. Rox's mind
and demanded full consideration. Harry, still in the
background, was only vaguely aware of E. Rox's thinking, but when E. Rox suffered a sudden jolt of extreme
anxiety, he became sharply concerned.

"What's happening?" he asked.

"Sana," E. Rox answered.

"Sana is dead! I guarantee it!"

"I know he is dead."

"Then what's the problem?"

"His father is Tanta . . ." E. Rox's thoughts faded to a
whisper. His anxiety became fear as he began fully to
realize the enormity of what had occurred. The son of
the leader of the Ancans lay dead, pinned to the ground
by his own spear among the rocks on this deserted
corner of the Rota Plain. Three of his cohorts lay dead

with him. All four had been killed by a single Orcan. A single Orcan named E. Rox.

"He asked for it," Harry said. "It was him or us."

"They, the Ancans—Tanta—won't see it that way."

"They'll call it murder?"

"They'll call it another example of Orcan oppression," E. Rox said.

"One Orcan defending his life against four? That's oppression?"

"When they tell it, it will become a force of fifty Orcans, all well armed, who trapped an innocent hunting party of Ancans and ruthlessly murdered them."

"I know what you mean. We call it propaganda."

"They will want revenge."

"Against you? Us?"

"If Tanta learns his son was killed by one Orcan, E. Rox—"

"And Harry Borg—don't forget me."

"—he will certainly want revenge. Blood for blood. And he will not rest until he has found the Orcan who killed his son. Found him and killed him."

"But that's not the worst of what's bothering you, is it?"

"No, it is not." E. Rox's mind was finding this almost too much to confront. "To understand what the worst of it can be, you must understand . . . how close we have been to war with the Ancans."

"Declared war?"

"Yes. Tanta has wanted a full-scale war. But he has needed something of great importance to rally his forces behind him . . . to begin the final conflict."

"Killing his son, the heir apparent—that ought to give him what he needs."

"And *I* am responsible. *I* murdered Sana."

"*We* murdered Sana," Harry said soberly. "Let's put it that way. *We* murdered Sana."

CHAPTER 7

"Guss..." Lori moaned. "Oh, no..."

Guss had killed the guard.

The Triss-nass had been hidden in a rocky depression a thousand meters from the ancient castle, all but invisible there in rain-swept darkness, where only an occasional ripping flash of lightning would find it, where it would be buffeted only by wind and rain and cannonading thunder.

The Triss-nass, their flying machine, had been safe there.

Guss and Sissi would be going back to it.

But not Lori.

That had been the plan.

Taking the crassal and the clumsy tripod, Lori, Guss, and Sissi had blundered their way up the dark road, groping and slipping and sliding, their faces lashed by rain, their eyes blinded by sudden lightning rips, their ears deafened by the thunder. They were frightened. What they had been doing, and were about to do, was forbidden. If they were caught doing it, they would be punished.

Guss had led the way, esso in one hand, the barrel of

the crassal in the other. The esso was a notoriously hair-trigger sidearm and always dangerous. Guss should not have brought the esso. Yet he had. To protect them, he had said. But it had been really to bolster his flagging courage. And then what had seemed a large rock, washed down to the road by the storm, had barred his way.

But it had not been a rock.

It had been a Jassan soldier huddled under a tarpaulin.

Guss, stumbling, had fallen over the soldier, and the soldier, frightened, had squirmed, fighting. The esso had flashed. One single bolt, accidentally fired, had gone through the chest of the soldier, killing him.

Mercifully, without pain.

"I didn't *mean* to!" Guss's whimper of regret had been useless. And too late.

In the misery of the steady, blowing rain, Sissi had tried to comfort him. That failing, she had helped Lori cover the soldier. Then, together, all three moved on.

They were almost crawling now.

No longer were they only trespassers, guilty of nothing more forbidden than going where they had been ordered not to go. Now they had killed. Now they would be severely punished if caught. Death—that would be the punishment. And not an easy death.

The converter...

They would be fed into grinding teeth, screaming, and, once living, pulsing beings, they would become meal, sacked and delivered somewhere to enrich worn soil.

But what could they do now but go on?

At a distance of about fifty yards from the castle entrance, they fixed the legs of the tripod firmly into the surface of the rocky road. Guss, working mostly by feel, rain-blinded, set the barrel of the crassal in place. Lori and Sissi erected the metallic shield that would protect them from reflected crassal rays. And they all crouched, waiting for a lightning flash that would permit Guss to aim with some precision.

Lori, rain-soaked yellow braids hanging like ropes about her neck, the lashes of her gray eyes weighted with drips, tried to locate the soldiers they knew would be guarding the entrance. Dimly, in light from a distant flash, she made them out: three misshapen lumps under back coverings beside great wooden doors.

"Three," Sissi said. "Two on the left, one on the right."

"I saw them," Guss said.

"Wait for better light," Lori cautioned. "To be sure."

They spoke telepathically: soft, urgent, whispered thoughts.

"Are you sure there will be an alarm?" Lori asked then.

"Very sure," Guss said.

"Absolutely sure," Sissi said, without hope.

Ten minutes . . .

That is what they would have, then, Lori thought. After they entered the castle, if they had not gotten done in ten minutes, they would be caught. The soldiers, summoned by the alarm, would have arrived, and they all would be arrested and carried away. If they had gotten done, Guss, Sissi, and Los Ross would be held, as before, as hostages, but they would not be killed.

Dear God, let that be so, she thought.

"You are mad," Sissi said, knowing Lori's thoughts. "Utterly insane."

"Hush," Lori said.

The lightning came, a brilliant flash that clearly revealed the glistening, rain-wet lumps of the soldiers. Guss pressed a button, sucking a hissing breath; the crassal made a soft *floop*, and a projectile was tossed to strike the door and explode. A burst of blue radiance bathed the bodies of the three guards. Lori, Guss, and Sissi, who had ducked down behind the shield, were not touched.

"Hurry!" Lori said.

They scrambled up, leaving the crassal and the shield, and ran to the castle entrance. They found the three guards paralyzed, but conscious. In a few minutes they would be normal again. Guss and Lori and Sissi bound the guards, left them covered out of the storm, and went into the castle, running.

Somewhere an alarm would be sounding.

Soldiers would be hurrying to flight-craft, boarding.

Every minute counted, every second...

First, there was a long stone corridor where their feet echoed hollowly. Then there was an empty room. Then a secret door that, since the police had last come, was no longer secret. After passing through this, they came to the brightly lighted laboratory.

It was empty.

"Los! Where are you?"

Lori's frantic call went unanswered.

The little scientist who had promised to be here was not here. Not visible, at least. Nor was there any answering telepathic response. Had he been arrested? Had he been taken away? Had it all been wasted? The soldier's life? Their lives, to be taken as punishment for killing the soldier if good cause could not be shown? Lori died a thousand little deaths in those first moments of uncertainty.

And then, finally, from an inner room, came Los Ross's telepathic voice, answering faintly. "Here... I am in here..."

They found him almost out of sight in a towering, intricate mass of electronic apparatus. He was a fussed and terribly worried little scientist. His smock, buttoned wrongly, was smudged and torn; his glasses were askew on his muzzle.

He was apologetic. "I'm sorry."

"Is something wrong?"

"The rissliss circuit. I can't be sure . . ."

"Zat!" Guss said.

"Guss!" Sissi scolded.

"Every lissing thing at once—"

"Shut up!" Lori cut him off. She turned to Los Ross. "Is it something you can fix? There isn't much time."

"I don't want to send you and have what happened to Mr. Borg happen to you."

"We haven't much choice."

"What do you mean?"

"She means I killed a guard," Guss said.

"Name of Osis—"

"He did not *mean* to!" Sissi said.

"I can't be here when the soldiers—the police—get here, Los!" Lori said. "Or they'll take you . . . Sissi and Guss, anyway, and then they will—"

"Don't say it!" Guss said.

"They will," Lori said.

"Probably will, anyway."

"*Not* if Los tells them he needs you—your *isslirs*—to keep Harry and me alive. It worked before!"

"I don't know. If a soldier has been killed—"

"It *must* work!" Sissi said. "We will *make* it work!"

"Tell a lie big enough, and I suppose . . ."

Guss was not hopeful.

"Come on!" Lori said, getting desperate. "Los?"

"Mrs. Borg. I've got to be honest—"

"Never mind honest! Lie to me! I've got to go!"

Los Ross's eight-fingered hands fluttered helplessly. "There is some possibility that—"

"Don't tell me about it! I don't want to hear!"

"You're insane," Sissi said.

"I know, I know!" Lori looked at Los Ross. "Well?"

He straightened his glasses on his muzzle, and his large yellow eyes behind them became thinking, sharp. "Some risk is acceptable. There is always some risk . . ."

"I'll take it! I'll take it!"

"Then, come."

The little scientist led the way back into the main laboratory. "Sit down over there, Mrs. Borg." He waved a hand at the comfortable chair in the alcove of gleaming metal, and he took his place at the console where dials and buttons came easily to hand. Lori ran to the chair and sat down quickly. This was no time for second thoughts. The decision had been made. Now was the time for *going*!

Sissi's golden eyes were agonized. "Oh, Lori!"

"Hush, sweetheart! I'll be all right!"

Guss couldn't even watch. He had turned his back and was facing the door through which the police, the soldiers, would come in just a few moments. Finding the dead soldier would delay them a moment or two, but then they would speed on.

He felt a soft humming vibration.

Then he heared Sissi's telepathic voice, almost breaking. "With Osis, Lori!"

"Not to worry—" Lori's voice ended abruptly.

When Guss turned, the chair was empty and Lori was gone.

CHAPTER 8

"They killed my son . . ."
Words so easily said.
A thought so swiftly formed.
But a fact monstrous beyond belief.
My son is dead . . .
Ran Tanta ut Krill.

He was the Krill of the Ancans, their leader. The warrior king. He was sprawled in a chair built of leather and wix, his great and powerful legs thrust out before him, hair-covered, yellow pillars of strength. His massive arms were supported by the arms of the wix chair, hands extended so that his orderly could lace on the micas that would transform his fingers, already cruel enough, into lethal weapons. His eyes, disks of smoldering red, had pupils gone to hair-thin slits.

"You don't know," his mate, Kana, said. "Not with certainty."

She was honing the accas she would soon fit over his gold-cased tusks, making them into even longer tusks, making them into cruel knives that would extend below his lower jaw, knives capable of slashing through flesh and tendon with ease. The *slick, slick* of whetstone on metal was a soothing sound.

"Sana is dead." Tanta's voice was a rumble coming from deep in his chest. "The Irno saw him lying dead, a spear through his chest. And he saw from a distance the Orcan who killed him."

"It may have been another."

"The Irno was sure."

The crippled Jantu finished lacing the mica on Tanta's right hand and began on the left. Kana, wife number one, wore a purple mane, which was most unusual, for most Anca females had no mane at all. Kana was regal in appearance, slim and tall; her six breasts were molded in golden cups connected by golden chains. She was trying to give Tanta comfort, but he was not to be comforted.

The Orcans had killed Sana.

The dressing room was octagonal, as all Anca rooms were, and was connected by a short corridor to the amphitheater, which, also octagonal, was huge and domed with a many-faceted roof of transparent cliga. The roar of the throng gathered there, waiting for the final event of Turning Day, came down the corridor now, like a wave beating on a near shore.

"The groll has been blinded," the wife said. She was still trying to give him comfort, trying to divert his mind away from sorrow and the fury she knew the death of Sana was bringing him. The blinding of the groll meant that he, Tanta, would make his appearance in a few moments. The throng was eager, thirsting. Blood would be spilled. Either Tanta's blood or the blood of the groll.

If the beast had been totally blinded, the chances were good that the blood spilled would be the groll's. But if even a little vision remained, the chances were better that the blood spilled would be the blood of Tanta, Krill of the Ancans. Tanta wondered if this would be the day

some underling, yearning to take his place, had dared
bribe the Tormentors into leaving the groll enough sight
to win the coming fight. Fate had taken the life of his
son. Why not his own life?

"Enta!" he growled.

"Sire?" An officer who wore insignia that marked him
highest in command of those present left a group of six
and approached fearfully.

"I want Sovan in ruins," Tanta said. "Not one wall
left standing. I want the head of every Orcan spiked.
Females, juveniles, old—spare not a single one."

"It has been ordered, sire."

Sovan was a small Orcan settlement. More than a
hundred would die there, if all were killed. As a beginning, Sovan would serve as an example of what was in
store for the Orcans. The pictures of the punishment
would appear on every Orcan vid-screen; the heads of
their young and their elderly on spears would serve notice to the Orcans that the uprising they had so long
dreaded had finally come.

They had killed the son of Tanta.

The time for talk had ended.

There would be no more meetings to discuss compro-
mise, where small concessions would be offered and rejected. There would be no more patient waiting. No
more enduring. They had brought it on themselves. After
centuries of treating the Ancans like beasts, denying
them equality, the Orcans were going to discover just
how powerful the Ancans had become. Intensive breed-
ing had increased their numbers until now they could
lose ten, even twenty Ancans for each Orcan killed and
still prevail in the final accounting.

"And then Rovas," Tanta said, naming another Orcan
settlement.

"Aye, sire."

Tanta called up visions in his mind of the two settlements in smoking ruins, the heads of all the Orcans displayed on the points of spears. But that still did not satisfy him. He needed more. It was just as well, then, if the death of Sana had been decreed by the gods, that it should have come on this day. On the Day of the Turning. The day of the groll killing.

It would serve him.

Not alone could he vent his rage and ease the pain of his torn heart—he could prove once more that none lived who had greater courage or greater strength than Tanta of the Ancans. And, because Sana had been revered by the warrior caste, the fighting Ancans would rally behind the strongest of the strong and the bravest of the brave to avenge the murderous death of their idol.

And thus Sana's death would serve the Ancan cause as well.

The crippled Jantu finished with the lacings. He backed away without lifting his eyes, then took up a thick drape of hide and held it up before Tanta. Tanta closed the fingers of his right hand around the grip of the mica and then, with sudden, swift movement, raked the three long saber-like claws that extended beyond the knuckles of that fisted hand through the hide, cutting the hide into shreds.

"Rako!" he said, voicing approval.

The cripple gathered the shreds and his tools and scurried away.

Now Kana touched Tanta's shoulder. The accas were ready. Tanta tipped his head back and allowed Kana to slip the accas over his gold-gleaming tusks and fasten them in place. He tested them, opening his mouth wide, causing his lower jaw to drop away and hooking the fangs into a slab of flesh brought and held for the purpose. The fangs sank into the flesh easily.

He was ready.

Rising, then, he stood tall and strong. naked to the waist, the powerful muscles of his chest and arms concealed beneath hair that grew thick, a cape on his shoulders. A brief, thick skirt of vidal protected his groin: vidal sandals covered his feet.

"Raaaaaw!" he roared, preparing himself.

"Kill, my sire," Kana said in encouragement.

The red disks of Tanta's eyes burned with a fierce glow. The mane that grew out of his strong neck was white where the others of his kind were yellow, and now, erected because of the combative rage burning within him, it made his fierceness somehow regal. With his muzzlelike facial conformation, tipped with black nostrils, and his gleaming tusks, he was a fearsome fighting beast by any measure.

A chanting cry of "Tanta! Tanta!" came down the corridor to the amphitheater. He strode to meet it. "Tanta! Tanta! Tanta!" The cry grew in volume and then into a sudden roar when he appeared on the red sands of the arena floor. He extended his long arms above his head in greeting.

"Tanta! Tanta! Tanta!"

They chanted not in reverence.

They hated him.

They hated him because of the work he had demanded of them, the sacrifices he had required. And they feared him. What need of reverence or of devotion, then, if fear served as well? All he asked was that they obey him without question. That they follow him wherever he might lead. And soon—he swore this as he looked up at the throng, thousands of warriors garbed in uniforms of red and gold, yellow manes tossing, rank upon rank—he would lead them into Orgas, the capital city of the Orcans, down streets lined with rubble and stinking with decaying dead.

No longer subjects!

Victors at last!

But now to the matter at hand . . .

The groll was on the far side of the arena. The beast was a powerful, oily-skinned creta, black in color, six feet high at the shoulder; it was raging. It had lifted its upper body and was standing on hind legs, pawing with its four upper limbs, claws fully exposed, snorting in air, questing for scent. Some said the groll had no need of eyes since its sense of smell was so keen. And at times, in the way even a blinded groll found and killed those brave enough to fight it, this did seem to be the truth.

Looking hard now, it seemed to Tanta that the eyes of the beast had been sufficiently wounded. Blood was streaming down from the sockets, across oily cheeks. And yet the beast had located him the moment he had strode out on the red sands. Was it scent alone? There seemed to be not the faintest breath of air moving. Or was there still a glint of sight in those bloody eyes? It was too late now to ask for more blinding. To call for it would be deemed an act of cowardice. He could only go ahead now, and if there was sight left—and if he sur-vived—work a most painful punishment on those re-sponsible.

He tipped his head back and roared a challenge.

The groll answered with a scream.

They rushed to meet each other, the groll using its four forward legs to carry its weight, holding the rear legs high, long tail whipping. A trail of red blood washed from its wounded eyes, back across its shoulders, and foam dripped from long-toothed jaws. Tanta bounded in long strides on powerful legs, each leap carrying high, each descent exploding a geyser of red sand when his feet struck again.

The claws of the micas and his saber-tooth fangs were his only weapons against the four clawed forepaws, against teeth like sharp saws embedded in vise jaws.

Tanta leaped a moment before impact.

The groll skidded under him, raised on its hind legs, raking the air with claws extruded in furious search. Tanta landed behind the groll and roared defiance. The groll spun, spraying red sand, and lunged in a half leap far more accurate than total blindness allowed. Tanta saved himself by a sideways leap, but groll claws scored his leg from hip to knee, and blood ran.

The scent of fresh blood was strength for the groll. The beast wheeled in sudden furious excitement, the long tail scythed knee-high across the sands unexpectedly, and Tanta found his legs cut from under him. Lying on the sands, for an instant helpless, he heard the sudden roar from the throats of his warriors. A roar of fear, of pleasure, or only excitement? No matter. They thought him beaten.

He cursed them . . . cursed them all.

Twisting to his back, surging, suddenly arching, he sprang to his feet, and a powerful leap carried him above the groll as the beast pounced, groping and scratching deep furrows, on the sand where he had lain helpless an instant before. Tanta landed several meters away. Infuriated, he turned his back on the groll and ran to the high wall that circled the arena, and then, holding his mica-armed fists above his head in a defiant, threatening gesture, his baleful crimson eyes searching out faces as if bent on remembering those who might have cheered his near death, he ran the circumference.

When he had finished, the only sound was the snorting, coughing, and roaring of the groll as it raged about, charging blindly in search of him. Now, leg streaming red, Tanta turned back to the fight.

"Raaawwww!" he roared.

The groll heard him and charged.

Again, they met in the center of the arena, the groll scratching air and Tanta leaping above him. Tanta's feet found sand again beside the groll; a powerful sweep by Tanta's right arm raked the sharp claws of the mica down the side of the groll, ripping flesh, cutting deeply, laying ribs bare. The groll screamed and spun, coiling upon itself. But Tanta had leaped away out of reach to stand at a distance, defiant, disdainful, while the renewed voice of the throng filled the amphitheater with booming sound.

Tanta ignored them.

Proud, his mane erected, a radius of white about his head and shoulders, he stood with his powerful arms at his sides, the claws on the micas touching the sand beside his feet. He seemed utterly without fear. But he was not without fear. His right leg, bleeding, flaming pain, told him how near to death he had been, how near he still was.

There was *sight* in the eyes of the groll.

Someone had betrayed him!

The groll turned and found him—perhaps only a dim figure seen through a red, blood-clouded haze, but clear enough to recognize as his tormentor—and charged, his four forelimbs scattering sand. The charge was dead on target. Tanta waited until the last possible fraction of time, then leaped again.

"Raaaawww!" His roar was a yell of anger.

Descending, he dropped astride the back of the groll, clamping his legs about the rib cage. The writhing muscles of the beast coiled and strained against the bands of Tanta's inner thighs, but Tanta held securely. He reached forward, loosed the fingers of his right hand from the grip of the mica, and hooked those fingers into the snout of the groll. His hold secure, he dragged the head of the groll back. The groll fought, screaming, shaking his head in a frenzy, but Tanta's strength was relentless. The head came back, folding on the neck. The groll fell to its side, its forelimbs beating wildly, its body writhing...

Its throat exposed.

Tanta's lower jaw dropped. His saber-toothed, acca-encased tusks, gleaming knives, were fully exposed. Without haste but with sure and inexorable intent, Tanta leaned forward and drove those knives deep into the throat of the groll. He dug and found the main artery. He knew he had found the artery, and had cut it, when hot blood gushed into his mouth, sweet-tasting and steaming.

He had only to hold and he had won.

He held.

A great sigh came from the spectators.

Tanta, drinking the blood of the groll, cursed them again. He hated them as they hated him. But he had proved himself again. And they would follow him, conceding to him the right to lead them anywhere he chose.

Kana cleansed the deep cuts in his leg. She sewed the flesh closed where sewing was needed and wrapped the leg tight with bandages. The wound would heal; the scar would join the other scars. Tanta seemed unaware of any pain. A large flagon of ruduso was brought, and he drank it.

A draught of the gods.

Liquid fire.

He ordered the Tormentors who had been responsible for the blinding of the groll brought before him. They stood with eyes downcast, knowing they had failed, knowing the penalty. No trial was asked, and none was needed. The hooked blade of a knife was inserted into their throats and ripped downward, opening them to the groin.

It was not a quick death.

Renewed, Tanta went to the *anticuum*. Ra, the mother of the Ancans, resided here, in an enormous, eight-walled chamber lighted by beams from recessed amber lights. Her head was the head of a huge ant; her body was an enormous, segmented, pulsing tube that rose higher than Tanta's head and was longer than ten strides. She was fed constantly by the letas, the giant ants, whose only task was to bring her a special nectar. She was fed by other scurrying letas, while still other letas, specially bred for the purpose, took the eggs that appeared with regularity under her afterparts.

Ra was not the *true* mother of the Ancans. She was the progenitor only of letas, which came in various function-ordained physical configurations. Some were nurses, some were nursery designated, some were workers, some were food gatherers and garden tenders, some were builders that constructed octagonal cells. And some were used as draft animals to be worked, and often ridden, by the Ancans.

In a past so distant none knew how long ago it had been, the Ancans had been used by the letas in a symbiotic relationship, sometimes as food, sometimes as warrior protectors. Evolution had favored the Ancans, giving them intelligence and the body structure they had now, and they had become a superior species in almost every way. But they had not abandoned the relationship. The Ancans and the letas lived together still.

Each Ra, the queen ant—and each exceeded a

hundred otis of age in their time—was given the homage due a god-queen by every Ancan.

Thus it had always been.

Thus it would always be.

Tanta, raised and conditioned to this way, was unfailing. He entered the queen's chamber with regularity. He stood silently until Ra became aware of him. They did not speak, but they did communicate by some means Tanta could not describe. Somehow he knew her thoughts. Somehow she knew his thoughts. It was enough.

"You have been near death," she said to him.

"But I did not die."

"Others will try to take your life."

"Yes."

"And now?"

"They have taken the life of my son."

"What does this mean?"

"We are going to punish those who killed my son."

Ra was silent a long moment, her antennae still. Tanta knew the wisdom of his decision was being questioned and that presently he would be told if Ra approved or not. Her thought came at last.

"You will die."

"One day I must."

"By the hands you think to punish."

"This may happen."

The white mane lay tightly against Tanta's thick neck now, giving him a subdued appearance. But the red disks of his eyes held undiminished fire, and his resolve was not in the least shaken.

"Until it does..."

He left Ra. His lieutenants, who had waited outside the entrance to Ra's chamber, fell in step behind Tanta as he strode through several octagonal chambers to reach a chamber with the appearance of an operating room. The eight walls here were metallic, shining, the light a merciless glare.

Lying broken on a flat table was the body of an Orcan.

It was Rux S. Ris, the young noncommissioned officer whom E. Rox and Harry Borg had thought killed in the attack at the discovery site in the desert cul-de-sac. He had been sorely wounded, but he had not been killed then. He was dead now. He had died here, on this table, after the most excruciating torment the Ancans had been able to provide.

"What did you learn?" Tanta asked.

The Anca surgeon, whose coat of blue rynal still bore the stains of the Orcan blood he had drawn during the questioning of S. Ris, was moderately proud of his success.

"The name of the assassin."

"Are you sure?"

"Only one Orcan escaped," the surgeon answered. "And that must be the one who killed Sana."

"Only one Orcan killed my son and three others?" The question held disbelief and pain.

"It was so reported, sire."

"And you know the name of this Orcan?"

"Yes. After a very long and difficult interrogation. This—this Orcan gave me the name of the one who led them, and who fled. The one hunted by Sana. Who killed Sana and the others."

"The name, fool!"

"E. Rox, sire. E. Rox, of Orgas."

Tanta turned his red, glowing eyes on an Ancan who wore the uniform of the Ancan Special Elite. After a moment of holding the officer in a steady, penetrating glare, he spoke quietly. "I want E. Rox."

"Yes, sire."

"I want him brought here alive."

"Yes, sire."

"Alive. Is that understood?"

"Alive, sire. I had anticipated the order." The officer was confident. "I have the necessary information. I have set craccos to the task."

"The craccos. You are sure of them?"

"These craccos are slaves to me."

"Good!"

"E. Rox will be brought here to face you."

"Alive."

"Alive, sire. I make that promise."

CHAPTER 9

They came out of the cool darkness of the building interior into the bright sunlight of the Orcan midday, the two of them together, walking in the body of one sadly depleted Orcan.

"What I need," E. Rox said to himself, "is about a lax of crox, dark, foaming, and ice cold." And then he added, as an afterthought, "It does not need to be cold."

He went down the steps in a stumbling run. They were kraxle steps, about a hundred of them, leading down and away from the imposing, many-columned, kraxle-faced building that housed the headquarters of the Orcan intelligence, which meant, more particularly, the Civilian Department of Intelligence as well as the Military Internal Intelligence.

E. Rox had been debriefed.

He had just had, as Harry Borg would have said, "the livin' hell debriefed out of him!"

Two solid days of being questioned!

A rescue EVAC craft had picked them up in Atoxia and had flown them to Orgas, the central city of Orca, to a medical station for a quick patch job—E. Rox's left arm had suffered a hair fracture of the *fornta*, his saucer-like china-blue eyes looked out of bruise-blackened flesh, and his left antenna had been so badly sprained that a splint and a restraining bandage had been applied. Then they had been taken straight to the debriefing and had been absolutely wrung dry by a relay of very sharp-minded, suspicious, razor-tongued officers of the military and civilian intelligence. They had been released, just now, under what they called "close arrest." And that meant, E. Rox had explained to Harry, that he was confined to a certain carefully defined area.

"I've got a hunch what crox is," Harry said. "But what's a lax?"

He was with E. Rox still, the uninvited guest who, like fish after three days, had grown a little burdensome and was being endured by E. Rox only with weary patience.

The question Harry had just asked, "What's a lax?" had not really been necessary. He knew from experience that the average person would be wanting a *lot* of something after an ordeal like the one they had just been through.

"A measure of liquid."

"Big. Right?"

"Very big."

E. Rox reached the street level and, ignoring the cruising craxis, hurried straight across the busy thoroughfare and entered a building on the far side. No matter that it was on the planet Orca, in a city called Orgas, populated by a strange-looking people who were ten feet tall and as thin as sticks, who had huge blue eyes, three-foot-long antennae that draped down their backs or stood straight up like jackrabbit ears as the need required—no matter all of that: This was a saloon.

"I knew it!" Harry said.

When the rather lithesome female Orcan had served

E. Rox a very large container of something dark and foaming and ice cold, Harry knew what it was going to taste like when E. Rox gulped it down. And he was right. It tasted absolutely great. And when a warm balloon developed in the stomach he was sharing with E. Rox burst, and sent a pleasant heat that flowed through all his veins, Harry knew all too well what that was, too.

"That's booze!" he said accusingly.

E. Rox had another long drink. "Whatever booze is," he said aloud, uncaring.

"Son," Harry said, "take it from an old hand, this stuff is poison. I should know, I was on it over forty years. Never took a sober breath."

"And?"

"It'll kill you."

"Way to go." He was beginning to talk more like Harry all the time.

"Come on, now!" Harry said. "I'm serious. I don't drink that stuff!"

"Leave. Any time. Now would be fine." E. Rox finished the tall glass and found the waitress looking at him strangely.

"Are you talking to yourself?" she asked.

"You might say that," E. Rox told her. He hiccupped gently. "Another one of these," he said. "Make that two more. And bring them to that table over there, if you would be so kind."

When they were seated, Harry was still trying to guide his host along the straight and narrow, talking like a kind of a friendly, understanding Dutch uncle.

"This is probably the worst time for a boozer," he said. "When he's been through some kind of an ordeal, the first thing your average bottle fighter is going to want is a drink. To nail him back together, y' know? To heal his bruises. Well, sir, that's where he makes his first mistake. One drink will lead to another. And then a third. And then he's gone right down the tube."

"Are you some kind of ica?"

"What's an ica?

"'One who preaches."

"I'm not a preacher. I'm just trying to give you some good advice. And I know whereof I speak, son. I've been there. Pretty damn near killed myself with booze."

"The worst kind," E. Rox said, his suspicion confirmed.

"What is?"

"The reformed sinner," E. Rox said.

The waitress came with a tray bearing two tall drinks. She placed one before E. Rox and the other across from him where another might sit. She still was not sure about E. Rox. He thanked her, paid her, and she went away.

"Always trying to reform other sinners," E. Rox said, continuing. "Whether they want to be reformed or not."

"In this case, I'm trying to do you a favor."

"Toya," E. Rox said. "To sin."

He lifted his glass and drank deeply.

The drink was pleasant, Harry found, as it bombed into the stomach he and E. Rox were sharing. Extremely pleasant, as a matter of fact. Even salubrious. It was easing the pain of the bruises to a very noticeable degree. It was steadying their nerves, knitting up their raveled sleeves, as it were. Harry found himself eyeing the glass across the table.

"That one is for you," E. Rox said.

"I don't drink," Harry said flatly.

"I will have it, then," E. Rox said. He drank at least half of it in several long swallows. The drink had a very substantial effect on both Harry and E. Rox.

"I can feel that, too," Harry said.

"Pleasant, is it not?"

"No, it is not!" Harry was lying, and he knew it.

"If you don't like it—"

"I can leave, right?" Harry was a little angry—with himself as well as with E. Rox. He knew he shouldn't be liking what the booze was doing to him, but, on the other hand, what could he do about it? "You can bet your bippy I'd leave if I could," he said, without much conviction. "In a flash, pal. In a flash."

E. Rox had another long drink.

"Now, now," he said. "I do not want to seem inhospitable. You are welcome to stay as long as—" He hiccupped. "—nec—necessary."

"You're getting smashed!" Harry said.

"Smashed?"

"Snockered!" Harry said. "Looped. High. In a word, drunk!"

"Oh. You mean intoxicated."

"Right!"

"And you are opposed to such behavior."

"Very much so!"

"Even though you are sharing in the result?"

"Absolutely!"

E. Rox finished the glass and pushed it aside. He sat looking at the empty glass while the waitress hovered nearby, waiting for a signal.

"Perhaps we had best stop now," he said.

Harry looked at the empty glass with E. Rox and found himself thinking, with E. Rox, of how well another one, tall, cold, and foaming, would go with the others. With E. Rox, he licked his lips.

"Well?" E. Rox said.

"Okay," Harry said finally. "One more couldn't hurt."

E. Rox agreed promptly and signaled the waitress.

And they shared a third drink.

There was, of course, a fourth and a fifth, and after

the fifth neither of them went on counting. Which did not
mean that Harry allowed himself and E. Rox to get
smashed out of their socks by any means. Mellow is
what Harry got. E. Rox got very mellow. And Harry
could not find a lot wrong with it.

If ever a person—two persons in their case—had a
right to get mellow, it seemed to Harry that they were
that person. Or those two persons—whatever. It wasn't
easy to keep things straight, what with him being a guest
in a strange body and all, and the situation being what it
was. And it became less easy as the afternoon wore on.

They did have a lot hanging fire, or up in the air, or
still unresolved—or something.

To start with . . .

If, as E. Rox had reported to the intelligence people,
he had discovered a huge illegal colony of Ancans; and
if, after his unit had been destroyed and all his troopers
killed, he had fled on foot across the desert pursued by
Ancans; and if, after being brought to bay by four
Ancans, all armed, and he, unarmed himself, had managed to kill all four; and if, as he had reported, one of the
slain Ancans had been Sana, son of Tanta, Krill of the
Ancans—and the Intelligence people, both civilian and
military had found ample reason to doubt that any of this
was true—then there was certainly going to be, to use
the words of Harry Borg, the very hell to pay.

War with the Ancans, for example, was among the
very real possibilities. War had been building—everyone
knew it. The Ancans had increased their numbers so
enormously that a minority representation in government, which had been offered, was no longer enough.
Tanta wanted full control.

Why mince words?

He wanted to become the Supreme Authority on
Orca, and that included over *all* of Orca. The people, *all*

the people, all the creatures, species, and kinds on the planet.

Total control of the Orcans by the Ancans, meant slavery for the Orcans and eventual extinction, make no mistake about that. Tanta hated the living hell out of the Orcans, and if it was true that his son, Sana, had been killed by an Orcan, Tanta now had all the excuse he needed to get a full-scale war going.

If it was true . . .

If it was true that one Orcan, an Orcan named E. Rox, who was described in the Orcan military records as being an academic, whose only physical achievements worthy of note were several footraces he had won—if this non-warrior had been able to slay four armed members of the Ancan elite, among them one whom the Anca believed to be the most fierce warrior of all time, Sana, the son of Tanta . . .

"They don't believe you," Harry said.

He was holding the glass of crox up to the light, viewing the world in a relaxed, contemplative sort of way through the rich amber fluid, taking the fact that he had fallen off the wagon more or less in stride. E. Rox, being a bit under the weather, had retreated, allowing Harry Borg, the more experienced boozer, to take control, while he wandered about, contemplating other more personal matters.

But he was following the dialogue.

"Do not believe it my . . . sself," he said.

E. Rox had begun to slur his s's, an unfortunate impediment of speech, Harry knew, often suffered by those unaccustomed to strong drink.

"Believe it," Harry said. "I personally spiked that sucker with his own spear. I guarantee you he is deader than a politician's promise the day after election day."

"Imagine that . . ." E. Rox murmured vaguely.

"There has got to be two of you," the waitress said.

She had come to stand beside the table with another tray of drinks Harry had ordered. E. Rox looked up at her with large round eyes gone larger and rounder. And seeing her through those eyes, in a world that had taken on a rosy glow, Harry Borg found that he was impressed by her lithesome appearance.

The Orcan females—who were very much mammalian, Harry had been gratified earlier to discover—were very tall and very slender, to be sure, but the better formed females were attractive in a lean, sinewy way. Very attractive, Harry decided, now that he was giving the matter serious consideration. This one wore a costume of nearly transparent material that glistened with a nice metallic sheen. Her face, artfully enhanced with cosmetic colors, could be called beautiful. She had very large blue eyes, a pert nose, and delicately arched, beautifully feathered antennae.

"You got a name, honey?" Harry asked, his eyes wandering.

"See!" she said. "Now you are talking with a different voice."

E. Rox's attention was suddenly caught. He made a very serious effort to sober himself up and to regain control. He pushed Harry aside inwardly, assuming the dominant position.

"A difficulty with my throat," he explained to the waitress. "An old war wound. Or perhaps a new one." He indicated his bandaged antennae. "I was only recently in battle. I suffered severe abrasions."

E. Rox gave the waitress money and waved her away. Then, to Harry, he said, "She is not your species."

"But, if I'm sharing your body—"

"No!" E. Rox said.

He said it with sudden vehemence that was near an-

guish, for he had been reminded with sudden forceful-
ness of a difficulty that confronted him now that he had
Harry Borg as a guest. The difficulty was rather enormous, now that he thought about it again.

Staggering was the best word for it.

How was he going to conduct his intimate personal
life? With Harry Borg, Earthman, huge, bearded, lusty
—obviously very lusty, as he had just demonstrated in
his pass at the waitress—with such a personality as that
inside him, sharing his consciousness, how was he going
to be able to do *anything*?

The Earthman, sharing his body, would be privy to all
thoughts and emotions. He would be able to hear all that
was said. And—Ixxil forbid!—experience all the sensations he experienced!

Impossible!

In a previous discussion, Harry had agreed to keep
his distance, his gaze averted, and all else that could be
done to ensure E. Rox every possible privacy. But now,
with Harry fairly awash with booze and his less than
gentlemanly urges showing signs of being on the rise, E.
Rox was having second thoughts.

"This is not going to succeed," E. Rox said.

"What isn't?"

Harry's eyes were still on the thinly clad waitress, his
thoughts dwelling lazily on various possibilities, none of
which were remotely concerned with proper matters.

"Our relationship," E. Rox said. "I am able to share
my body with you. And to a certain extent my life. But
my *personal* life? Harry! You can't be serious!"

"I promised to keep my distance," Harry protested.
"And I'm a man of my word!"

"It is just not possible!" E. Rox had a quick gulp of
crox, then wiped his mouth with the back of his hand.
"How can I talk to O. Rani, how can I even face her with

you looking on, listening, waiting for me to—" He broke off, shaking his head in despair.

Harry could sympathize. "I keep telling you—get me out to Ursal, wherever that is, and let me get a few seeds of that ursis plant, take me back to Atoxia, and I'm gone! Gone back to Earth. Out of your life. Forever!"

"You know I can't do that."

"Why not?"

"I'm under close arrest—that's why not!"

"Come on! I don't see any cops! How are they going to know if you slip away for a day or two?"

"They would know. And if I am caught for violating a close arrest—yaaak! Execution! Or, at the very least, imprisonment for life." He shuddered violently at the thought. "That means both of us, you know!"

"Doesn't scare me."

"You haven't sense enough to be scared."

"I can get as scared as anybody," Harry said. "The trick is, you don't get caught. Listen, I know more ways to outsmart an enemy force than you would believe. Trust me! I can get us there. And I can get us back."

"No! I wouldn't dare!"

Disgustedly, Harry used E. Rox's hand to lift the lax for another drink of crox. "Then you're stuck with me," he said. "Sorry about that."

"What is Rani going to think?"

It was a rhetorical question, a plaintive rhetorical question, for this, too, was a subject E. Rox and Harry had discussed at some length before.

O. Rani, the young female Orcan whom E. Rox dreamed of some day taking as a mate, had been most difficult in the past months. She did not, first of all, approve of E. Rox's service in the "volunteer" forces of the Orcan military under any circumstances. She was against a military solution to *any* problem. More importantly, since the problem the military was using E. Rox to solve while he was in uniform was the "Ancan Problem," she had been most forceful in stating her objections.

O. Rani, Harry had learned, was an "Ancanic," which meant that she sympathized very strongly with the Ancan species. She also sympathized very strongly, Harry had learned after further questioning, with the rassles and the urssles, who were even "more oppressed" to use her language, and with the plight of the traaco, which was a flightless avian species nearing extinction, and with various other causes of one kind or another.

Harry had known a few like that.

O. Rani was very beautiful, if half of what E. Rox had told Harry was true. Beautiful and tender and caring. And she smelled absolutely great. But beautiful, tender, and caring as she might be, when it came to worthy causes, she was a bar of lixle, unbending, inflexible . . . and thus far E. Rox had not been able to persuade her that he was a cause as worthy as any of those others.

"I can help you with this," Harry had said when he had been first apprised of the situation. "Y' see, females are pretty much the same everywhere, be they Orcan or human. And when it comes to females, you aren't going to find a man who knows better how to handle them than I do. You let me take charge and I'll straighten her out for you in no time at all."

That had been simply an offer of a concerned guest made to a host who seemed to be having a problem. Harry had not been able to understand the near hysteria the offer had generated. E. Rox had practically jumped out of his socks, panting, sweating, and yelling. It had taken ten minutes to quiet him down.

And Harry still couldn't understand it.

But if his host did not want his help or his advice, why, that was fine with Harry. Harry had agreed to stay out of it. How he was going to stay out of it, being resident in E. Rox's body, had not been worked out in detail at that time. Since E. Rox had been in such an emotional state, Harry had thought they should leave the problem until later.

Now was later.

And now it was still not clear to Harry how he was going to stay out of it. One thing was sure: He was not going to leave E. Rox's body until he was back in Atoxia, the ancient city where the "receiver station" was located, with the seeds of the ursis plant packed and ready to go home.

"No way!" he muttered. "I'm staying!"

And for a couple of reasons. He *knew* E. Rox—that was reason number one. E. Rox was *family.* And on a strange planet, in a strange country, among aliens, family—a secure relationship—was important. A second reason was he had no way of knowing if he *could* get into another Orcan. Maybe E. Rox was his type or something. Like type O blood. And if he could not get into another Orcan, if he *were* rejected, for one reason or another, for even a short time, would he be able to retain his identity, or would he dissipate like a belch in a high wind?

No way of knowing, right?

And if a man didn't know double-damned sure, he would be a sucker to take chances. No chances, thanks. Things were tough enough already.

He was going to stay. Close enough, at least, so he could get back into E. Rox, if he had to, like a prairie dog down a hole when a hawk came over.

"That's a buy!" he said.

To seal his fierce determination, he had a couple of swallows of crox. And to make double sure it was sealed, he had a couple more, losing track, in the process, of how many that made altogether but not caring much about it one way or the other. There were more important things to be concerned about.

He had come all the way here to Orca to get that ursis plant, hadn't he? Betcher life! And for good cause. If he could get home with that plant, Los Ross, the little Jassan scientist, would be able to distill an antivirus, an interferon of some sort, from it that would prevent all sorts of diseases in humans—from the common cold to AIDS—and save lives.

Lives of grown-ups.

And little babies . . .

He had another drink for the little babies.

He was getting moody, he could tell. This here crox went down easy, he thought, but it had a lot of wallop once it started working.

Where was he? Oh, yes, he was worrying about E. Rox and his girlfriend. And how E. Rox was going to explain him to her.

Where was E. Rox, come to think about it?

Gone off to sleep somewhere . . .

Okay. He could go it alone in this dinky body, this bundle of sticks. Which wasn't all that bad, this body, come to think of it. Kicked the hell out of those Ancans, didn't it? All it took was a little know-how, and a man could do just about anything with any body . . .

Thinking about bodies reminded him of his own body. All right! He had to drink a toast to a great body like that. After drinking a toast to his great body, he looked up to find the waitress was watching him, an odd look on her face. He waved to her. She came over and asked if he would like her to bring him another drink.

He said sure.

She went away to get it.

He went back to thinking about his body.

Then he wondered how she, the waitress, would like the body, the real body, of Harry Borg. A body like that, he was willing to bet, would turn her on like a tree full of lights—and Los Ross had *lost* it?

Could you *believe* that? A great body like *his*? And Los Ross had lost it somewhere in outer *space*? In-flipping-credible! That's what it was! And here he was now, hanging around in some dinky Orcan's body—a ten-foot-tall bundle of galvanized pipe, was all it was—without a body to call his own.

Talk about a mess of hard luck!

Talk about lonesome!

Man, he was *far* from home.

He was surprised, then, in the midst of these realizations, to feel tears rolling down his cheeks. Or down E. Rox's cheeks, anyway.

He hadn't even known Orcans could cry.

"Roxie," he called inwardly. "Roxie, baby."

E. Rox came blearily to the fore. "Huh? Whatdchu say?"

"Let's get outa here," Harry said.

"Whazzwrong?"

"I'm bagged!"

"Bagged? Wha's bagged?"

"Stiff."

"Stiff?"

"Never mind. I can handle it."

Harry pushed E. Rox's body to his feet. But when he found that the room had suddenly taken a hard slant to the left, he decided he had better not get up. No way. In his condition he could very well run into something. He sat E. Rox's body down with a thump, jarring E. Rox awake again.

"Huh? Whazzamatter?"

"You drive," Harry said.

CHAPTER 10

The city of Orgas, the capital city of the Orcan nation, had been built to a specific design during a century when the Orcans had been obsessed with orderliness. Perfect straights and perfect circles had been their religion. The major streets radiated from a central hub in straight lines; the cross streets were concentric circles broken into major segments by the perfectly straight major streets, segments which in turn were broken into smaller segments by perfectly straight minor streets.

The buildings—some very tall, some not so tall—all fit their allotted segments perfectly. Since all of them were relatively new—built in the last century of that most durable of building materials, kraxle—they were tidy in appearance as well as orderly. There were growing things—trees, bushes, and the like, some flowering, some not—but since the growing things had been planted in an orderly fashion and were kept extremely neat by pruning and trimming, they looked more artificial than natural and more like each other than like anything else.

The whole city was very beautiful.

And monotonous.

And boring. Very boring.

But that was not the most difficult part about Orgas. The most difficult part, Harry Borg had discovered, was that one could get lost without half trying. Hell, everywhere looked the same as everywhere else. And the designations were impossible for an Earthman to understand. The bottom line was you had better depend on a craxi driver to get you where you wanted to go.

If you knew how to tell him where that was.

Harry had been able to get E. Rox to write down the address of the building where O. Rani lived before he had passed out entirely. "Rag 10, Tixt 405, #" was the way it came out in human terms, which wasn't even close to what it looked like when written in Orcan. But Harry didn't want to go to O. Rani's place yet.

They were too dizzy—him and E. Rox both.

"Of course I can drive!" E. Rox had said.

A bunch of bull! He hadn't been able to get them out the door.

Harry had taken over, finally. And he had gotten them out of the saloon only one jump ahead of the craccotypes who looked, or at least acted, like police—probably called in by the shapely waitress about the second time E. Rox had walked them into the broom closet he had thought was the way out. Out in the street, Harry had managed to flag down a craxi.

"Where to?" the driver had asked.

"Someplace where we can sober up," Harry had told him.

"We?"

"Me. Us. Whatever..."

In a country where they had saloons, there had to be a place where the folks who used the saloons—the drunks like himself and E. Rox—could go to get right-side-up again. Or so Harry had figured. And he had figured right, as it turned out.

The craxi driver took them to a spa in a mall beneath one of the taller buildings and turned them over to a doorman there. The driver explained to the doorman, a friend of his, that E. Rox and Harry were one soldier on leave so smashed that he thought he was two soldiers and it was causing him to talk funny.

Crox did that to a lot of people, the doorman said.

He said he would see to it this soldier got well in a hurry. A big bruiser, he took E. Rox by the arm and turkey-trotted him down a flight of steps into a locker room. Harry just went along. Another big bruiser in a tight shirt got him and E. Rox undressed and settled into a steamy kind of a cooking pot—some kind of a health bath.

There they soaked in a slickery, mudlike soup and drank about a gallon of some bitter-tasting drink that burned their throat on the way down and stung their nose on the way up. It seemed to work, though. After a couple of hours, Harry began to feel halfway normal again. E. Rox, however, became sure he was going to die. His head ached, his hands shook and his stomach quivered. To someone who hardly ever took a drink, those would seem like symptoms of a terminal illness, Harry supposed. But to a man who had spent the best part of his life fighting the bottle, they were hardly anything at all.

"You should try the DTs once."

"Krissilo," E. Rox moaned.

"What's that?"

"A dirty name."

"What'd *I* do?"

"Drank to excess . . . got us intoxicated."

"Me? You were right there, drink for drink!"

"Not willingly."

"Horse pucky!"

"Well, perhaps at first. But then you took over."

"So I did. After you started it. So now it's *all* my fault." Harry was pretending a lot more injury than he felt. "That's still no reason you should call me dirty names. Krissilo! That have anything to do with my mother? Like she lived under a porch and barked at strangers?"

"Never mind."

"My mother and father were married."

"Forget it. I apologize."

"I wouldn't have done *any* drinking," Harry went on, "if you'd left it up to me. I tried to talk you out of it, remember? I'm a *reformed* lush. What I said was—"

"Please . . . I don't want to hear."

They took an elevator to ground level and started toward the street door. Suddenly, Harry stopped them and moved behind a pillar. The three cracco-types who had almost nailed them at the saloon were on the walk outside the entrance, talking to the friendly craxi driver. That could mean only one thing: The craccos had traced the craxi driver, and the driver had brought them here. Why? Never mind why. They were here, they were armed, and they looked like they meant business. Harry was in no mood to be arrested, and E. Rox was in no mood to argue.

They stayed hidden.

"What, exactly, is a cracco?" Harry asked.

"A subspecies. A lower branch, servants mostly."

They looked almost like Orcans—same big kind of eyes, same antennae, but smaller and blockier—and these three wore sidearms.

"I thought they were cops."

"They are. But not government. Not city."

"Private eyes."

"Whatever that is."

"They work for anybody who'll pay them."

"Something like that."

"What do they want with us?"

"I don't know."

"Don't like it," Harry whispered inwardly. "Don't like it at all."

They stayed hidden until the three craccos entered the building and went down the stairs that led to the locker room, and then they went down a hallway to a different exit and found a different craxi. E. Rox was in control, scared but sober, and Harry was willing that it should be so.

"Where're we going?" Harry asked.

E. Rox didn't answer. He sat stiffly, staring out the window, trying to keep himself separated from Harry, who began to feel like a three-day-old fish again.

Unwelcome.

"Look, old buddy," he said. "I'm not *happy* here."

"I could drop you off—"

"You could take me out and get me that plant I came for. I'm not going to leave either your or this planet until I get it. The sooner I get it, the sooner I'm gone."

"Harry . . ."

"Tonight," Harry said. "We'll do a fade out—"

"I can't, Harry!" E. Rox was a little desperate. "You don't know how serious an offense it would be for me to leave the city when I've been placed under close arrest."

"Keerist, Katy!"

"What does *that* mean?"

"Means I had to pick a Nervous Nelly—" Harry broke it off in disgust. "Look. Take me back to that receiver station, that old city—what's its name?"

"Atoxia."

"Yeah. Take me back to Atoxia, and if Los Ross has

sent my body, I'll get out of you. Believe it, baby! I won't ask you for another thing. I won't even have to *see* you again."

"Harry! You're making me feel terrible!"

"*You* feel terrible. How d' you think *I* feel?" Harry was angry now as well as hurt. "I saved your ass out there in the desert. Killed that Sana sucker when you were ready to let him whack your head off, and this is the thanks I get. Get lost, Harry. Take a hike!"

"Oh, Lixxia!" It was a curse.

"You all right, soldier?" It was the craxi driver. He had been watching his agitated passenger in the rearview mirror, and he was concerned.

"Yes, I'm all right! Just take us...*me*...to Tixt 405 #."

"Yes, sir!"

To Harry, then, E. Rox said stubbornly, "It was your ass, too."

"What? Oh . . . yeah, all right. It was my ass, too. But I was the guy who got us out of it, okay? It was me pinned that rascal to the ground. So you owe me one. We *both* owe me one, when it comes right down to the bare facts."

"You sure you're all right?" the craxi driver asked again.

"Just tend to your business," Harry said.

"All right. Go ahead and talk funny," the driver said. "But there's something else you should know."

"Like what?"

"We're being followed."

Harry and E. Rox looked back. There was another craxi behind them with three occupants in the passenger seat. The passengers looked like the same craccos who had been at the saloon and at the health spa. And there they were again.

"What the hell's goin' on?" Harry wanted to know.

"I don't know," E. Rox said.

Harry was worried. "You in some kind of trouble you haven't told me about?"

"Trouble?"

The craxi driver said, "I can lose them...for a hundred nicks."

"A *hundred*?" E. Rox repeated.

"We got a hundred—whatever it is he said?" Harry asked.

"I—I think so."

"Better give it to him. I don't like the looks of those guys back there."

E. Rox found the required amount in his wallet—just about all he had left—and gave it to the driver. The driver settled back in seat. "Better buckle down," he said. And when he was sure E. Rox—and Harry—was secure, he touched a couple of buttons, moved a lever, and the craxi was suddenly transformed into a rocket. E. Rox and Harry were rammed into the back of the seat, then whipped hard to one side, then hard to the other, then up against the driver's seat, then back against the seat back again. Then he did it all again. Several times. He scared the living wallop out of E. Rox. He scared Harry, too, as far as that went. When it finally ended, they were limp as one rag.

"Where are we?" E. Rox asked groggily.

"Where you wanted to go." The driver was smugly unconcerned. "Tixt 405 #, I believe you said. And that will be thirty nicks more."

E. Rox looked back in search of the pursuers.

"Gone," the driver said. "Crashed into a divider."

Tixt 405 # was a tall building, no different from any other as far as Harry could tell. "What's here?" he asked.

"This is where Rani lives."

"Oh, sure. You gave me the address."

E. Rox gave the driver the rest of his money, and they went through an entrance into an atrium planted with shrubs that were strange to Harry and suggested carnivores. They had spike-fringed petals that were open wide enough to consume a horse. The atrium was lighted by a skylight above, and it was filled with delightful fragrances, or what the antennae Harry was sharing with E. Rox described to Harry as something that smelled very, very good.

There were lifts to take them to upper floors, but instead of going directly to them, E. Rox went to stand beside a pool and stare down at the fishlike creatures swimming there.

"What the hell?" Harry asked.

"I do not understand 'What the hell?'"

"You're acting funny again," Harry said. "One minute you're so antsy to see your girlfriend you can't stand it, the next you're standing around looking at fish. If they are fish."

"They are fish."

"Well?"

"Harry, I want to ask you a favor."

Harry was feeling magnanimous, among other things. And fatherly. "Sure, son," he said. "Ask away."

"I haven't seen O. Rani in almost six dicos . . ."

"Six dicos would be like six months, our time," Harry said. "And that's a long time, son. A *very* long time."

"And while Rani and I *do* disagree about certain things . . ."

E. Rox was nervous, fidgety, embarrassed, which said clearly to Harry that E. Rox was trying to address a delicate subject and didn't quite know how to go about it. Harry knew what the subject was, but, perversely, he wasn't about to give E. Rox any help.

As a matter of fact, he was grinning to himself. "But you don't disagree *all* the time. Right?" he suggested.

"There *are* some things...things of...ah, a rather *personal* nature...about which we *do* agree."

Harry relented. "I know, son. I know."

"You do?"

"Of course I do! It's the same with us humans. You take one of us, and we've been in the service, say, six months, and we finally get home on leave, and there's the wife, or the girlfriend, the first thing we're going to want to do is—"

"Harry!"

"Okay, okay!" Harry said. "I just wanted you to know I understand—"

E. Rox was relieved. "I am glad to hear that."

"—and I can hardly wait."

"*What*?"

"I said I could hardly wait. Since I'm more or less livin' in here with you, I guess whatever you do, or smell, or feel is going to come through to me, loud and clear."

"And you mean you—" E. Rox couldn't say it.

"Yeah!" Harry said with relish. "It should be a ball!"

E. Rox was shocked. "Harry! How *could* you?"

Harry was unabashed. "I dunno. I guess what people used to call me is true."

"What did they call you?"

"A dirty old man."

When E. Rox found out exactly what "a dirty old man" was, he couldn't have agreed with Harry more. And he was more than shocked; he was horrified. Such behavior, such an attitude, was, he told Harry, totally unacceptable. He was too much of a gentleman to embellish "unacceptable" with profanity, but an icy hauteur can sometimes serve as well.

"Shucks," Harry said.

He said he was just curious about how Orcans did it. It would only be a kind of an independent biological survey that might be useful—in a purely scientific sense, of course—to the folks back home who made a business of recording the various customs of species everywhere.

"Under no circumstances!"

Translated into American, that would have been, Harry knew, "No, flippin', damned way!"

And E. Rox went on to describe Harry as crude, rude, and about as far from couth as a person could get, which, again in American, would have been a lot spicier. With more sting.

"You talk *dirty!*" Harry said, pretending shock.

What E. Rox wanted was for Harry to disembark, as it were, here in the atrium and wait until morning. The atrium was pleasant enough and warm, with greenery and fish to look at. It was softly lighted all night. First thing in the morning, E. Rox promised, he would come back and pick Harry up again.

"How many times have we been through this? The answer is still the same: No way!"

"But, Harry!" E. Rox pleaded. "I'm not asking you to leave permanently! It would be only for a little while! And if you began to fade or feel ill, you could come right back. I promise! Just for an hour, Harry? Or two or three?"

"Sorry," Harry said flatly. "I can't take a chance like that."

"But, Harry—"

"Too many things could go wrong."

There were those damn craccos, for instance.

Remember them, he said. Suppose they came back

and sneaked up and caught E. Rox while he was in the sack smooching, or whatever it was Orcans did when they were fooling around. Where would yours truly be then? Harry wanted to know. He and E. Rox hadn't figured out what it was those craccos wanted so bad they would chase them so hard, had they? Hell, no! It wasn't because they wanted to pin a medal on anybody, you could bet your ass!

Shoot holes in them was more like it.

"All right, Harry! Say no more!"

E. Rox's surrender was complete. He strode to the elevator, his antennae hanging limply down his back, a thoroughly subdued and defeated young Orcan. Which was to be expected. There was nothing in the Orcan culture that might have conditioned him to cope with a human personality like Harry Borg, who, by Orcan standards at least, could be as abrasive as a kraxle crusher.

"But you *are* going to be disappointed," he said.

"Why is that?"

"I can wait another six dicos," E. Rox said. "Or twenty!"

"Before what?"

"Before I will perform for a pervert."

"Party pooper," Harry said.

O. Rani lived in a very nice apartment. Not upper crust but comfortable. Very. There were deep-cushioned carpets, warm colors, and sofas and chairs large enough to accommodate the ten-foot-tall Orcans. Floor to ceiling draperies billowed gently in scented air. After gaining admission into these pleasant surroundings with certain pressures on a security control, E. Rox called out to announce his presence.

"Rani! I am home!"

He was answered by a delighted squeal. "Rox . . . darling!"

She came from another room in a rush, a slender creature, lightly clothed, beautifully scented. She threw her arms around E. Rox's neck, pulled his head down, and entwined her antennae with his antennae ...

Whammo!

Harry's lights turned *on!*

His bells chimed!

Entwined antennae, Harry had just discovered, was a marvelous embrace. Better than kissing. Much better. More stimulating. Sweeter. Tender as flower petals. It wasn't really like kissing. It was more like—

"Never *mind!*" E. Rox yelled.

"Oh, sorry," Harry said.

Their intercommunication was silent, heard only by them. But the messages got through, loud and clear.

O. Rani ended the embrace.

She disengaged her antennae, though she held to E. Rox still, her wonderfully warm body pressed against him. Smiling, she looked up into his face. Looking down at her, seeing her as E. Rox saw her, Harry was impressd.

This girl was a keeper! No doubt about it!

Her delphinium-blue eyes were absolutely huge. Her mouth was a plumlike treasure, her little ski-jump nose a sheer delight. And she felt so warm and pliant in E. Rox's arms ... so ... so *promising!*

"It has been so long, Roxie," she murmured.

"Yes! Yes, it has," E. Rox said rather crisply. He disengaged her arms, turned her, and guided her to one of the sofalike lounges. She was surprised, prehaps even a little hurt, at what seemed to be rather abrupt behavior for a lover after such a long separation.

"What is wrong, Rox?"

"Wrong? Is something wrong?" How do you tell your best girl you have brought along a visitor who wanted to be a spectator. Spectator, *rozzoto*! This Earthling was a visitor who wanted to *share*!

"You act so strange," she said.

"Strange . . . oh, strange. Yes! Well, it must be the wounds."

"Wounds?"

"My war wounds. I, uh . . . had rather a bad time . . ."

They sat down, holding hands.

Harry chuckled. "War wounds! What a crock!"

O. Rani was all sympathy. "You poor thing!"

Her gentle fingers caressed the bruises on E. Rox's face and touched his bandaged antenna. "You stay right here and I will bring you something good to drink."

"Really, I should not—"

But she was already gone to another room.

"Wow!" Harry said.

"Please," E. Rox said wearily.

"Y' know what you got there?" Harry asked. "Class! That's what that lady is—pure class!"

"A compliment, I presume."

"You better believe it!" Harry was all eager enthusiasm. "And listen. That business of entwining the antennae—absolutely great! Never felt anything like it in my life. Went all through me. Wham! Bam! Thank you, ma'am!"

"Harry—"

"Can't wait to find out what the rest is like!"

"Harry—"

"Be a blast!" Harry said. "Gotta be!"

"Fissle!" E. Rox said.

O. Rani came back with a tray of drinks. They were tall glasses of something that looked like crox, only fizzier. Harry decided that at a time like this, it wouldn't hurt if a man on the wagon dragged a foot for a while. He was glad when E. Rox—for an entirely different reason than partying—reached quickly for a glass and gulped the contents.

"I think I will get intoxicated," E. Rox said to no one in particular. "Very intoxicated."

"Not too snockered," Harry warned. "Not with what we've got coming up!"

E. Rox decided that his only hope was to get himself snockered—whatever that was—enough so that nothing could happen. And he set about doing just that with a vengeance. The last thing he remembered, when he awakened later, was standing in the bedroom with O. Rani helping him out of his clothes. And when he awakened to stare blankly at the ceiling, he suddenly realized that he and O. Rani were alone.

Very much alone.

Harry Borg was gone!

Thank Osmos!

The visitor from Earth, that uncouth barbarian, had *some* decent sensibilities, after all! E. Rox reached for the warm and pliant O. Rani, the love of his life. She turned at his touch. Her voice was sleepy but warm and willing.

"Again?" she asked.

CHAPTER 11

Those enormous characters out there wearing lion fright-masks were up to *no* good. Lori knew that for sure. They were just waiting for her to show herself again, and when she did—*zap!*, they were going to knock her out of the sky like a duck on opening day. And probably have her for dinner.

Why else would they dress up like that?

There were six or eight of them. They had silver-metal-fabric uniforms with scarlet insignia; they had overgrown automatic pistol-looking weapons, and curved knife-type swords at their belts, and they'd come in some kind of air-ground battle vehicle. So they were warriors. And warriors wore fright-masks when they were out to kill people, right?

Everybody knew that.

She had arrived on this "godfordammit planet"—her words—early that morning, after a ride that had scared "the holy hell"—again, her words—out of her.

She had felt no pain during that ride. None at all. Just the weirdest, zaniest stretching out, stopping, going bunch of sensations she had ever dreamed of experiencing in her

128

wildest nightmares. Sometimes cool. Sometimes hot. Racing through some kind of a black emptiness . . .

A ride like that would be worth a lot in an amusement park, she thought. It would make millions.

"Hyah! Hyyah! Hyah! Step right up, children of all ages. Get the thrill of a lifetime. Just one dollar, one tenth part of a sawbuck. See outer space with your very own eyes!"

A real gas! She would guarantee it.

But don't go, would be her advice now.

For a number of reasons, not the least of which was when you got where you were going, to this planet Orca, for example, the first thing you would have to do would be to use a facility. The ride would have scared you that much. And then you would find, as she had found, that there were no damn facilities.

When she'd arrived on this planet she'd found herself in a weird vault. The walls and the ceiling had been of some strange glowing material, like metal, and she had found herself lying on a kind of a table with glasslike rods that pulsed and radiated warm light all around her. When she had tried to move, she had found she could move fine. All her parts had been in excellent working condition, except there had been a couple of problems.

When she had tried to walk, it had been as if her feet had come unglued from the floor—as if she were floating. With every step she had tried to take, she had bounced. Her head had even hit the ceiling twice before she had caught on to walking carefully. The other thing was that she had needed to go to the ladies' room.

But there had been no ladies' room. No men's room. No damned nothing! What a way to run a see-the-universe ride! Those next ten minutes had been agony. Hop on one foot, then the other, knock her knees together. Cuss . . .

To add to her troubles, there had been that confounded little quiss. A *quiss*, already! Like the ones they had on

Essa. And where the heck had *that* nasty little critter come from? The quiss had kept running at her feet.

She had finally found a rack of buttons, and pressing one had opened a door to the great outside. A fast, bouncing run to a rock a safe and sanitary distance away —she had been in time, barely.

Only then had she looked around . . .

What a country! Old! Old, old, old. Older than Methuselah! The buildings were red, crumbling ruins. There hadn't been anybody living around here for a thousand years, maybe two thousand—it was that empty.

Everybody was absolutely *gone*!

A desert wind was blowing. A red sun was shining.

Hot! Hot, hot, hot.

And so, where was Harry?

There was no Harry. No Harry of any kind.

Here she had been, about a block from the underground room with all those pulsating glass tubes, feeling physically very much relieved, almost human again, and then, suddenly, there *they* came!

Whoosh!

The aircraft had appeared out of nowhere. Once on the ground, those huge characters in lion fright-masks had gotten out and had begun poking around. She had hopped up to see what they were doing. Just a little hop. A *little* hop! She'd forgotten about the weak gravity, and the hop had carried her about thirty feet into the air— some hop! And there she'd been, way up in the air, waving her arms, trying to keep her balance, when one of them had seen her and had yelled at the others.

"Raxxi!" Or something like that.

Now they were about a hundred yards away, hiding behind the crumbling red walls of an old, old building, peeking out, jumping back. Trying to think what to do, she supposed. Like what was the best way to blow her into a million bits and pieces.

Along with their fright-masks, they each wore a head-dress that made it look as if they had manes. Lion's manes, growing out of the backs of their necks and shoulders! And, as if that weren't enough, they had armed themselves up with fangs! Regular tusks, sticking out from under their upper lips. Holy saints, what next?

And that was the situation—there they were, the warriors on this strange planet, and here she was, Lori Borg, Earthwoman, and she didn't know what the hell they were going to do next.

And to top it all off, she'd had nothing to eat for the Lord only knew how long. She was *famished*! Add famished to scared, and add both to lonely, and you had one very miserable lady.

They didn't come after her, they didn't go away...

What Lori didn't know was that the Ancan patrol that had discovered her was in a fix of their own. A fix that was, in ways that were peculiar to them, as difficult as hers.

They didn't know what she was.

They had been searching through the ruins of Atoxia in the area where they had been told there had been an outpost of Orcans—probably the outpost from which the Orcan who had killed Sana had come—when, after landing for a ground search, they had seen, rising up into the sky, this strange creature.

A tansy.

That is what Rogo the Elder had said it was.

Rogo was a reader who had made a study of ancient myths and who believed in tansies, and glifts, and toths, and other such magical things. If he said that what they had seen flying above the ruins was a tansy, well, all right. No one was going to argue with him. Certainly, it had been like nothing any of them had ever seen before.

No matter.

Whatever it was, magical or not, military law required that they report what they had seen to Higher Authority, and after reporting it, they had to wait until Higher Authority thought it over and had decided what ought to be done. That was what Higher Authority was doing now: thinking it over.

And the patrol was waiting.

Finally, over the field communication system, the patrol was informed that Higher Authority thought what they had encountered was undoubtedly a tansy. If it was in fact a tansy, and not a glift, it was the first tansy anyone had seen since the reign of Ranta IV, a thousand recos ago. If it were a glift, it most probably would have killed them before this. Therefore, if they were still alive and not dead, they could presume it was a tansy. Since it was a tansy, then, as it seemed to be, they were to make every attempt to capture the creature, being careful to do it no harm, so that it could be studied by Higher Authority.

They were also informed that a tansy, when alarmed, displeased, or in any way frightened, had been known— according to a legend often recounted but never verified —to have the power to obliterate an entire village with the mere pointing of a wand.

The Ancan patrol, after a prolonged discussion among themselves, discovered that there was none among them who wanted to be the victim of a pointed wand. Having discovered that, they decided that a show of reverence was perhaps the best way to go about beginning the capture of the tansy.

Thus it was that when Lori Borg, who was more frightened and tense than she knew, gave another little hop up so she could see what the warriors were doing and, because of the lesser gravity of Orca and her tenseness, soared thirty feet again into the air, to hang there twittering—waving her arms to keep balance, actually, and only *seeming* to fly—saw the Ancan line themselves up on their hands and knees, facing away from her, in a posture that was considered by them to be one of craven obeisance but which seemed to her to be preparation for a dreadful kind of attack.

Skunks did it like that, didn't they?

She panicked. Three terrified hops took her back to the entrance to the underground vault that housed the receiver station. One more hop—it was really more like a dive—took her back inside the vault, sprawling across the floor, banging into apparatus. She regained her feet, scrambling, got back to the control panel, and pushed the button that closed the door.

She was standing with her back against the vault door, feet braced, for perhaps five minutes before she became aware that the apparatus was humming softly. Now the humming grew gradually louder. The glowing tubes of light took on a violet tinge that deepened to red. They began to pulse very hard, straining, as if in some way strange to them they were going to give birth.

"Harry?" Lori asked hopefully.

Then, becoming certain, she yelled, delighted, "Harry! It's about time! Where in the hell've you *been*?"

A figure was beginning to take shape on the table beneath the pulsing red lights, obscured for the most part by the eye-blinding radiance, and Lori's joy at the prospect of being rescued by Harry Borg faded as she began to see the shape was not nearly big enough to be that of her beloved Harry.

Who, then? What, then?

Watching with a frightened stare, one hand at her throat, the other at her mouth, she watched as the eye-blinding radiance dimmed and faded and the newcomer assumed a recognizable shape. Then her joy returned in an almost equal magnitude.

"Sissi!" she yelled.

Sissi was dressed in the battle fatigues Harry had had made for her during the war between the Jassans and the Ussirs on the planet Essa, complete with the Red Flame shoulder patch, belted short sword, and sidearm. Her huge, vertically slitted golden eyes were concealed behind the gray inner lids, and the delicate tips of her forked tongue were just visible, quivering under her nostrils. Her color was not good, Lori thought. There was usually a faint blush under the gray, almost imperceptibly scaled skin, but now her face had a purplish, compressed look. Before Lori could develop a real concern, Sissi's golden eyes popped open to stare directly into Lori's eyes. Her first words were quick and urgent:

"Where's the ladies' room?"

Lori's answer was a yell of delight. "There isn't any!"

"What do you mean?"

Lori was hugging her, laughing and crying at the same time, so happy to find a friend, someone she knew, loved, and trusted that she didn't know what to do.

"Sissi! Sissi! I'm so glad you came! You came? Why'd you do it? You silly dope! Oh, I'm so glad you did! It's terrible here. There's a bunch of bad guys outside. Big bandits! They're wearing lion masks. And these great big headdresses! You wouldn't believe how scary—"

"Lori!" Sissi's plaintive telepathic cry. "I have to *go*!"

"Yeah, I know. Me, too." Lori wiped at her happy tears. "I mean—well, anyway. There's no ladies'. No men's, either. I went outside. But you can't. Those bad guys, they got down on their hands and knees and aimed their—"

Sissi pushed Lori aside with a strength born of desperation. Her feet touched the floor, she bounced up, and her head hit the ceiling, and she yelped—telepathically, to be sure—and when her feet hit the floor, she scurried down a short hallway out of sight. Lori waited, afraid to think, and presently, when Sissi returned, straightening her uniform, sighing with relief, she couldn't help being shocked.

"Sissi! You didn't—" she began, and then thought better of it. "Never mind. Don't tell me. I don't want to know."

"What about those bad guys?' Sissi asked.

"There's six or eight of them."

Lori rapidly recounted all that had happened to her since her arrival on Orca—her troubles, her solutions— and Sissi listened with sympathy and amazement.

"Lion masks! Imagine!"

"Manes, too!" Lori said, gesturing. "All around their heads. And, Sissi, they're wearing fangs. They stick way down, like this, below their chins!"

"Name of Osis!" Sissi got her sidearm out of its holster and checked the load. It was fully energized, its rays capable of burning a fist-size hole through almost anything.

"I didn't think to bring one," Lori said enviously.

"You can use my sword," Sissi offered.

Lori took the sword and swung it, doubtfully, a couple of times to try it out. It was better than nothing. She decided to keep it.

Then they heard a voice addressing them telepathically.

"O Queen. O Queen of Tansies," the voice said. "We beg of you. Hear us. Come forth so that we may honor you . . ."

There was more—a lot more.

And while what they said was not exactly those words—indeed, they were only thoughts and not words at all—the meaning of what they said was plain enough. The telepathic voice went on at some length and in even greater detail, while Lori and Sissi stared at each other, their eyes growing round with wonderment and disbelief.

"You hear what I hear?"

"I think so . . ."

The bad guys outside were Ancans, they said. They were honored that Lori, a tansy—whatever that was— had come to their land, now, in this time of great need. They had not meant to frighten her. They meant her no harm. In all truth, what they wanted was the privilege of paying her homage.

"Homage? To me, *homage*?"

"They think you are a queen or something."

"Why would they think a thing like that?'

"You were flying."

"I can't *fly*! I just jumped up, and zowie! I could hardly get down again. It's the gravity!"

"They *thought* you were flying."

The telepathic voice from outside came on again. The bad guys out there had the idea that she was a tansy, some kind of a fairylike creature with magic powers, they said. And they kept begging her to come out so she could wipe her feet on them, or thoughts to that effect. They were so sincere that it was hard *not* to believe they were telling the truth.

She could even bring her handmaiden, they said.

"What *handmaiden*?"

"They mean me," Sissi said.

"But you're not a servant!"

"I'll be your servant, your handmaiden. I'll be anything I have to be to get us out of here. We haven't a thing to eat or drink, you know. We can't *stay* here! We can look. If they are not what they seem to be, I can make holes in them."

Lori was unsure. "Harry might come back . . ."

"When?"

"Well, he . . . you know . . . if he's around he might—" She broke it off. "Y' got a point there. Maybe never."

"We could at least open the door and look."

Lori went back to the panel of buttons, found the right one, and pushed. Before the door swung open, she took a position in front of Sissi, her sword gripped firmly in her right hand. And since the chamber was an underground one, there was a short ramp and a flight of crumbled old steps to climb. Once these had been negotiated, and she and Sissi were at ground level, they found themselves looking out over a flat area where seven Ancans were on their hands and knees, facing away.

"Watch it!" Lori warned Sissi.

When she explained why, Sissi said, "Rubbish!"

"If you knew about skunks, you wouldn't be so smart."

"I know about these."

"So what do we do now?"

"You are the queen."

"Yeah, sure." Lori found that her knees were shaky. She took a deep breath to get steady, then, in what she hoped was an imperious tone, she addressed them. "Arise, vassals!"

"All right!" Sissi whispered admiringly.

The seven Ancans remained kneeling, shivering for a moment. Then one of them with special insignia on his uniform—probably the equivalent of a sergeant's stripes —said something in a guttural language to the others. They remained kneeling while he got slowly to his feet.

"Holy torpedo!" Lori whispered.

"Big," Sissi agreed.

Big, nothing! He was colossal! He was nearly ten feet tall, counting the headdress, which for some reason was kind of laid back at the moment, combed down. He had wide, hair-covered shoulders and long arms... *Long arms!* He could scratch his ankles without stooping!

Lori was terrified.

But since he was acting meek, and since he had said

she was a queen tansy or something, she thought it best to brave it out. She squared her shoulders and assumed a regal air.

"Those masks," she said. "They've got to go!"

To lend emphasis, she had unconsciously, in the manner of a mother shaking a scolding finger, shaken the sword at the Anca sergeant—and at the others, who had been peeking—with an absolutely astonishing result.

"For heaven's sake!"

They had *flattened*!

All of them. If it had been possible to dig under, they would have done that, too, but as it was they were as prone as giants could get, shivering, faces pressed to the ground.

"What happened?"

"The sword scared them," the ever-observant Sissi answered.

Lori was shakily delighted. "Hey, that's okay!"

"If you can control them with it, we're in business."

"Looks like I can."

To test her authority, she ordered the giant Anca to their feet, waving the sword in a commanding way, but being careful not to point it directly at them.

And it worked!

They all got up very carefully.

It must be said that Ancans were as brave as any species under normal circumstances—in the face of known dangers. I was only the unknown that frightened them, things like magic wands—and they had, in fact, assumed the sword was the magic wand they had heard about—or religious dogma. And this pretty little fairylike creature was so utterly different from anything any Anca had ever *really* seen that common sense dictated they shouldn't take chances.

"O Queen of Tansys," the sergeant begged humbly. "Your smallest wish is our command."

"Okay," Lori said, all business. "The first thing we're going to do is get rid of those masks."

"Masks?" the sergeant asked. He seemed honestly puzzled.

Lori, perhaps a little giddy with her success, certainly not as tentative as she might have been, advanced on the giant Anca, gave a very tiny hop—she was beginning to learn about the Orcan gravity—fixed her fingers into the hair above the Ancan's eyes, and gave it a hard tug.

Nothing happened.

The mask stayed in place.

And Lori found herself staring, eyeball to eyeball—hers startled, wide, and gray; his equally startled, huge, and glowing red—into the eyes of the Ancan. Her sudden shriek quite possibly frightened the Ancan as much as it did Sissi. The Ancan stood frozen. Sissi followed the sudden, whipping flight of Lori back into the vault and helped her get the big door clunked shut again.

"Lori! What in the name of Osis—"

"They're *real*!" Lori gasped, almost gibbering.

"Real? What is real?"

"Their faces!"

"Masks?"

"Faces! Those are their *real* faces! Lion faces! Fangs! Manes! Even bad breath! They are *not* wearing masks, Sissi! Those are their *real* faces!"

"So?"

Lori stared at Sissi. "What d' you mean, so?"

"I mean, so what if they've got lion faces?"

Lori was shocked. "I'm not going to be queen for anybody with faces like *that*!"

CHAPTER 12

They came out of darkness, a legion of them, stalking out of the plain, ponderous in their battle gear, hulking dark shadows, the gleam of whitened fangs a promise of savagery, the lancing purple beams of their weapons reaching out and exploding all that moved or threatened.

They were huge, with hair-covered shoulders and powerful arms so long that fingers trailed the ground. Their manes, already frightening enough, were dyed shimmering colors and stiffened to stand erect and radiate about their heads. Bandoliers crossed massive chests; wide big-buckled belts held curved knives designed for no other purpose than to decapitate.

Inexorable. Merciless. These were the warriors of Anca.

A. Bir, an Orcan who made a decent living in irrigated fields raising twoll, the grain that was the staple of the Orcan diet, was on his way to his fields when he saw them coming. The four moons that ringed the planet Orca had already set, and the enormous red sun was still only a promising glow on the horizon when he saw the hulking shapes bobbing with their shuffling strides in the deep shadows.

"Kammos!" was his first, mistaken thought.

A herd of kammos, enormous grain-eating beasts, could destroy a field of twoll in a hour's time, and with the twoll would go a deco's work and the savings of years. That would be a catastrophe almost beyond enduring.

This was far worse.

As they neared, A. Bir, his antennae erect, quivering with anxiety, caught the stinging, acrid scent he knew too well and realized that they were not a herd of kammos, not simply the end of a deco's work and the savings of years, not simply a catastrophe.

They were the end of life.

They were Anca, finally risen.

There could be no mistake about that now—the long-dreaded Final Days had begun. And in this moment of sudden clarity, he knew that there had never been any doubt in his mind, or in the minds of others like him who gathered evenings in the latos for a convivial cup of steaming crox, that this moment would—*must!*—one day arrive.

The mathematics were inescapable.

Each Orcan like himself produced, on average, one young, while each Ancan produced, on average, *eight* young. The number of Orcans, then, remained constant, while the number of Ancans increased by a multiple of eight: each Ancan young producing eight more Ancans, and each of these eight producing another eight, and each of these yet another eight.

And they *all* lived a long, long time.

No reasoning, no bargaining, no compromising could hope to stay the inevitable result of this disparity. *They*, the Ancans, would eventually prevail. They *must* eventually prevail. And when they did prevail, then *they*, gross and savage, and not the slender, gentle, and caring

Orcans, would guide the destinies of all living things on the planet Orca. All the inequities of past centuries—a few real and a multitude only fancied or invented by the Ancans to serve their purpose—would be called into accounting. The debt would be found to be enormous. Full payment would be demanded, and full payment would mean obliteration.

Death to all Orcans—a special kind of death.

For the Ancans had found that only one kind of death would satisfy the hate-lusts so long held—first in colonies nurtured by the giant letas when they were few, then in caves of their own, then in skin tents, and, as the centuries wheeled and their numbers began to increase enormously, in cities built in the hexagonal shapes of leta dwellings—a hate-lust that could be satisfied only by a powerful stroke of the hook-shaped sword, a head lifted by antennae held in a clenched fist . . .

A final retribution.

A. Bir turned and ran back to his home, his long thin legs carrying him in bounding leaps. He knew he was going to die. And he knew that his family was going to die. And that all in the small community of Sovan were going to die.

Nothing could save them.

The gunships of Orca would come after the alarm had been sounded, and they would exact a terrible revenge for whatever crime had been committed, scything down the Ancans with bolts of purple light for as long as the bolts and the Ancans lasted. But they would come too late. The community of Sovan, and all the inhabitants, would have suffered total obliteration.

A. Bir ran on.

His wife, T. Bir, met him as he came in. She knew at once that the final day had come—he had returned from the fields, running, even before daylight had fully come, his face gone white, his enormous blue eyes full of pain. The disks of her light-blue eyes became huge and round with anguish; her antennae, lovely and expressive fronds, so loved by A. Bir, fell, broken with her anguish, one to this side, one to that.

He caught her in his long, frail-seeming arms. His antennae sought hers, entwining, comforting. They were only a moment thus, giving and taking support, and then they broke apart. They had planned for this moment, yet there was much to be done.

"Tris! Trix!"

The half-grown children came. The four of them ran to a redoubt A. Bir had built and stocked with the few weapons the government allowed—long-barreled tovas capable of firing a dozen bolts of zun with reasonable accuracy. Token weapons, capable of only limited destruction. And the family waited.

With the huge red sun at their backs, the Anca came striding. Unhurried. Powerful. Inexorable. A few Orcans, like A. Bir and his family, chose to fight. A. Bir watched as the thin bolts of zun from the weapons of the defenders cut into the ranks of Anca, cleaving an arm, a leg, even a head, but slowing the enemy not at all. Others simply walked out and knelt, accepting their fate.

The Ancan had no understanding of mercy.

An Ancan cared nothing for life—not his life, not the life of any other. Life, itself, was not a concept an Ancan understood. One was, or one was not; it did not matter. What alone mattered was doing exactly what one had been told to do by one who had the authority to tell one what to do.

They had been told to behead all Orcans. This they would do.

When an Orcan knelt before them, or when one was shot, or when one was caught fleeing, the ritual slaying occurred—the gripped antennae, the head lifted, the neck stretched, and then the sweeping stroke of the hook-bladed knife that severed the head.

"Araaaaaaagh!"

The deep-throated, bellowing roar, with head tipped back, enormous mouth agape, and tusks gleaming, came while the severed head, blood spurting, was held high. And this, too, was ritual, ceremonial, and a battle cry known to strike terror to every Orcan who heard it.

The family of A. Bir heard it, and they knew terror. But they did not run. Neither did they cross into the street and wait, kneeling, for their turn under a hooked-bladed knife. They fought, kneeling at a wall, firing their meager weapons down the street. Among them they killed perhaps three Ancans and wounded several others. But what was three among hundreds?

T. Bir was taken first.

A. Bir was forced to watch as her fragile-seeming antennae were caught in a huge, bloody paw, as her thin and lovely neck was stretched. He heard the shrill, meaningless whimper of her voice in soft protest, then heard the *snick* as the hooked blade cut through, separating head from body, then watched as head, eyes weeping, was held high, and he heard the ceremonial roar.

"My love . . ." he whispered.

The two children were next. And he followed.

The entire settlement of Sovan was brought to smoking ruins as ordered by Tanta, and the severed heads of every Orcan—too many to count—were mounted on spears and shafts and staves cut for the purpose and set in an orderly row about the circumference of the ruined village.

And it was then, only then, that the warships of Orca came to exact vengeance. The horrible truth of the attack—the fact that the long-dreaded Final Days War had actually begun, for such an attack could mean nothing else—had been most difficult to admit. Once admitted, the dreadful reality had to be accepted, and once the reality had been accepted, Orca would be committed to a conflict that could very well mean the end of life for their species . . .

But they did accept the reality. And they did come.

In the space of an hour they had, with their darting ships that flashed through the skies like avenging angels above the lumbering Ancans, found each and every fanged-tooth warrior and turned each one into a smoking cinder.

Too late.

Too late to save A. Bir. Too late to save T. Bir. Too late to save the children. Too late to save any other of the several hundred Orcans of Sovan. Too late to save Sovan.

And they were too late to save Rovas.

Rovas was the second small community ordered destroyed by Tanta of the Ancans. Destroyed, he had said, as payment for the murder of his son at the hands of an Orcan named E. Rox.

And that was true. He had wanted vengeance. And some healing of the disgrace incumbent in the fact one Orcan, unarmed, had somehow slain not only his son, known to be the most fierce warrior of Anca after himself, but three other Ancan warriors of almost equal ability.

But even more than any of that, he had wanted to announce that his species, the Ancans, had waited long enough, had bowed long enough, had been subservient long enough.

The Final Days War had begun.

CHAPTER 13

E. Rox was not coming back.

Why would he? Why would anyone, once rid of a second personality, willingly accept that second personality back, particularly when—and Harry Borg had grudgingly come to this admission, because, after all, fair is fair—the second personality had been something of a bastard. An irritating, coarse, crude bastard—at least, by the standards of an Orcan gentleman.

Harry Borg had to concede that E. Rox was that, all right—an Orcan gentleman. Courteous at all times. Polite. Not patronizing, not condescending—simply of higher quality than most. Better goods. And he, Harry Borg? What was he?

Face it, Harry baby, he said to himself, what you are —and what you are cannot be exactly specified in polite society—is not, repeat *not*, the *front* end of a horse. Admit it! he told himself morosely. Harry Borg, you're an obscenity.

Unwashed, uncombed, uncouth.

Sure, he had a college degree. Sure, he could read, write, and do arithmetic. Knew a lot of big words, too. Even owned a tux once. But when it came right down to the nitty-gritty, he was coarse, he was vulgar, he was full of bad jokes and dumb sayings.

Nor was that the worst of it.

Even though he was on the wagon, he could get stinking drunk—that was the worst of it. How about that? Bluenose Harry Borg had gotten as drunk as a sailor on a Saturday-night shore leave. He made passes at females he didn't even know. Even a barmaid. Even on distant planets, he did those things. Females of a different species . . .

So why would E. Rox come back? A nice guy like E. Rox shouldn't even *think* of taking a schlonk like Harry Borg back as the second half of a dual personality.

Such was the thinking of Harry Borg as he spent the long night in the atrium of the address where E. Rox's girl, O. Rani, lived. It was a long, lonely, cold night for a sorry and sad Harry Borg, full of remorse and self-recriminations, with only the small water creatures in the fountain pool to keep him company.

And he could have added to his catalog of self-denigrations one thing else. One great big thing else: He was nothing but a wraith! That's what he should have added. Nothing but a wraith. Invisible. Without a body to call his own. Sitting here on the edge of the fountain pool, not even the little waterdog kind of fish could see him.

The little lizardlike creature, the Orcan excuse for a goldfish, Harry supposed, was swimming near the surface, searching for food, and Harry, bored out of his socks, with nothing better to do—it being about three in the morning, with a lot of the night still to go—began trying to tease the little critter.

His finger, being the finger of a wraith, with no substance at all, couldn't really tease the little waterdog. He was sure it couldn't. A finger, without substance, could not dimple the water, could not make a ripple. It could not scare the little beastie.

Then why did it?

Why did the water dimple and ripple where his wraith finger touched it? Why did the little waterdog suddenly whip away, scared to death, to hide under a waterplant that grew in the pool.

Startled, Harry looked around.

The atrium, a beautiful, softly lit little parkland of greenery, comfortable benches, paths, and fountain, was deserted—except for himself, of course, a wraith—and the only sounds were the soft whispering of the spraying fountain and the sleepy cheep of some small insect.

There was nobody here except himself.

Then, what had scared the waterdog? What had dimpled the water? What had made the ripples? His finger? Come on, Harry! Your clutch is slipping! It couldn't be! Could it? Cautiously, he tried it again. Nothing happened. Then, concentrating very hard, he tried it yet another time. And he dimpled the water—*he made a ripple*!

How about *that*?

Now he had something to do. Something to occupy his mind, something besides self-pity and self-recriminations to fill the lonely hours. By using deep concentration and a great force of will, he found he could do other things besides dimple water and make ripples. He could, he found, after much effort and many failed attempts, move a leaf on an overhanging shrub. And then, finally, after hours of experimenting, trying, learning, he was able to pick the leaf, carry it through the air, and drop it into the pool!

Holy smoke! Like Cary Grant in one of those old Topper movies.

All *right*!

"Harry?" It was E. Rox's voice. Tired and a bit tentative, but it was E. Rox's voice, sure enough. "Harry? Are you here?"

Harry turned away from the shrub and the fountain and found that it was morning and full daylight and that E. Rox was standing in the entrance of the atrium. His enormous china-blue eyes were a little bloodshot. His antennae were erect and searching, though a bit wobbly. But there he was, E. Rox, an Orcan gentleman to the death, searching for the wraith of Harry Borg, the crude interloper from the planet Earth who had caused him so much trouble.

Harry was overcome with emotion.

If he'd had eyes, he would have had tears in them.

A champion, this Orcan. A real champion.

Harry moved quickly, and then, gently, so as not to frighten E. Rox or to cause him any more discomfort than he had to, he reentered the person of E. Rox. He didn't know how it was done, nor did he care how it was done. He had to get in out of the cold—that was all that mattered. And he was immensely grateful when he was again snugly inside.

There was a moment's shock. E. Rox's knees buckled, and he had to sit down on a bench and steady himself in a world that had suddenly started spinning.

"Wow!" Harry said, when he was plugged into E. Rox's circuits again. "Have we got a headache!"

"You're back," E. Rox said tiredly.

"Yeah, I'm back. But, good lord, man! You can't drink like that. A hangover like this could kill an ordinary man. Could even put *me* in bed for a week!"

"Tell me about it," E. Rox said. He had picked up a lot of Harry's way of talking.

Harry was at once contrite. "Sorry. I go on being a thoughtless bastard." He made a few small adjustments to finish settling in. Then he said, "I didn't think you'd come looking for me, Roxie. I surely didn't."

"I did not want to."

"Why did you?"

"As you would say, I owed you one."

"Yeah, I suppose you could say that," Harry agreed. "But it was my head, too—at least, the one I was using at the time—that sucker was going to chop loose."

"Still, a debt owed is a debt that must be paid."

"A lot of people owed me and never paid," Harry said. "You're first class, Roxie. A real champ. And I want to say, right now, as soon as I get those seeds that're gonna save a million lives back home, I'll walk right out of your life and stay out!"

"Harry..."

"Yeah?"

"There is something..." E. Rox's inner voice, shaky at best, faltered and stopped.

"Yeah? Yeah? What something?"

After a long moment, E. Rox said, "I do not know how to say it."

"Come on, give it a try. Anything."

"Last night..." E. Rox began slowly. "I—I, uh, drank rather more than I should have."

"That's a buy!"

"Buy!"

"It means I agree," Harry said. He was being gentle and understanding, perhaps in a belated attempt to right past wrongs. "You're not used to that kind of drinking," he said. "I could tell."

"True," E. Rox said. "As a usual thing, I drink very little."

"Makes a difference."

"When I overindulge—" E. Rox waved his hands weakly. "—I sometimes have difficulty remembering everything what—that I did, or did not do, while under the influence."

"Don't feel bad about *that*! Happens to a lot of people."

"I remember drinking, talking to O. Rani. And being in the bedroom, getting undressed. Then—nothing. Until this morning."

"Passed out," Harry said. "You'd had a hard day."

"Passed out?"

"Went to sleep standing up," Harry said. "After all you—we'd been through, I'm not surprised. That debriefing alone would wring out the best of 'em. Then we got smashed in that saloon. Then we got at least halfway sober in that massage parlor, or whatever it was. Anyway. Then we got chased by those cracco-characters, whoever *they* were—"

"Yes. I remember now. The craccos—"

"They ran into something, the cabbie said."

"I wonder why they were following us."

"No matter. They're gone. And then, when you got here, finally, to see your gal, which you hadn't seen for six months or so, with me along looking over your shoulder, you got smashed all over again. It was a strenuous day, son. You don't have to apologize to anybody."

"Harry..."

"Yeah? Now what?"

E. Rox was very tentative now. And embarrassed. "I do not know how it passes with you humans...but with we Orcans—I mean to say...Well, when a male Orcan is forced by circumstances to be away from the female of his choice for an extended period of time, certain biological urges—" He waved his hands, his wheels spinning.

"You don't have to spell it out," Harry said. "I know what you're talking. It's the same with us."

"It is?" E. Rox said, relieved.

"Believe it!"

"Oh."

It seemed now that E. Rox was not so relieved as he had been. It seemed, rather, that he was now, after thinking it over, perhaps more concerned than he had been.

"You are like that, too," he said dismally.

"Very much so."

"And you have been away from your female."

"Yeah. For a while, anyway."

"Crixx!" E. Rox swore softly.

"There's nothing wrong with it!" Harry protested. "Being antsy, I mean. It's the way the race is propagated! If it wasn't for that old urge, there wouldn't be any little humans. Or any little Orcans, for that matter!"

"I know it."

"So what's buggin' you?"

E. Rox kept his eyes on a distant wall. Even his uninjured antenna was bent and sagging. His voice was faint.

"When I woke up this morning," he said, "I couldn't remember if I had—had—" He couldn't say it.

"Made love?"

"Yes. Or not."

"Like we said, when a guy is really snockered, he can forget."

"O. Rani thought I had."

"There y' go!" Harry said.

"Harry..."

"Come on, now! If she says so, that's the way it was! Who would be in a better position to know? No pun intended."

"You don't understand.

Harry was puzzled. "You're right, I don't. So, do me a favor, Roxie. Clue me in."

"You were gone when I woke up, Harry."

"What you wanted, wasn't it?"

"Yes. Yes, of course..." E. Rox bogged down again. After a moment, he took a deep breath and blurted, "I don't know when you left!"

"Oh. Now I get it!" Harry said, finally catching on. "You don't remember...she said you did...you don't know when I left...so you think maybe it was me... before I left..."

E. Rox could only nod numbly.

"How could you think a thing like that? We're not even the same kind of a race!"

"In the bar...with the waitress..."

"I was only foolin'!"

"You seemed serious...You said when we entwined our antennae that you—"

"Oh, *that*! For laughs, Roxie! Just kidding around!"

"You seem to feel what I felt. You...you—"

"Roxie!" Harry said. "I'm *shocked*!"

"*You* are shocked..."

"Mad is maybe a better way to say it." The inner voice Harry was using held all the hurt outrage he could manage. "Okay. I'm a crude bastard. A peasant. A yokel. But come *on*! I'm not that kind of a stinker! My *host*? Would I do a thing like that to my host? I mean, with *his* girl? Hey! You're more than my host. You're my best friend! You know that, don't you?"

"I—I would like to think so..."

"You *are*, Roxie! You are!"

"Then you didn't..."

"Believe me, Roxie! When you two started for the bedroom, I—" Harry paused a moment for dramatic effect. "—*watched* you go!"

E. Rox was beginning to feel giddy with relief. "She said I was better than she ever remembered—" The relief vanished.

"Roxie!" Harry scolded quickly and perhaps a little

desperately. "It had been six months, remember! You *had* to be a superman!"

"Oh. Yes, to be sure." Relief again. "That *would* make a difference."

"You better believe it!"

After a moment's thought, E. Rox said, "I am sorry Harry. It was very rude of me to have...I mean, I should have known better than to think for a moment—"

"Forget it!" Harry said. "Don't say another word!"

"If you say so."

Now Harry was relieved. And maybe a little proud of himself.

If a man could not control himself when faced with overpowering temptation, he had to be—and this was the bottom line—he had *better* be a damned convincing liar.

Whatever it took, he seemed to have it...

"O. Rani is preparing food," E. Rox said. "Are we hungry?"

"Starving," Harry said with a deep sigh of relief.

CHAPTER 14

The scream was thin and high and very frightened.

They heard the scream as they approached the entrance of O. Rani's living quarters. E. Rox knew at once that it was O. Rani who had screamed. His antennae had erected, stiff and trembling. His knees were suddenly watery, and the surge of emotion that flashed through him was like the sudden jolt of an electric shock. He stopped, sagged, and reached a long arm out to a wall for support.

"What the hell?" Harry asked.

"O. Rani," E. Rox moaned.

He seemed paralyzed or too weakened to move; he could only stand, staring at the entrance to her living quarters.

"That was *Rani*? Christ!" Harry Borg felt the fear and pain E. Rox felt, but he reacted in a different way: While E. Rox was stunned, apparently unable to move, Harry wanted to leap into action instantly. When it became obvious that E. Rox could not gather himself to do anything, Harry took command.

"Get the hell out of the way!"

In command, he got what E. Rox thought of as his

body and Harry thought of as a collection of galvanized pipe, into sudden violent motion. He took the ten-foot-tall Orcan down the remaining length of the hall in giant strides and hit the closed entrance of her quarters with a slam. The door was closed, locked.

"Damn!"

The scream sounded again, high-pitched, wailing. Muffled by the closed entrance, it came from a distance now. And there was a shrill whine Harry did not recognize.

"What the hell is *that*?"

"A twill."

A twill, Harry came to understand, was an aircraft capable of vertical takeoff and landing. The rising sound meant that it was about to take off. Harry sent the angular body of E. Rox at the entrance of O. Rani's apartment in a shoulder-down charge.

"Yaaaaaah!"

It was a yell of pain from E. Rox as his shoulder burst the entrance open and he sprawled, moaning, across the floor of the living quarters. Harry wouldn't let E. Rox lie, shocked and dizzy though they both were. Harry drove the body of E. Rox to its feet, eyes searching, antennae erect, vibrating, and saw, with E. Rox's eyes, through a wide-open door that led onto a roof garden, an aircraft a rooftop away with multiple rotor blades spinning, on the verge of lifting off.

"Eeeeeeeee!" It was another shrill scream from O. Rani.

Now Harry Borg saw her. She had eluded her captors and had been caught again, just now, and she was struggling with them. Her captors were craccos, four of them. They were the short, stockier versions of the Orcans, similar to the ones who had pursued E. Rox and Harry the day before and who had been lost when they had crashed into a divider.

Harry used E. Rox's voice to yell at them.

A meaningless sound.

They heard, turned. One of them lifted a long-barreled weapon of some sort and aimed it at E. Rox. Instinct, honed in battle, caused Harry to drop E. Rox's body instantly. Falling, he saw a brief flash and heard a *snick* as a projectile of some sort bit into the wall just behind where he had been standing.

E. Rox was panting, "Kovic . . . get the kovic . . ."

Harry understood that to mean a weapon. He allowed E. Rox to direct him, running, to a closed chest. A lid thrown back revealed a handgun. Harry grabbed it. Both he and E. Rox fought for dominance as they turned back toward the roof garden.

"This thing got a safety?"

"Here . . . on the side."

"Let *me*, damn it!"

Harry finally gained control of the weapon, and of the body they were sharing, and raced back to the roof garden. At a distance of perhaps a hundred meters, the craccos had finally gained control of the struggling, kicking O. Rani and were dragging her into the aircraft. Harry came to a skidding stop. Brace-legged, holding the handgun in both hands, he took aim at the last cracco who was still on the rooftop, shoving O. Rani into the aircraft. There was a hiss as Harry pulled the trigger, and a ball of something purple raced across the rooftop to strike the cracco in the small of the back. The cracco shrieked, fell, and lay kicking.

"Got the bastard!"

He took aim at a second cracco, who had leapt down to assist his fallen comrade, and pulled the trigger. Nothing happened.

"No more," E. Rox moaned.

"Whaddayuh mean, no more?" Harry, outraged, clicked the trigger again and again. "A one-shot shooter? Jesus!" He threw the useless weapon into the bushes.

The aircraft's whine became shrill, piercing. The machine vaulted straight up into the air, leveled off, and whipped away. Harry cursed in frustration while E. Rox wept in anger and despair—both in the same body, both at the same time.

"Of all the cockamamie, good for nothin'—"

"Look at this!" E. Rox was using their eyes now to stare at a small, dark projectile that lay at their feet. It was the projectile that had been fired at them by the cracco—the projectile that had missed and had struck the wall and had fallen. Picking it up, E. Rox turned it slowly in his fingers.

"So?" Harry asked. "It woulda killed us. Right?"

"It is not intended for killing."

"What then?"

"Capture," E. Rox said, puzzled.

"Why would they want to capture us?"

"I do not know."

"Or your girlfriend?"

E. Rox did not answer.

Harry realized, then, that E. Rox's attention had shifted again. Now he was staring into the living quarters of O. Rani—a thoroughly wrecked living quarters—but he was not staring at the destruction.

"Oh, jissa," he whispered.

Harry realized that he was seeing—with E. Rox, through E. Rox's eyes—a video screen on which was depicted a scene of absolute horror. A row of heads had been mounted on the blades of spears, on tall sticks, or simply staves, the butts thrust into the ground. Not just a few—there were perhaps as many as a hundred in this one view. Young and old. Even little children. Male and female. Empty eyes were staring sightlessly, the lovely blue of them gone dull. Blood had dripped down the shafts, long, twisting, drying, red strings. The antennae of each perished Orcan, so expressive in life, were hardly less expressive in death. The long fronds hung limply, framing each face dolorously, infinitely pathetic.

"Oh, my God, my God . . ."

Harry's whisper had added human shock and grief to the devastation E. Rox was feeling at the scene portrayed on the screen. He heard, with E. Rox, the voice of the vid-reporter, choked with emotion, as they moved in closer to the screen.

". . . found on arrival. Our forces eliminated the Ancans here in Rovas, as they did in Sovan, but not before this small community had been destroyed and every inhabitant slain."

The message was clear.

E. Rox collapsed onto a couch and caught his head in his hands. He was devastated, in a state near screaming, struggling to hold on to himself. Harry, caught in the same maelstrom, fought to retain some stability, but it was like being tossed on a raging sea.

"Bloody bastards! What happened?"

"They—they killed them, beheaded them."

"Who? Why?"

"The Ancans—Tanta's soldiers."

"They killed *civilians*? *Kids*?" Harry was incredulous.

"Every living creature. It is their way."

"Good God Almighty."

With E. Rox, Harry was fighting nausea. His eyes strayed back to the vid-screen, where, thankfully, the grisly view of the slain Orcans had been replaced by the figure of an elderly Orcan—obviously an official of great importance—whose face showed great sadness and who was speaking almost in resignation.

"Who's he?"

"Our leader . . . listen."

"We shall fight them . . . but there will be a long and bitter struggle in the times ahead. Blood and sacrifice will be the lot of every one of us . . . In the end, Osmos willing, we shall triumph." He did not say the last with any real conviction.

The Final Days War had begun.

"Because of me!" E. Rox moaned.

"Whaddayuh mean, because of you?"

"I—I killed Sana. This is Tanta's revenge."

"Rot!" Harry said. It was almost a curse. "If Tanta's started a war, it's because he *wanted* a war! His son's death was just an excuse!"

"*I* will be blamed."

"Come *off* it!"

"They will defeat us . . . we are lost!"

"Who's we?"

"All of us—my race. They will behead every last one of us before they are done . . ." E. Rox's voice had collapsed into a hysterical moaning.

"Of all the stupid crap I ever heard!"

"It is true!"

"The war's just started—*if* it's started—and you've lost it already? What kind of bull is that?"

"There are too many of them!"

And with that E. Rox broke down completely.

Guilt.

Harry was made to suffer the same guilt, since he shared equally with E. Rox, and there was much to share. There was the feeling that the war had begun because he had killed Sana, son of Tanta. A feeling that he would be responsible for the enormous loss of life, both

Orcan and Ancan, sure to follow. The feeling grew until he became certain that he would be responsible for the end of the Orcan race.

And there was still more . . .

Because of him, E. Rox, because of something he had done, O. Rani had been taken to suffer some terrible abuse.

And because of him, E. Rox, the creature from a distant planet—and Harry realized that this was himself—who had come to Orca in search of seeds from the plant Ursis, a plant from which an extract could be taken that would save the lives of millions of what the creature thought of as "little babies"—this creature would fail in his mission of mercy and most certainly die . . .

"Jumpin' Jehosaphat!"

Harry, awash in the self-pity and fed to the teeth with the defeatism, finally, figuratively speaking, to be sure, took E. Rox by the back of the neck and shook him until his teeth rattled.

"Enough!" he roared in a voice that almost blew the circuits of their intercommunication system. "Stop your damned sniveling! Be a man for a change!"

"Please . . ."

"At ease!"

Harry was back to being Old Iron Balls again. Though he lacked the physical aspects of the hard-bitten old campaigner, his personality had lost none of its force.

"Atten—hut!"

E. Rox jerked to his feet—he was wobbly, he was sniffling, but he braced his shoulders and sucked in his gut. "Sir!"

"Now hear this! You're nothing but a spineless wimp!"

E. Rox stared straight ahead.

"Let's hear it!" Harry yelled at him.

"Spineless wimp, *sir!*"

"And don't forget it!" Harry snarled without mercy. "From now on, *I* am the backbone of this operation! Got it?"

"Got it, *sir!*"

"There will be no more blubbering in the ranks!"

"No blubbering, sir!"

"No surrender!"

"No surrender, *sir!*"

"When I say stand, you stand! When I say sit, you sit! When I say run, you run! When I say fight, you fight!" And then, again figuratively speaking, Harry shoved a cold, snarling face into the wide-eyed, almost frightened face of his host and yelled, "Is that clear?"

"Clear, *sir!*"

"All right! Stand at ease!"

E. Rox seemed to know instinctively what that meant —or perhaps basic military training is the same everywhere, even on distant planets—for he braced his legs apart and clasped his hands behind his back, his stance not quite so rigid.

And he seemed relieved.

"I want answers!" Harry said.

"Answers, *sir!*"

"Why did those craccos take O. Rani?"

"I have no idea, *sir!*"

"No idea? None at all?"

"None, *sir!*"

"Then I'll tell you," Harry said, after brief thought. "They didn't want her, they wanted *you!* But they ran into her. She put up a fight. They panicked and took her. A botched operation is what that was. You'll hear from them."

"Sir!"

"Now to my operation . . ."

In his own mind, Harry was scowling, pacing before a subordinate officer, a swagger stick clamped beneath his arm. "I didn't come here to get involved in a war," Harry said. "I came here to gather the seeds of the plant ursis. That was, and still is, my first order of business! Understood?"

"Understood, *sir*!"

"Where is that plant?"

"In the Seco of Lara, sir. A long day's journey by air."

"I want to go there, now. Today."

"It is not possible, sir. I—"

"It *is* possible!"

"Correction, *sir*!"

E. Rox gulped. He was suddenly, inexplicably, seeing ways of doing things he would not have imagined, even in his wildest dreams, that he could have done a few moments before.

"I can steal an aircraft at a port near my home. We can fly under the cover of darkness. The seeds can be obtained from plants growing in the Leeta Valley..."

When E. Rox had finished roughing in a plan of action—a plan that was sheer madness when only a few of the risks and obstacles were considered—Harry Borg relented to a small degree.

"Once I have the seeds, I'll help you get O. Rani back. Shouldn't be any problem. They want you. We'll give them you, and *me*. And between us, we'll take their clocks apart."

"Clocks apart, sir?"

"We'll bust their asses!" Harry yelled.

"Their asses, *sir*!" Then, hesitantly, E. Rox added, "But the war, sir. The war with the Ancans..."

"All right. *That* war. We'll take care of it, too."

He didn't say how he would take care of a war that

the leader of the Orcans clearly thought was of such a dimension that it could very well—and most probably would—result in the end of the Orcan race.

"How, sir?"

"How what?"

"How are you—we—going to take care of it? *That* war."

"Don't know yet. Need time to think about it."

"There is not much time."

"A couple of days, maybe a week?"

"Not even a few moments," E. Rox said. His antennae, directed toward the hallway, were picking up signals that Harry had been too preoccupied to notice.

"Who's that comin'?" he asked.

"The government police," E. Rox said.

"What do they want?"

"They want to arrest me," E. Rox said. "They believe now that I killed Sana, son of Tanta . . . that I am responsible for the war." He sighed resignedly. "I shall probably be executed."

"Oh, balls!" Harry said.

"Balls, sir?"

CHAPTER 15

"Scary . . . scary . . . scary . . ."

Lori Borg whispered those words softly as she was ushered into the *anticuum*, the huge octagonal chamber where Ra, the giant queen mother of Ancans, resided. The enormous size of the creature alone was enough to frighten a grizzly bear. Lori guessed the wormlike, segmented body to be fifty feet in length and at least twenty feet high. It was a pulsating tube that changed in color from pale violet to purple and back again as the inner convulsions flowed from one end to the other in slow waves. The head seemed very small, though it was in fact three feet across, not counting the bulging disks that were her many-faceted eyes. Tall antennae rose gracefully from the head; two small mandibles projected above the mouth parts.

"Osis preserve us!" Sissi whispered, as frightened as Lori.

"That's a *queen ant*!" Lori whispered.

"Whatever a queen is."

"We've got 'em at home . . . they get into things."

"That big?"

"Lord, no! Nothing's *that* big!"

165

"Shhhhh . . ."

There were letas, the giant ants, scurrying in and out of the chamber. One size and kind brought large spheres of amber-colored fluid to the forepart of the queen, feeding her, while another size and kind carried away eggs that emerged with regularity from the afterpart. A third size and kind climbed about her pulsating body, stroking, grooming. They gave no attention whatever either to the Ancan females who had brought Lori and Sissi here or to Lori and Sissi themselves. They had their tasks, and the haste with which they went about them suggested that they were always behind with no time for such foolishness as being curious about visitors.

Not so with Lori.

"Outa sight!"

She had kept saying that in awe, staring round-eyed, unbelieving, at the incredibly strange sights she had been seeing during the past few hours. And now this! It was some kind of a giant, eight-sided chamber—every darned building and room she had been in had eight sides—where an enormous queen ant, flashing colors like a neon sign, was laying eggs like some kind of a factory, one every four or five minutes . . .

Pfuuuuut! There came another one!

The four Ancan females who had brought Lori and Sissi here were clearly very much in awe of this creature they called Ra, and, though they had backed away a considerable distance, leaving Lori and Sissi to stand here before the creature, they were watching nervously, as if afraid that Lori and Sissi might commit some kind of a boo-boo that would get them all in trouble. They were in awe of Lori and Sissi, too, of course—very much so!— but this queen ant was apparently the grand panjandrum.

Bigger even than a Tanta, whoever, or whatever, *that* was.

The Tanta was next on their list, they had been told.

The Ancan females, Lori and Sissi had been relieved to discover, were not nearly as repulsive as the males. The males, big, hairy buggers with arms so long their fingers dragged the ground, with faces like lions, were too much. But the females were not so bad. They were big too, of course, and you wouldn't want one for a pet —good lord almighty! A female lion lying around the house?—but they were kind of cute. In a female lion sort of way. And they weren't mean-natured. They were nice. Generally speaking. At least, they hadn't tried to eat anybody yet.

The female Ancan named Kana, the one who bossed the females who had taken charge of Lori and Sissi, was apparently somebody important. Very important. And had she looked regal! Her mane had been purple—*purple*, for heaven's sake!—and when she waved her hand, the other females jumped. Not, it had seemed, because they were afraid of her but because they loved her that much. She was the best-looking female Ancan they had seen so far, but, like the others, she was unusual in certain ways.

"They've all got six dugs," Lori had whispered to Sissi when they had first seen the female Anca. "Have you noticed that?"

"What are dugs?"

"Titties, y' dummy!" Lori had said. "Three on each side!"

"Oh. They are mammals! And you have—"

"Just two, baby. Just two."

"Very strange."

"And they have *litters*! Six, eight kids at once!"

"How do you know?"

"I asked."

"Six are too many!"

"I should hope so!"

But all that had been before.

Now their attention was absorbed entirely by this enormous queen ant—Ra, they said her name was. And on the question of why they had been brought here to Ra's chamber by the female Ancan.

"Who are you?" a quiet voice asked.

Lori jumped, startled.

"Huh? What? Who said that?"

"Don't look at me," Sissi said, startled, too.

Nor was it any of the Ancan females, Lori discovered, for they were looking toward Lori and Sissi with extreme apprehension—as if, just as they had feared, the tansy was not going to show the respect owed the queen mother.

"It was *her*?" Lori asked incredulously, pointing.

The four Anca females nodded in unison.

"Well, how about *that*?"

It was a stupid thing for a person to say at such a moment, and Lori knew it. But, holy smoke! She could communicate with a *queen ant*? It had been strange enough to discover that she could communicate with the Ancans—they used a telepathy that was translatable by the receptors given her by the Jassans, the one that enabled her to communicate with Sissi and the rest—but she would never in this world have expected it to work with a . . . a bug.

The queen ant was a bug, an insect . . . wasn't she?

No. Apparently not.

Not like back home, anyway.

"My name is Lori Borg," Lori said with respect. "I'm a human being . . . from the planet Earth. I came here looking for my husband, Harry. He's a big—well, not as big as you folks, maybe, but he's big—and when I find him—"

"You are a tansy?"

"Well, really, I—"

A sharp dig of Sissi's elbow reminded Lori that their lives might depend upon the Ancans believing she was a tansy, some mythical fairylike critter with super powers. Lori used the old throat-clearing dodge to cover the blunder.

"Well, yes. That, too. I'm a tansy, all right. Among other things. What I do best, though, is—"

"I do not think you are a tansy."

Lori and Sissi exchanged glances.

"You're entitled," Lori said resignedly.

"I do not believe in tansies."

"Some do, some don't," Lori agreed.

Ra, the queen, was silent for a moment, perhaps preoccupied with egg laying, for one was laid in the interval. *Pfuuuuut!* Then, in a tone of one issuing an ultimatum, she spoke again.

"I declare you to be a tansy."

"You mean, you—"

"Yes. You are now a tansy."

"Gee, thanks!" Lori was genuinely relieved. "It *was* kind of expected of me. I hated to disappoint these . . . these people. Y' know? Could've been harmful to my health."

"The females of the Ancans have need of you."

"Is that so?"

"Their need is very old. Very great."

"Can you tell me what it is? Their need, I mean."

"Not at this time. Much must be done . . . done in great secrecy. And when the time is right, you will be told. Until that time comes, you are to do all things a tansy is expected to do."

"Could you give me a for instance, Your Majesty?" Lori asked. "I'm a little rusty at this tansy business, y' know? Maybe if I knew what they expected. I could use a hint—"

"Go now," Ra said. "I grow weary..."

"One other thing," Lori said. "My Harry. I'd sure like to—"

"Go, now."

"I gotta find him, see? It's why I came here—"

"Liss...liss..." Sissi hissed.

The Ancan females had hurried forward to usher Lori and Sissi out of the chamber. They did it quickly and firmly but with respect. Their respect, as a matter of fact, verged on reverence.

Lori felt a little silly being given that kind of attention. She was not, after all, that kind of important. Finding Harry and staying alive, her and Sissi both, was the only kind of important she gave a hoot about.

That and keeping her feet on the ground.

There was something about this planet that when she walked, she practically floated. No gravity, she supposed. Not the usual Earth or Essa kind, anyway. It was absolutely amazing. Both she and Sissi could, if they wanted to, jump a quarter of a mile. Easy. And strong? Shades of Paul Bunyan! They both had to be careful what they touched and how they touched it. When they wanted to move something or lift something, it was like magic what they could do.

It *looked* like magic, anyway...

Lori and Sissi were taken once again to the quarters of Kana, she of the purple mane. The tall and regal Ancan female was holding court in her chambers. With her were six female Anca whom Lori and Sissi had not seen before. These, too, had manes, which seemed to be the prerogative of only VIP Ancan females—they were soft yellow in color, not purple—which set them apart from other females. And they seemed older than most.

Two were quite old.

They were very interested in Lori and Sissi. While Lori and Sissi were still at a distance, the Ancan females stared at them with their huge, red, disklike eyes and exchanged whispered comments among themselves.

Sissi became uneasy. "Do some magic," she said. "Impress them."

"Like what?"

"*You* are the tansy."

"Thanks a bunch!"

Still, Lori shared the uneasiness. People looking at her, whispering among themselves, had always given her the yips. She agreed with Sissi that she ought to do something impressive. But what? Her best shot had so far been the appearance of flying, so, more or less out of desperation, she decided to give that a try.

She gave a small spring upward.

The small spring shot her upward so far, she knocked her head against a ceiling that was maybe thirty feet high. She seemed to hang there forever—actually it was only an instant or two—before she started down again, waving her arms to keep her balance.

It sure looked like she was flying.

And it worked.

The ladies *were* impressed.

They oohed and aaahed, nodding in confirmation, eyes getting bigger and rounder and redder. The regal female with the purple mane seemed pleased at what Lori had done. She motioned Lori to approach.

"What are you called?" she asked.

"I'm Lori. This is Sissi—"

"Your handmaiden," Sissi reminded her, whispering.

"—my handmaiden," Lori continued, stumbling only slightly.

"We are honored that you have come," Kana said.

"You are the first tansy to have come to us since ancient times. We tussas have been waiting for you. Even praying for you."

"My pleasure, I'm sure," Lori said, wondering what a tussa was.

Tussas were female Ancans, Lori was to learn.

But not until later...

At this juncture, there proved to be time only for a few exchanges, with Lori and Sissi trying to maintain an appearance of being sort of supernatural and trying to steer the conversation around to their most urgent question—"Has anybody here seen Harry? Big fella, dark blue eyes, short beard, great teeth?"—before a messenger came to take them to another place.

"Great Essnia..." Sissi whispered in awe.

"Likewise," Lori whispered back.

It was some kind of a place!

It was a great hall—eight-sided, to be sure—with windows high up that let in long rays of red light from the Orcan sun. Silken banners were suspended from giant spears thrust into the walls. The floor was tiled, brightly colored. There were rows of huge benches, like pews, a narrow aisle that led to a dais at the far end. And the place was crowded with the huge, hairy, lion-faced warriors in full military garb. All males. With manes. The only females were the ones who had brought Lori and Sissi here.

And there were ten Orcans.

These were new to Lori and Sissi, creatures they had never seen before. They were prisoners in chains. Very tall, very thin creatures, with huge, disklike blue eyes and antennae—

"Antennae? Really?"

"What else could they be?"

The antennae were long fronds, like rabbit ears, broken and forlorn now, hanging down around vacant, beaten faces.

"Poor things," Lori whispered.

Sissi went, "Shhhhh!"

There was a throne on the dais at the far end of the great hall, and sprawled there was the biggest and most ferocious-looking male Ancan that Lori and Sissi had seen yet, with a *white* mane and *gold* fangs!

"Got to be the king," Lori whispered.

"He is Tanta ut Krill," Kana said. "He *is* king of the Ancans."

Lori thought she detected something strange in Kana's tone. Something that might have been more like anger and resentment than respect. But she thought she could have been mistaken. And when she watched Kana move out now and walk down the aisle to take her place on a throne beside Tanta ut Krill, she knew she *had* to have been mistaken.

If Tanta was the king, Kana had to be the queen.

"La dee da!" Lori said. "Aren't we the one!"

"Hissst!" Sissi said, and jabbed Lori's ribs with an elbow.

Lori and Sissi had been the focal point of many eyes from the moment they had entered the hall. There had been humming, moaning sounds of interest and awe. But now the audience's attention was drawn away by the sudden booming of a gong.

Tanta ut Krill, the king of the Ancans, arose from the throne. He tipped his head back, dropping his lower jaw so that his long, golden fangs were most prominently displayed, and filled the hall with a booming roar.

"Arrrrrragh!"

The sound scared the hell out of Lori.

Sissi, too.

And it seemed to frighten all those assembled almost

as much. It got their full attention, at any rate. All assembled turned their eyes back to the throne and to Tanta. He made a signal, and at the signal a most awful ritual was begun.

A huge, hairy, white-fanged Ancan warrior, red-eyed, heavily bemedaled, strode forward, pulling one of the lanky, almost stiltlike prisoners forward into a sort of basin that was sunk into the floor before the throne. Now, he shifted his hold from the prisoner's arm to the prisoner's antennae, gripping the two frondlike appendages in a powerful hand and lifting, stretching the prisoner's neck. With his other hand, the Ancan drew a long, hook-bladed knife from a belt scabbard. Now he waited for a signal from the king.

The king lifted a casual finger.

The blade was swung, and *snick!*—the head was cut off.

The body of the prisoner fell into the basin, blood spurting, and the head was held high, blood dripping, for the king to view.

The king viewed it and signaled for another.

"Oh, my God, oh, my God!" Lori whispered.

"Cruel," Sissi whispered. "Cruel . . . cruel . . . cruel . . ."

The bloody rite went on, with one after another of the prisoners losing their heads and bleeding into the basin before their bodies were carried away. The Ancan warriors who filled the hall seemed to share the enjoyment of Tanta ut Krill, their king, for whom this ceremonious slaughter had apparently been staged.

"Death to the Orcan!" they chanted.

"Kill! Kill! Kill!"

"Evil ratans!

The females who had accompanied Lori and Sissi here did not join in the chanting. They did not seem to enjoy the bloody slaughter at all. Instead, they seemed infuriated by it—actually, they growled softly in unmistakable anger as each head fell. And when they became aware of the horror that Lori and Sissi were obviously experiencing, they pressed closer to the two strangers.

Not in anger—in sympathy.

In answer to Lori's questions they whispered that the victims were Orcan, members of a race who had ruled the Anca—all of the planet Orca, in fact—since the beginning of memory, and that these who were being decapitated were prisoners who had been taken in a war that had just begun.

A war that Tanta had long wanted.

A war that was going to end the Orcan race.

"Good Lord!" Lori wailed. "What have we gotten into?"

A war to the death, she was told.

Again, not with pride but with anger.

Now, when all the Orcan prisoners but one had been killed, that one, a female, was brought forward to stand before Tanta. The female Orcan was rather attractive, and even though she had just seen so many of her kind put to death, she had strength enough to face Tanta with defiance. The questions Tanta put to her, as well as her answers, reached Lori and Sissi.

"What is your name?" he asked.

"I am O. Rani," she answered.

"O. Rani. The mate of E. Rox of Orca?"

"I am that one."

"E. Rox, who murdered my son, Sana?"

"I know of no such murder."

"You lie."

"It is not my way to lie."

"Then you will learn the truth!" Tanta growled.

In a voice deep and rumbling with anger, he told the

young Orcan female that E. Rox, her mate, would soon be standing here in her place. He would come in search of her, if for no other reason. And when he came, when he was here, he was going to pay for the murder of Tanta's son.

"He will pay with blood!"

He went on then, to describe in some detail how E. Rox was going to bleed. It was going to be slowly, and it was going to be with much pain, and Lori, hearing it, felt a terrible fear that she could not quite explain.

"Who is E. Rox?" she whispered. "I don't even *know* him."

CHAPTER 16

3333 3333 3353 3333 3333 . . .

A single digit out of order.

A 5 instead of a 3 in a row of 3s.

The variation was hardly worth noticing. What could it matter? One small part of an array of digits. One small disorder. Why not let it go? Why worry? Why not go on to other, easier problems? Why not seek easier answers? Was orderliness so important? Symmetry so necessary? Was there not something to be said for randomness?

"Oh, crap!" Chad Harrison whispered.

He rubbed shaky fingers against eyes burning and grainy with the strain of staring hour after hour through the lens of a powerful microscope. First he stared at that damnable row of 3s—minute little ducks in a stubbornly defiant row, peering up at him from a small window embedded in a tiny circuit board—then he stared at infinitely convoluted imprints on minute microchips, searching for possible breaks, possible contaminants, possible misconnections; carefully checking, blowing away, reconnecting, then returning, after each alteration, to that damnable row of 3s, hoping to find it pure at last, unsullied by the ugly 5, but finding the ugly 5 each time, still stubbornly in place.

The hour was very late.

Except for the occasional lash of rain on some distant slate, a low, far-off, muted bowling-alley rumble of thunder, and the gentle breathing of his men sleeping on cots nearby, the laboratory was almost still. The only other sounds were little: the soft hum of fans blowing cooling air across circuitry, distant dynamos, the drip and *spleet* of a single water drop, the quiet, mewling protest of Los Ross, caught in some dark dream in the alcove where he had collapsed, utterly exhausted, several hours ago.

3333 3333 3353 3333 3333 . . .

Damn . . . Damn . . . Damn . . .

Were they only digits?

Not by any means.

They were distances beyond imagining.

They were coordinates, of time, of space, of matter.

As if a rainbow had been straightened, Los Ross had said, trying to conjure up images that the mind of Chad Harrison, a human being, could use in place of formulas constructed by the Ancients. A rainbow, the colors of the spectrum from ultraviolet to infrared and all between, a rainbow that represented the components of *life* unbraided, a rainbow laid straight, beginning here and stretching far, far, far, dwindling in width to a singularity and somehow growing smaller even than that—if Chad could envision such geometry, he would have, Los Ross had said, a grasp of what had been needed, and what had been done, to transport Harry Borg from Essa to Orca, the distant planet.

The process that had somehow minutely gone wrong.

Not for Lori Borg or Sissi—only for Harry Borg.

Somehow something had unconnected.

A ray, perhaps in the band of purple, had been broken and had gone wandering. The digit 5 told of that. If that 5 could be changed to a 3—more exactly, if whatever fault the digit 5 was representing could be found and corrected so an unblemished line of 3s could be established—then the body of Harry Borg could be recovered and redirected to the planet Orca.

A gentle hand touched Chad's shoulder. He turned to find Illia, holding a steaming drink.

"Something to warm you," she whispered.

She had not slept as the others had, though she had to be as worn as they. She had curled up at his side, as if to give him strength from her body, that of a bassoe, not a human. This bassoe was a lovely creature, near human, with larger than human copper-colored eyes and incredibly gray soft fur that covered a body that was human in all other respects: She had the body parts of a human, and a human mind, fully intelligent, capable, and caring. And she was Chad's wife.

"Can you rest soon?" she asked.

"Soon?" he said. "Yes, soon."

It had damn well better be soon, he thought, if the body of Old Iron Balls was ever to be found.

He sipped the hot drink, then turned back to the microscope. An infinitely careful turning brought a new circuitry into focus. He held his breath as he searched. A young man, not more than twenty-one, a powerful athlete, at the moment engaged in most delicate adjustments. His hair was white, his face was deeply tanned, his eyes were cold, cold gray.

"Come on," he whispered. "Come on..."

In the city of Larrisa, in a cell in a government jail, Guss Rassan, the renowned sissal-player, was being held prisoner, under the threat of death. It was not an idle threat. It was quite serious. It was a threat that seemed certain to become a reality before many more hours had passed.

Guss had become sure it would.

This cell was in the building that housed the Converter, which would be the instrument of his death when the final moment came. He would be taken, manacled, from this cell and ushered down a short hall—"Please, Osis! Let me not scream!"—to the room that housed the Converter, that evil machine that turned the flesh of living creatures into fertilizer for plants. He would be lifted and shoved, headfirst, into a blur of flashing knives that would slice him, bone and skin and flesh and blood, into tiny bits. Then the bits would be heat-dried into meal and finally neatly sacked.

He, Guss Rassan, the creator of symphonic fragrances, loved by millions, idolized—Harry Borg had called him the Elvis Presley of Jassan show business, whatever that meant—a national hero, presently to become a product to enrich the soil of potted islips? Was such a villainy, such a despoilment, such a *sacrilege* possible?

Indeed, it was.

Now that he thought about it—inevitable.

He was being held hostage for that purpose.

Well, perhaps not specifically for that purpose. He was being held hostage against the eventuality that certain promises would not be kept, but the possibility that the promises *could* be kept became more remote with each passing moment.

Los Ross had promised that the Earthman, Harry Borg, the Earthwoman, Lori Borg, and the Jassan female—his own beloved mate, Sissi—would be returned safely from some distant planet and, most particularly, that *no further scientific experimenting would be done*!

Fools! Idiots! Imbeciles!

Guss sagged back against the wall.

He drew the gray inner lid across his golden vertically slitted eyes, his tongue fell out the side of a mouth gone half-open, and the delicate forked tips, usually so expressive, were now limp and mute. His color was ash-gray. He wore prison clothing, a drab sexless sleeve of coarse weave. Misery and fear shrouded him.

Why had he volunteered?

What manner of a fool would stand and say, "Take me, if it pleases you, kill me if you must, but do not forsake those brave Earthlings to whom we of Jassa owe so much!"

Not Guss Rassan!

Surely, he had not said *that*! Oratory? From a sissal-player? Heroism? From an errant coward? He must have been out of—as Harry Borg would have expressed it—his cotton-pickin' mind!

He'd lost an oar...

Gone bananas...

True, the need had been great, the time for careful consideration of all possible alternative avenues non-existent. The criss-headed authorities, caught in a vise between the jaws of Old Laws and Peacekeepers, had been on the very verge of striding into the towering, winking, blinking mass of electronics that was Los Ross's laboratory equipment, flailing with bludgeons and swords in a mindless orgy of destruction that would have condemned Harry Borg, Lori, and Sissi to an eternity of wandering through the dark, cold reaches of outer space.

The humans? If it came to the worst, don't ask.

Sissi he could not spare.

Of such crises are heroes made. Or sissal-players turned into mindless idiots. He could not now, thinking about it in a blue fit of mental flagellation, be sure which.

Hero, senseless idiot—whatever—he had at least suc-
ceeded in holding the criss-headed authorities at bay,
saving Harry, Lori, and Sissi for a little time from a horrible death.

How little?

A few days at the very most.

Word had come, finally, from the president, Ros Moss
himself, who, while he certainly owed Harry Borg a very
great deal, was an astute and battle-tested politician and,
like all politicians, placed first things first, and had agreed
to stay the destruction of the laboratory and scientific
equipment for only a limited period of days, agreeing to the
execution of a national idol in the person of Guss Rassan if
Los Ross failed within that period to recover Harry Borg
and his mate, Lori Borg—and only incidentally the female
Jassan known as Sissi—after which the scientific apparatus would be smashed to smithereens.

Oh, yes! Smashed!

The fear of scientists and scientific experimentation
and exploration was indeed that great. With ample reason, it was easy to argue. And it was so argued by many
millions, most vehemently by the Peacekeepers. Had not
the entire planet of Essa been brought to the very brink
of utter annihilation four centuries ago by what the scientists at that time had declared was the greatest scientific
achievements in the history of science?

Yes, the planet had.

That "greatest scientific achievement" had been
turned into a weapon, a weapon that turned out to be the
greatest *annihilator* in the history of scientific achievement.

Before the weapon had been finally controlled, much
of the planet had been rendered unlivable for a century
and the population—on both sides!—had been reduced
to a bare few.

So much for "great scientific achievements"! So much for scientists and their experiments! One more like *that* achievement they did not need.

Scientists and scientific experimentation had been outlawed.

Tinkerers, like Los Ross, who aspired to no more than keeping the devices presently in use in working order, were tolerated; but those who exceeded those limits—those who ventured to send anyone or anything into outer space, for example—were subject to punishments ranging in severity up to public execution.

It had been the prospect of being able to execute a personage as renowned as Guss Rassan for violating the law—thereby bringing public attention to the law and once again demonstrating the seriousness of breaking it—that had persuaded the criss-headed authorities and the Peacekeepers to allow Los Ross the seven days with which to attempt to bring back those lost in space.

After the attempt had failed, and after the famous sissal-player had paid with his life, and after the laboratory had been destroyed, the whole insanity of science and scientific experimentation would then be safely buried for all eternity.

And good riddance.

"I did it, I did it," Chad Harrison whispered. Then he jumped up from the microscope and yelled, "By the living gods! I did it!"

"Did what?"

The question came from all sides.

"Changed that damned five to a three!"

They came with a rush, the four members of Harry Borg's cadre who had been sleeping nearby, and then

Los Ross, the diminutive Jassan scientist, glasses askew on his short muzzle, soiled smock buttoned two buttons wrong. Chad stood aside, trying not to appear too triumphant, though he in fact felt as Sisyphus might have felt had he ever rolled his rock clear to the top of the mountain. Los Ross put his eyes to the microscope's lenses.

"The tenth chip in the third row to the left," Chad said. "Do you find it?"

"Yes."

"There were three bent pins—two on the left side, one on the right. I straightened them and reseated the chip. *Bingo!*"

"Bingo, what?" the knuckle-faced Arnie Garrett asked.

"Changed the five to a three, dummy," Eddie Cole said. Then, realizing he had been too quick, too hopeful, added, "Didn't it, Chad?"

"That it did," Chad said quietly.

Homer Benson turned and hit Sam Barnstable a solid punch on the shoulder, a punch which the enormous button-nosed youth seemed not to notice, since he was busy tipping back his head and going "Yoweeeee!" in a cry of relieved triumph.

Now the body of Old Iron Balls, misshipped to a distant corner of the galaxy, could be located. Or could it? The young men suddenly sobered and looked intently at Los Ross, who now lifted his eyes from the lenses. The Jassan scientist seemed only cautiously relieved. He rubbed his forehead with eight shaking fingers.

"Well?" Arnie queried anxiously. "That's it, isn't it, sir? You can find his body now, can't you?"

"I think I can," Los Ross said.

But to himself he said, "I hope I can."

He had known the kranuss, of which the board Chad had been searching had been a minor part, had contained the flaw that had caused Harry's body to go astray. He had used a different kranuss to ship both Lori and Sissi, the same smaller kranuss he had used to ship the quiss in earlier attempts. And now that the trouble with the board had been discovered and corrected, he had only to compute the direction the body would have taken and the probable destination at which the body would have arrived as a result of such a malfunction—a numbers-grinding task of monumental proportions...

And so little time remained.

He went quickly to the keyboard of the tryanuss, an enormous computer, zero-cooled, and began to key in the necessary figures, his eight-fingered hands flowing swiftly, his long forked tongue caught in the side of his mouth in a gesture of intense concentration.

Behind him, the young earthlings still exulted.

"Chad, baby—you're a winner!"

"Give you a leather medal. Hero, first class!"

"Make that a steak dinner if you don't mind."

"Say!" It was Arnie, sometimes a worrier. "How about Iron Balls's body? Y' think... I mean, it's been sort of *dead* without him in it... for like three or four days now. Hasn't it?"

"Y' got a point there."

"Not to worry. I asked Los, and he said it's okay."

"What would keep it from, y' know, spoiling?"

"It's *cold* out there, man!"

"Deep froze, right?"

"Not exactly. It was disassembled before it was transmitted."

"Then, when he finds it, and ships it to the right place, it gets reassembled. Okay. So while it's waiting for Iron Balls to come pick it up at the lost baggage counter, what then? It's still gonna keep like fresh meat?"

"Arnie! For God's sake! Y' have to be so gruesome?"

"I'm just asking questions, all right?"

"Think of it like this," Chad said. "His body will be like a new car sitting in a garage, the motor running. Everything in fine shape, all parts working, just waiting for the driver to slide in and get behind the wheel. Okay?"

"Okay."

"I hope so."

"Or," Homer said, "a house at night. The lights are on, the water and power are on, the furnace is running, but there's nobody home. All it takes is for the owner to come in the front door, and it's a home again. All right?"

"I like that better."

"A car doesn't make it with me. It's machinery, sort of yuk. But a house, now—with a house, we're talking people."

"All right, a house."

Eddie Cole, the black from south central Los Angeles, where life was never easy, had been listening but not taking part.

House, car, he thought, if it's just lying there with nobody watching, how long is it going to be before somebody steals Old Iron Balls's body? Or eats it?

But he didn't put his thoughts into words.

He didn't want to spoil the fun.

Los Ross, aware of the voices as he sat through the intervals of waiting necessary while the numbers crunched, could only marvel at the humans. They were believers. They believed if they wanted something badly enough, and worked hard enough, they could achieve whatever it was they wanted.

Even wildly improbable things.

Like finding a wayward body lost in space.

And keeping it alive indefinitely...

CHAPTER 17

The body of E. Rox was bathed in sweat. His muscles were trembling with fatigue. The long-bladed machete-like knife he had been swinging with such desperation the past hour and more had begun to weigh a hundred times its normal weight. But he could not stop. He could not even rest for a few moments.

"You take five and we're dead!" Harry warned.

They were in a jungle of reechee plants, fighting to chop a clear path to the plain they had seen moments before they had crash-landed in this remote part of Latia. Behind them, gaining steadily, were three podpuii in unrelenting pursuit.

"Elephant-size garden slugs!"

That was the way Harry, in stomach-churning disgust, had described the giant mollusks now intent on devouring them. The podpuii traveled on a slick path of slime of their own making, flowing rather than charging, but flowing swiftly, their stalked eyes weaving above their foreparts, keeping their intended prey in view.

They were not more than three hundred meters away.

Or was it only two?

E. Rox finally *had* to stop.

187

He was going to collapse, he was sure, if he did not stop. His lungs were sucking and billowing at a frantic speed but still could not draw in enough of the sweet-laden, almost cuttable gas that passed for atmosphere in this rotten jungle. He simply could not lift his arms or force another stride from his legs.

Three meters tall and so very thin, his uniform torn and bloody, his antennae gone lifeless with weariness and hanging down his back like a pair of frayed rags, his huge, china-blue eyes agonized—E. Rox was, in fact, within moments of death from exhaustion, his will to live, his flame of life, faded to no more than a dying ember.

"Please, Ixxi! No more!"

"No more, your *ass*!" Harry snarled.

"Harry! I cannot lift my arms—"

"Give *me* the con, Goddamn it!"

Perhaps E. Rox was too weak, perhaps he was beyond caring, but he surrendered control of his body to the personality of Harry Borg. This despite the furious ultimatum he had laid down before this journey had begun:

"I shall take you after those ursis seeds, yes!" he had said. "But *only* on condition that *I—I*, alone—shall be in command of my body! At *all* times. Is that understood?"

He had communicated a rage unimagined in the usually compliant Orcan.

Harry had been impressed. "I copy," he had said.

To himself he had said, "Let him have the con. Maybe this loosely stacked collection of galvanized pipe has some sand in his bottom, after all."

Sand he had proved to have—up to a point.

But now, exhaustion had drained the lean Orcan of the will to live: exhaustion and what must have seemed to him to be the inevitability of defeat. An Orcan, Harry had found, had total courage, up to a point. But when there seemed no longer a chance of survival, the courage melted to hopelessness.

"Just get the hell out of the way!" Harry barked.

He shoved, bull-shouldered, into the fore of E. Rox's consciousness and forced new strength into the limp, almost lifeless grip E. Rox held on the haft of the cutting blade. He began again the sweeping strokes that lopped off the stinking, stinging, sucking arms of the reechee plant.

An arm came, unseen from the left, to coil about E. Rox's leg, stinging most painfully, sucking. E. Rox moaned with the pain. Another arm joined the first. Others, barring the way, became agitated, eager. If only one or two more made contact, they would at the very least slow E. Rox enough so that the loathsome podpuii must surely catch up.

"Bloody hell!" Harry cursed.

He chopped the two arms free and plunged on. He was only a second personality, a visitor, an interloper, a trespasser in the body and mind of E. Rox, but somehow he managed to bring to the struggle the *person* of Harry Borg. The man with the short-cut brown beard, the heavy jaw, the burning dark blue eyes, the smile of white teeth. He of the booming voice, the roaring laughter, the raging curses.

Earthman.

American.

E. Rox wanted to turn his head as Harry drove forward, wanted to look back and measure the distance they were ahead of the oncoming podpuii, but Harry would not allow it.

"No, y' don't!"

He forced the huge blue eyes of E. Rox to remain fixed on the task at hand. They had a hundred meters of reechee plants still before them, and their lives depended on cutting a way through. The plants themselves were lethal.

They were carnivorous.

The body of the plant was a huge, tuliplike cup, bright crimson in color and taller than a man. Its petals were fringed with arms able to search out and grasp prey at a distance of four meters, apparently guided by body heat. If the prey was finally caught, it would be drawn into the cup, which would clamp into a tight bud, and it would be bathed with an enzyme in a digestive process that would turn living flesh into a putrescent soup that would finally become the yellow sap that passed as reechee blood.

The podpuii, which lived safely amidst the reechee plants, protected by a film of repellent excrescence, promised a death no less agonizing. Once E. Rox had been caught by the podpuii, a veil of slime would envelop him and the mollusk would then extrude a stomach that would engulf the Orcan in folds of wet, sucking flesh, drowning him and finally consuming him.

"Not by a damn sight!" Harry promised savagely.

He fought the reechee tentacles with a relentless ferocity, chopping with a strength E. Rox never knew he had, cursing, savage, almost demented.

The tentacles were black in color. They stuck like hot glue when they touched cloth or skin. Their stingers, like the nettles that grew in the wet places of Earth, held a poison that hit like a hammer—enough stings could paralyze.

"It is so hot," E. Rox whimpered.

"Shut the hell up!"

But it *was* hot, steaming hot, with almost total humidity. It couldn't have been wetter at the bottom of a lake. Harry was sure that if he held an egg in his bare hand, it would boil in three minutes.

This jungle of Latia was a pestilential place. Since their aircraft had been forced down by the torrential downpour of hot rain, they had been either soaked with rain or almost suffocated by the clouds of steam that rose from the saturated vegetation like hot, liquid air.

This was the excremental orifice of the Orcan planet. Pure hell for animals. Pure heaven for plants.

It was no damn wonder the ursis plant preferred this place to any other on the planet Orca. This was plant paradise. Heat, water, nutriments—all in superabundance. A steaming Amazon jungle intensified by a factor of ten . . .

"Dirty, filthy bastard of a place!"

The severed ends of the tentacles, shorn by the swinging blade, squirmed on the ground. He stamped on them as if they were living snakes. He whipped and chopped more. The stalks bled a yellow sap the consistency of soft glue. The parent plant whined at the loss, whether from pain or from frustration in not being able to catch and hold, Harry did not know.

Behind them, the giant podpuii, eyestalks waving, glided on their slime roads in relentless pursuit. All around them, and particularly before them in a dense growth, the reechee plant tentacles waved and groped hungrily. Yet, as the unyielding will of Harry Borg drove the desperately tired body of E. Rox at the seemingly hopeless task of fighting a way to safety, there was still time to wonder however in the hell they had managed to get into a fix like this.

It hadn't been easy . . .

The departure from the living quarters of O. Rani— was it only a day ago?—had been more than sudden. When Harry had learned that the government police coming down the hall were coming to arrest E. Rox—for purposes of later execution, E. Rox had been sure—

Harry, who had been the personality in control of E. Rox's body at the moment, had acted with an immediacy of which only Harry Borg was capable.

At once. Instantly.

"Harry! No!"

"No, what?"

"To avoid arrest is a capital offense!"

"Tough turkey!"

Two giant leaps, powerful enough to flatten E. Rox's antennae straight down his back, had taken the long and slender body of E. Rox out of the living quarters and into the roof garden with the speed of a thrown spear.

"Ixxi help me!" E. Rox had wailed.

To no avail whatever.

Additional, even longer leaps had carried them to ever more distant rooftops, and by the time the government police had entered the living quarters of O. Rani, it seemed to them that everyone who had ever been there had been gone for at least a quarter of an hour—it was *that* empty.

While the kidnapping of O. Rani by the craccos for reasons as yet unknown, and the discovery that the Ancans had brutally slaughtered all the occupants of the Orcan farming community in the opening engagement of the Final Days War were vividly in Harry's mind, he had never for a moment lost track of his purpose for coming to the planet Orca:

He had come for the seeds of the ursis plant.

And he was going to get those seeds!

War or no war.

Craccos or no craccos.

Orcan police or no Orcan police.

First things were going to come first, if he had to take the planet apart piece by bloody piece!

"Y' got that?" he had asked E. Rox.

"I have it," E. Rox had answered wearily. "I read you, as you would say, loud and clear."

"Then let's get on with it," Harry had said. "Now!"

They had been in a craxi at that moment, a safe distance from O. Rani's living quarters and the Orcan police, and they *had* gotten "on with it" to the exclusion of all else.

There had been difficulties, of course.

Difficulties in finding a place where they could hide throughout the remainder of the daylight hours. Difficulties in approaching at night an airfield that, because of the war newly begun, had been placed under tight security. Difficulties in obtaining a fully fueled aircraft. Difficulties in falsifying their purpose and destination. Difficulties in obtaining takeoff clearance when only top-priority flights were being allowed use of the runways.

All these were difficulties that E. Rox managed to solve through the use of his military rank, an arrogance that comes of being born to an upper class, and a credibility that can be gained only if the demands made are *so* outrageous that they *must* be valid.

"A feat of skill, bravery, and deceit without precedent," E. Rox said, allowing himself a moment of giddy congratulations after it had been accomplished. "I did not know anyone in my family was capable of such knavery. We are basically honest citizens."

"You're also bull-futz lucky," Harry said.

They were flying at night high above a dark landscape. During the day, they had managed a safe refuge in the state library, and while there they had spent the hours poring over botanical encyclopedias, acquiring all necessary information concerning the ursis plant and maps and charts that would guide them to the remote corner of Latia where the plant grew. What they hadn't learned was that the weather in that locality at this time of year was a constant, drenching hell of hot rain, or that the aircraft they were to use was unsuited to flying under water.

An exaggeration, to be sure.

Harry had been flying the aircraft in those last moments before disaster had clobbered them. "Here, let me," he had said when E. Rox had begun to panic. "I flew P-38s in World War II in zero-zero weather over Holland, and compared to *that* this weather is almost CAVU."

"CAVU?"

"Ceiling and visibility unlimited."

Stupid, bragging bastard—him and his big mouth. The next thing he had known he was flying through a solid wall of hot water.

"Goddamn waterfall!"

Or was it a geyser—a waterfall going *up*?

Whatever it had been, it had drowned the engine of the aircraft, and from there on it had been all horse-bobble. Harry had managed to put the craft between two trees which had slowed and stopped the aircraft very effectively and without harm to the pilot but which had neatly removed the wings of the craft while doing so.

"I could have managed *that* well," E. Rox had said, miffed.

"I didn't say I could fly submarines," Harry had said defensively.

They had remained in the craft, consulting maps, planning, until the cloudburst was over, and they had decided—actually, Harry had done the deciding, and E. Rox, the host, had wearily assented—that as long as they were in the area and this close, a mere mile or so from the small valley where the ursis plant grew in certified abundance, they would hike it, harvest a sack full of seeds, hike back, and then torch signal for help.

Or not signal, as they might deem wise when the time came.

Nothing to it?

"Keerist!"

Harry chopped at the arms of the reechee plant, the breath he needed sawing into the exhausted lungs of E. Rox, the long, spindly legs of the Orcan wobbling with fatigue. Harry was an unrelenting demon. He had to be. The strength of E. Rox could not last much longer, no matter what the will driving it. The rush of rain runoff, now ankle deep, now thigh deep, cascading down the slope—that runoff alone was enough to exhaust a giant. And he had at least another hundred yards of this growth of reechee to cut through.

He swung the blade with a demented fury.

The bloody things wouldn't quit. When they were cut off they kept wriggling, like the cut-off tail of a lizard, splashing in the water, if there happened to be a pool where they landed, or splashing mud. The mother plant whined as if it were alive and injured.

Hell! The plant *was* alive, all right. They all were alive. They had to be—searching out, grabbing, trying to drag him in the way they were—but what kind of life did they have? What kind of life *could* a plant have, for God's sake? Not like an animal! Did they *think*? Did they have *brains*?

Two on the right . . . another on the left . . . a mess of them, reaching out to form a barricade in front of him. They *were* thinking! The dirty, filthy, cruddy bastards! They could plan ahead! They could lay traps!

Harry chopped, he ripped, he tore . . .

His feet slipped out from under him, and he went down on his ass. A long snakelike arm wound round his neck, stinging, choking. He tore it loose, sawed the blade of the knife across it, threw the cut-off piece at the parent, and saw it drop into the gaping petals.

"Eat that, y' bastard!"

A sudden burst of rain came down, pounding, blinding. For a few moments, E. Rox's lungs could find no air at all. Then, gasping, Harry got his legs under him, shoved himself up, charging, and gained another few yards, whipping the machete blade back and forth, a blur of shining steel before him.

His antennae caught a new sound.

Huff...suck...huff...suck...

"What the hell is *that*?"

A glance over his shoulder told him. The first of the three podpuii was no more than a dozen yards away and gaining. The eye stalks had lowered, pointing straight at him like a pair of spears, the eyeballs, round purple globes, glistening.

"It is no use...it is no use..." E. Rox wailed in despair.

Harry, measuring the distance left to the open plain and the number of groping reechee arms yet to cut before reaching it, couldn't argue—at the rate they were going, the way the bigger beast of a slug was closing on them, they weren't going to make it.

Not this way.

He turned suddenly and lunged back through the way he had cleared. A few long strides brought him up against the forepart of the slime-wet creature, and a single hard slash of the machete cut through both eye stalks, which fell away, squirming, down the slope. Blinded, the podpuii convulsed, seeming to turn inside out, and began thrashing aimlessly among the reechee plants.

Harry turned and ran, slipping and sliding to the end

of the path he had cleared, chopping furiously again with a strength somehow miraculously renewed by the victory over the slug.

"Harry . . . Harry . . . Harry . . ." E. Rox's voice, babbling in the back of the conscience they both shared, held wonder and a growing hope.

"Hang in, laddie!" Harry panted. "Gonna make it! Goddamn, we're gonna make it!"

And, indeed, a dozen more slashing strokes were all they needed to break out of the reechee plants and onto the clear plain. The knee-high grass here was no hindrance, and the ground was drained of standing water— E. Rox's long legs could drive them in long leaps that carried them safely away from the reechee plants and far beyond reach of the two remaining podpuii.

"Made it," Harry gasped.

Totally out of breath, he let the slat-thin body of E. Rox fall to a hands-and-knees position, chest heaving, mouth sucking air hoarsely, antennae, filthy with mud, hanging uselessly down from the sides of his head, like the ears of a badly abused basset hound.

"Roxie, baby," Harry wheezed. "We whupped them sombitches . . . we whupped 'em good . . ."

He gave the con back to E. Rox.

Going the rest of the way proved to be much easier. A walk of less than an hour across open country to a higher elevation brought them to the grove of ursis plants the maps had promised. The seedpods hung in clusters easily reached. They were like giant beans. Each pod contained a dozen or more seeds the size of marbles, and many of them were ready to burst open at the touch, proving they were ripe for harvest.

"You are very lucky," E. Rox said.

"Whaddayuh mean, lucky?" Harry yelled from his

corner of E. Rox's mind. "After what I just did to get us through those goddamn man-eating bushes, you say I'm *lucky*? Good lordawmighty, man! I *fought* our way of there! I *earned* every bloody inch of the way!"

"To find the seeds ripe—*that* was lucky."

"Oh," Harry said. "Okay, so I don't lose 'em all."

He filled a sack the size of a GI duffel bag.

"There y' go!"

He was proud when he finally buckled the top shut. "Shows what a human can do!" he said, strutting a bit, if an inner voice could strut. "When a human sets out to do something, he, by God, gets 'er done! An *American* human, that is."

"And I presume that is the very best kind?" E. Rox asked.

"What is?"

"An *American* human?"

"You better believe it!"

E. Rox rolled his eyes heavenward.

"So what's the matter, wise-ass?" Harry asked. "Didn't I just prove it? When the going gets tough, the—"

"Tough get going," E. Rox finished for him. "You have told me that on several previous occasions."

"So?"

"You *are* tough," E. Rox said. "Modest you are *not*."

"I don't see what the hell that's got to do with—"

But time had run out.

Now, coming fast, skimming over the distant forest of reechee plants, obviously following the path Harry and E. Rox had cleared, coming on with the tenacious certainty of bloodhounds on a hot trail, were three military aircraft. They zeroed in on E. Rox, whipping overhead, splitting their formation, and began to circle in the manner of hunters who have found their quarry and are preparing for the kill.

"Who are they?" Harry asked.

"They are ours," E. Rox said tiredly.

"What do they want?"

"Us," E. Rox said. "Me."

CHAPTER 18

Ran Tanta ut Krill was bats, Lori was sure of it.

Back at home on Earth she had known about a few like him in her lifetime. Maybe not as big or as ugly. Maybe not with arms so long their fingers dragged on the ground. Or with front teeth you had to call fangs. But bats, just the same. Idi Amin was one she remembered. Marcos and Baby Doc Duvalier were a couple of others. And Pop had told her about Hitler, Mussolini, and Stalin. Dictators were what those characters had been. All those guys. What was it the eggheads called them?

Megalomaniacs?

Something like that.

Anyway, they were all going to conquer the world.

What they were was nuts, bats, fruitcake.

Why would anybody want to conquer *any* world?

All that trouble?

All those nay-sayers coming around telling you you were doing it wrong? Who needed *that*? All those assassins trying to blow you away? All those poor types you had to feed? All those rich types trying to pick your pockets? You wanted *that*? Just so everybody would salute you? So you would have somebody drive your car for you? Wash your windows? Mow your lawn?

And the dead people—don't forget the dead people.

If you were going to be a dictator and rule the world, any world, you had to kill people by the millions, and that meant you were going to have dead people up to here.

Grown-ups and little kids.

Lying on that fine, soft bed they furnished her, staring up at the eight-sided ceiling where dim light from outside cast strange shadows, lying there remembering the great hall and all those poor, sad creatures getting held up by their ears and getting their heads cut off—and most particularly remembering that brave female one who had the same as told the Tanta character to stuff it—remembering all that, she had come to an inescapable conclusion.

"Take it from me, Lori Borg," she said to herself, "he's certifiable squirrel food."

Nuts.

"Sissi," she whispered telepathically. "You awake?"

"Who could sleep with you rattling on?" Sissi answered wearily.

"He *is* mad. You know that, don't you?"

"I know it."

"Well?"

"Well, what?"

"What are we going to do? I mean, you've got somebody bonkers like that, and you've got a whole different bunch of circumstances you have to deal with."

"Sleep first," Sissi said. "Get some rest—that's important."

"I can't sleep."

"Try."

"Oh, shoot!"

"Lori!"

"Well, I don't know how *you* can sleep. Remember that little female . . . what did they say they were, those people they beheaded?"

"Orcans."

"Wasn't she brave? So many of her people got their heads cut off right there in front of her, and she stood up to that awful beast and the same as told him to go in his hat."

"Go what in his hat?"

"Never mind."

"Go to sleep."

"I can still see the blood running into the tub—it was awful, Sissi. How can you sleep?"

"I can't. I can just lie here trying."

"What kind of people did we get associated with?"

"Monsters. The males, anyway."

"We should have stayed in that lab thing—whatever it was."

"You expected to find Harry there?"

"Well, no."

"These Ancans were the only people on this whole yizzi planet, as far as we knew, and if Harry was anywhere, he had to be somewhere with them—isn't that right?"

"Almost."

"Or dead."

"I wasn't going to *say* that!"

"Sorry."

"Oh, Sissi . . ."

"Where else could he be?"

"I don't know. But you shouldn't say 'dead' like that," Lori said.

"I unsay it."

"Sheez! *That* helps."

"You could hide your head under the pillow."

"It doesn't help."

"You tried it?"

"About an hour."

"For a tansy, a magic fairy the Ancans think is a queen of some kind, you are being a big baby."

"I know it."

"Stop, then."

"How about you?"

"*I* am scared witless," Sissi admitted.

"Makes two of us."

"You can't be scared tomorrow, Lori."

"Don't remind me."

"Have you thought of any magic you can do? He will expect something special, what you call glitzy."

"No, I haven't."

"Get busy, Lori."

"I've been trying to think."

Silence.

"Sissi?"

"What?"

"I don't think he believes in tansies. I mean, really."

"Why is he having this big meeting tomorrow, with all the chiefs there, to show you off, if he doesn't believe in you?"

"To show them I'm *not* really a magic fairy."

"Would he do that?"

"Sure. Most of the Ancans believe I'm a tansy, and they're scared of me. He doesn't want anybody scared of anybody but *him*."

"That is possible."

"Certain."

"Ixxi!"

"Swearing won't help."

"Helps *me*."

"Listen, Sissi. There's something else."

"What else?"

"The lady Ancans, the women of this country."

"What about them?"

"They don't think Tanta is all that great. Did you sense that like I did? I mean, especially with his wife, or whatever she is. Kana, I think her name is. I don't know if he knows it or not, but she hates his guts."

"How do *you* know that?"

"I'm a female, and I can tell."

"I'm a female, too, you know."

"Yes, but maybe I'm closer, you know, evolutionarily speaking."

"Oh, boy!"

"No, I'm serious. They've got tits, I've got tits. See? We're mammals, both of us. We feel the same way about things."

"They must feel a lot more than you do, then."

"Why?"

"More tits. Three on each side—"

"Smarty!"

"Go to sleep."

In the morning, Lori Borg and Sissi were first taken to baths where they were washed down by giant ants. That's what the letas, large and small, were to Lori —they were ants. The smaller types, about the size of Shetland ponies in her frame of reference, were the cleaners. They cleaned the big queen, so why shouldn't they clean tansies and handmaidens and people like that?

"It figures," Lori said as two of them worked on her.

"I say it tickles," Sissi said.

"That, too," Lori agreed. "That, too."

When they were finished, they dressed again in the clothes they arrived in—Lori in gray whipcord slacks,

knit sweater, and soft hiking boots, and Sissi in the cam-
ouflage combat uniform of the Red Flame Brigade,
weapons belt, short sword, and all.

Lori's face had a scrubbed-clean look—wide-set gray
eyes, good cheekbones, strong brows, and a wide,
friendly mouth. She wore her wheat-colored hair in a
single, shining braid down her back. Sissi's eyes were
enormous disks of gold, cut vertically by the narrow
lines of her dark pupils; her almost imperceptibly scaled
skin was gray, blushed with pink, and her slender
tongue, always flickering just beneath her small nostrils,
was split-ended and lovely.

"We're the best-looking girls in the house," Lori whispered.

"That's not saying much."

True, by ordinary standards the Ancan females were
sort of horrendous. The shortest of them stood head and
shoulders taller than Lori. They had shorter incisors
than the males—though they were still closer to fangs
than to teeth in Lori's book—and, except for a regal few,
they lacked the manes that the males had growing out of
their necks and shoulders. The regal few, Kana and several others, wore shorter versions which were actually
false manes, dyed a variety of colors, and were worn to
show they were among the privileged class. Like the
males, the faces of the Ancan females were definitely
lionlike, with large, red eyes, short muzzles, and black
noses, though they were softer and less brutal than the
males' were. Their torsos—and their many breasts—
were covered with garments artfully ornamented with
embroidery and bangles, shells, small bells, and the like.
Their arms were quite long, of course, but more gracefully managed—they did *not* allow their fingertips to
drag on the ground.

Lori and Sissi were fed.

"If that's not ambrosia," Lori said, "it will just have to do."

A liquid similar to delightfully spiced honey—what else could it be but the food of gods? It was served in silver bowls, garnished with flower petals, and lightly scented.

Loaded with calories, Lori was sure.

"But worth every pound," she said to Sissi. "Right?"

"Oh, absolutely," Sissi answered, trying to sound sincere. She would honestly have preferred a couple of mice.

They were taken, then, by Kana and three of her handmaidens to their confrontation with the king of the Ancans, Ran Tanta ut Krill himself.

Since Tanta's primary interest at the moment was getting the war with the Orcans successfully under way—a war that was to gain for the Ancans rights "equal" enough to enable them to obliterate the Orcan race entirely—he was inordinately busy.

He had converted his throne room into a combat headquarters, complete with enormous vid-screens, map tables, hurrying message-carrying subordinates, large urns brewing what seemed to be coffee but probably wasn't, and a number of female Ancans busily one-finger-tapping at devices that looked like writing machines and probably were.

"Have you thought what you were going to do?" Sissi whispered anxiously as they waited for Tanta to tear himself away from a group of officer-types who were debating something of crucial importance in front of a vid-screen. "What kind of magic, I mean?"

"Sheesh!" Lori said. "Magic, already! Me?"

"You're a tansy."

"Like heck I am."

"*They* think you're one."

"*He* doesn't!"

"Convince him."

"What's a tansy *do*?"

"Magic, you dummy!"

Lori was getting a little desperate. "What *kind* of magic?"

"Something! Anything!"

"Give me a f'rinstance."

"Fly once."

"Fly, she says! Well, okay ... here goes ..."

With that, Lori gave a spring and her Earth muscles vaulted her once more a very considerable distance up into the air. To further the illusion, she wafted her hands about gracefully and managed to appear to be flying before the astonished eyes of the Ancans.

On becoming aware of her fluttering up near the ceiling, some of the Ancans shrieked, some fell to the floor on their hands and knees, and some only went, "Ah ... ah ... ah" in frightened wonder.

Tanta appeared to be moderately impressed.

He yawned as she settled back to ground.

Then, with exaggerated patience, he waved at his staff to clear a way for Lori and Sissi, and beckoned them to approach while he took his place on the throne. Kana moved to sit in the throne beside him, alert, her purple headdress impressively arrayed. Her red eyes, like Tanta's, were fixed on the strange-looking little creature that the scholars had said was the long-awaited tansy of ancient times.

After staring at Lori for a moment, Tanta tipped his head back, dropped his lower jaw, and skinned his upper lip back to expose the full length of his gold-encased fangs. And if that was a gesture meant to scare Lori, it was hugely successful.

"He could bite a person in two!" she whispered to Sissi.

"Shhhhh!" Sissi said.

"Well, he could!"

"Hush!"

Tanta's voice, as it came through the Jassan-implanted receptor in Land forth inside her head like a soccer ball kicked in a closet.

"I am told you are a tansy," he said.

"That's the story," Lori agreed.

"I do not believe in tansies."

"Well, I guess you're entitled, being king and all."

"*Are* you one?"

"Are I—*am* I—what?"

Sissi dug her in the ribs with an elbow.

"A tansy," Tanta repeated.

"I'm *trying*!" Lori hissed at Sissi. To Tanta, she said, "You saw me fly, didn't you? Sir."

"That might have been only a trick."

"You got anyone else can do it?"

Kana leaned over to whisper something to the king beast. Tanta nodded, listening, and then directed his attention back to Lori.

"We do not mean any disrespect," he said. "But these are difficult times—dangerous times, since we are now at war with the Orcans—and we must be very careful."

"Naturally," Lori said. "Sir. Your Highness."

"We want to give you all the honor a tansy should be given. To grant you every favor in our power to grant—"

"Speaking of favors," Lori said quickly, interrupting, "there's a male tansy around here somewhere—his name's Harry, he's big, wears a beard—and I was wondering if you, or anybody else, might have seen him, or maybe heard something—"

"Before we can grant favors," Tanta said, interrupting her, "we must be sure you are the tansy you claim to be. And not an imposter. Or possibly a spy of the Orcans."

"Hey! Come on! I'm no spy!"

Tanta consulted with Kana again. While listening to her, he kept his eyes on Lori and he opened his mouth wide again, possibly to remind Lori of what might happen to her if she were found to be a spy.

Not that she needed any reminding. She hissed desperately to Sissi, "Get ready to run!"

"Don't be silly!"

"They shoot spies! Or worse!"

"Don't panic," Sissi hissed back. "Just ... don't ... *panic*!"

"Easy for you to say!"

"If you would be so kind"—Tanta was rumbling again, trying to sound respectful, when he sure as hell was not—"as to show us some further demonstration of your ability, our worries would be laid to rest."

"You want some more ... uh ... "

"Magic," Tanta said. "If you would be so kind."

"What sort of—of magic?"

She was stalling. She knew it, and Sissi knew it. And probably they knew it, sitting up there, skinning their teeth, a couple of big cats getting ready to pounce on a couple of little mice.

Lori could feel cold sweat forming on her back.

"Anything at all," Tanta said, almost gently.

"What am I gonna *do*?" she hissed at Sissi.

"Something! Anything! Even if it's *wrong*!"

"Okay ... Okay ... Okay ... "

An inspiration came to Lori. She looked around and found something that would serve her inspiration. It was a large table on which a mass of glowing electrical equipment of some kind was sitting. And then, with all the elaborate ceremonial gesturing of a stage magician, she moved to stand beside the table.

"Abracadabra!" she said. Not very original, but it was the best she could do.

After a last series of gestures meant to include everyone in the room, all of whom had fallen silent, she ducked down and slipped out of sight under the table.

Then, suddenly, there was a terrific crackling and sparking of torn electrical connections, and the table lifted from the floor, straight up, to reveal Lori standing erect under it, shoving the table skyward until her arms were extended full length. And then, with a grunt not at all ladylike, she heaved the table halfway across the room. It landed on top of another table with a bang and a crash.

The huge room was stunned into silence.

Lori dusted her hands. "You wanted magic," she said. "You got magic."

The Ancans in the room fell on their knees, facing away. All but Tanta and Kana, of course—they couldn't very well kneel to anybody, being royalty and very high class. But Tanta *was* obviously impressed. Not even he, the strongest of all creatures on Orca, could have done what Lori had done.

She had about ruined his headquarters.

"You must be a tansy," he admitted.

"You better believe it!" she told him.

"All honor to you."

So she had won one.

"You did it!" Sissi hissed gleefully.

"I suppose I did," Lori admitted modestly.

"You got us out alive!"

"And that's not all I got."

"What else?"

"I think I got a hernia."

CHAPTER 19

It was very dark. They were in some sort of tube, as nearly as Harry Borg could tell. A shipping tube, or some kind of a protective device that also served to immobilize.

Harry had been out of the body and mind of E. Rox briefly for a look around, and he had found they were in the cargo hold of an airship that was flying very high and very fast. He had no sure way of knowing where they were going, but he had a pretty good idea that they were going somewhere in Anca.

He would almost take it to the bank and ask for money.

Since there was nothing much he could do that didn't mean he would have to leave E. Rox stuffed in this tube alone, as helpless as a pickle in a jar, he had decided he had to ride it out and see what was going to happen.

He and E. Rox had been heroes one minute, then prisoners the next. What could you depend on anymore?

Lying quietly inside the shipping tube—and inside E. Rox—Harry had nothing better to do than to think back on how things had been going for them. He and the lad had been leading a very active life. No doubt about that. Look what had happened . . .

E. Rox had awakened to find that he had become a dual personality, for openers. There had been his own self, which he was used to, and there had been this other "self," which he was never going to get used to—the personality of some guy from a planet called Earth who had moved in, an uninvited guest.

"Just for a few days . . ."

Oh, yeah?

Harry had to admit that it hadn't been easy for E. Rox. That guest, Harry Borg, was a rough character. Harry could see how it would be living with a guest like himself, particularly when you were a different kind of person entirely, ten feet tall, very slender but whippy, with enormous light blue eyes, three-foot-long antennae, and a gentle, educated nature.

It would be difficult, to say the least.

Right after the guest had moved in, E. Rox had lost his patrol. Then he had—with a certain amount of help from his guest—fought and killed an Ancan named Sana, who had just happened to be the son of Tanta, the king of the Ancans, who had been looking for a reason to start a war with E. Rox's people and who had figured the killing of his son was reason enough for anybody.

And Tanta had gone for it, as they say. He had started the war.

The next thing, the craccos had run off with E. Rox's girl.

And then his guest personality had insisted he go after some ursis seeds that his guest was sure were going to end diseases and save lives on his home planet. E. Rox had nearly gotten himself swallowed by man-eating plants and a bunch of giant garden slugs, trying to do this favor for his guest, somebody he didn't even know real well.

Never do favors for strangers, right?

But it hadn't *all* been a downer for E. Rox. How often did a young kid, hardly a year out of officer-training school, a kid who had had his first command wiped out by enemy fire, get a medal pinned on him and the same as a ticker-tape parade down the main street of his home town?

Never mind that what E. Rox had done had started a war. The war had been going to start anyway. What E. Rox had done was kill, in single-handed combat—as far as anybody knew—Sana, the second meanest, toughest Ancan on the whole planet. That victory had earned him a ticker-tape parade, a medal the size of a dinner plate, and the rank of one-star general.

Funny, how things could turn out sometimes.

Win a few, lose a few...

Harry thought now that he, as a guest personality, had perhaps in the final analysis taken unfair advantage of his host when he had persuaded him to take him from the ursis seeds they had gathered together back to the receiving station in the ancient city of Atoxia. E. Rox had been dizzy with all that adulation and probably had not been able to argue sensibly against going at the time.

But he, Harry, had to know if his body had arrived yet, hadn't he? And if his body had been there waiting, Harry would have gladly left E. Rox and gotten back into his own body, and E. Rox would then have been rid of Harry for good and all, so the business of taking Harry and the ursis seeds to Atoxia had been to E. Rox's advantage, after all, hadn't it?

Going alone—*that* had been E. Rox's idea.

And a serious mistake, as it had turned out.

So Harry's body hadn't arrived. They'd found nothing

alive in the receiving station but the quiss, the little rodentlike reptile Los Ross had sent earlier, squeaking and running about. All they had been able to do had been to leave the ursis seeds tied safely out of the quiss's reach for later shipment—if and when. The disappointment of not finding Harry's body had hurt Harry more than it had E. Rox, when you came right down to it. Hadn't it? Maybe his body was *never* going to arrive—would E. Rox want *that* for a future?

No way!

But they should not have been arguing about who was the big loser on their way out of the receiving station— that was their big mistake. They should have been alert. When there's a war going on, every man in uniform should be alert at all times—lesson number one, for Christ's sake! Instead of being alert, they had been jawing at each other inside E. Rox's head when the dart had hit them.

A cracco dart.

The craccos had finally caught up with E. Rox. Those same nasty little buggers who'd kidnapped O. Rani, his girlfriend, had shot E. Rox with that same kind of tranquilizer dart just as he had reached the top of the steps from the underground chamber.

Harry had regained consciousness first to find E. Rox and himself packed in this shipping tube. On their way to Ancaria, he was willing to bet, and while E. Rox was still out, as of this moment, he seemed okay otherwise, breathing normally, heart beating, blood circulating—all systems go.

They were prisoners of war.

Targets for a firing squad, Harry thought, if you wanted to be exact about it . . .

* * *

In the ancient castle that housed the once-clandestine laboratory of the Jassan scientist Los Ross, there was some cause for celebration.

Los Ross had found the body of Harry Borg.

"In the fourth pirissium," he told Chad and the others. "In the lissia tekuss, beyond Tomiss Twelve."

"I'm glad," Chad said, trying to appear knowledgeable.

"It is all right?" Arnie asked. "The body, I mean?"

"Perfectly all right," Los Ross said. He went on to explain that Harry's body was in a condition known as Fluss Four, which was one of the several stages a solid body went through while being disassembled for transport through time and space, and that it could be reassembled at the receiving station on the planet Orca without too much difficulty.

"Glad to hear that," someone said.

There were other matters for concern, to be sure. Whether or not Harry Borg would be there to reclaim the body when it arrived was one of those other matters. And once in possession of his body, whether or not he would be able to get the seeds of the ursis plant was another. And still another was whether or not, after obtaining the seeds, he would be able to join up with Lori and Sissi. And even beyond these was the matter of whether or not, after informing Los Ross they were ready, Los Ross would be able to bring them home.

Nor were these matters all. Perhaps the most crucial of all the matters was the fact that *all* the matters had to be resolved within a severely limited amount of time. If they exceeded the time allotted, the Peacekeepers would come and destroy the laboratory, and Guss Rassan, their much-loved friend, would be fed into the Converter.

"How much time we got left?" Sam Barnstable asked.

"Three days," Eddie Cole said, his black face shining with the sweat of anxiety. "And that is not very much."

"It's enough," Arnie said. "Right, Mr. Ross?"

"It should be," Los Ross said.

"So what's to worry about?"

"Who's worrying?"

Los Ross said, "The body of Mr. Borg will arrive on Orca within the hour." His spectacles shifted crookedly on his muzzle, and he straightened them. "Not within the hour in our time reference," he added. "They are a little more than twenty turns to the oss of us. It will be—let me consult my notes . . ." He took a calculatorlike apparatus from his smock pocket, and pushed several buttons. "It will be a rass wiss from now. Or perhaps sooner." He looked hopefully at their anxious faces, his slender, forked tongue flickering.

"Sounds about right," Chad said.

"Give or take a couple of wiss," Homer agreed.

"When he arrives in the receiving station, we will be able to make voice contact with him again."

"How can we do that?"

"The zissi beam is centralized on the niss at that point."

"Oh, I see . . ."

Los Ross turned away, knowing that they did not see or understand a fraction of what he said. There was so much they didn't see and understand, these Homo sapiens. And perhaps it was just as well. If they knew all there was to know, they would be worried to distraction.

He knew all there was to know, and he was very worried.

He knew there was not nearly enough time left to do comfortably and safely all that had to be done—if, indeed, it could be done at all. Guss, sitting next to the

Converter that would turn his flesh into fertilizer when time ran out, was in extreme peril. The laboratory was in extreme peril. And if the laboratory was destroyed before Harry, Lori, and Sissi were returned, those three would be lost forever.

Nor was that all.

There was the more immediate problem of the quiss.

While the quiss, the small reptilian creature he had sent to Orca to test the apparatus, was well suited for experimental work, it did have a very high metabolic rate and required an amount of food equal to its own body weight every twenty-four hours.

A ravenous little beast.

Insects were the usual food of quisses. All kinds of insects. And it was very adept at catching and killing these. It would also eat other prey. Worms, for example. Small birds. Even fish. And, should the supply of these become exhausted, the quiss was known to eat other quisses. And when the other quisses were gone, it would eat anything else it could find. If the quiss had not starved to death before the body of Harry Borg arrived, fresh and warm, utterly defenseless and rich in protein—

Ah, but there are some things best not thought about at all . . .

E. Rox recovered consciousness gradually, shuddering. Harry Borg took control of the long, thin body, afraid his Orcan host might thrash about in the shipping tube and injure himself if the drug from the cracco dart were to induce severe withdrawal symptoms. E. Rox did jerk and buckle, knocking his knees against the sides of the tube, pumping his head about.

"Steady, steady . . ." Harry whispered gently.

E. Rox gasped. "Uh . . . uh! Ah . . . ah . . ."

"Hang on, son."

Harry experienced some of the pain E. Rox was feeling, and saw some of the bright flashes that flickered behind the eyes of the Orcan. And he knew there would be blind panic during those first few moments. To awaken in total darkness, to find oneself constrained totally by some enclosure—what more frightening awakening could there be?

As full consciousness came, E. Rox's body became rigid.

"Easy now," Harry whispered. "It's all right . . . you're okay . . ."

"Harry!"

"Yeah, Roxie, right here."

"Oh, thank Osmos!"

"You're okay, we're okay."

"Where *are* we?"

"We're on a plane. En route, you might say—"

"The craccos!" E. Rox said suddenly. "They caught me!"

"That they did. Hit us with that capture dart as we came out of that receiving station."

"Crixx!"

"You can say *that* again."

"Do you know where they are taking us?" E. Rox asked after a moment.

"Five'll get you ten it's Ancaria."

"It must be." E. Rox paused. "Why? Why, Harry?"

"Come *on*! You know why."

"Tell me."

"We killed Sana, remember? Makes you their number one bad guy. Be a reward on your head that'd keep your average cracco in luxury the rest of his life."

"And that means—"

"Yeah."

"Oh, jixxo."

"Take it easy!" Harry said. "We're not dead yet by a long shot. There's something about you they don't know, remember?"

"What is that?"

"You're really two people—you and me."

"Oh."

"Makes a difference," Harry said. "I don't know what the difference'll be, but it'll be enough to convince 'em they've tangled tails with the toughest Orcan alive, I guarantee it!"

E. Rox was silent for a long moment, his rapid, frightened breathing gradually slowing down to something approaching normal. Then he spoke softly. "Harry?"

"Yeah?"

"Why are you still with me?"

"It's where I belong, you knucklehead."

"You could have left."

"Why would I do a thing like that?"

"You did before."

"Yeah . . . yeah, but then you needed privacy."

"You are in extreme danger now."

"Nah! Anyway, I'm in love with your girlfriend, O. Rani. They're probably taking us where they took her. Got to do what I can to get her back."

"I don't believe it."

"Don't believe what?"

"That you're in love with O. Rani."

"Sure, I am. Figuratively speaking."

"Whatever that is."

"It means I care, y' dummy!"

"Oh."

"And besides, it's cold out there."

There was silence. Finally E. Rox spoke again. "Harry?"

"What?"

"Thank you."

"Aw, f'r . . . all right! What the hell? You're welcome."

They were met by a squad of ten Ancans, a kind of a
SWAT team of soldiers, all bigger than most, all heavily
armed, a row of lion faces, a bank of huge red eyes,
glaring malevolence. And they gathered, snarling hatred,
around E. Rox when he was dumped out of the shipping
tube and onto the stone flagging of a courtyard.

"Orcan filth!" an ugly voice roared.

The owner of the voice was the squad leader. His fury
was like fire in his red eyes as he shoved his lion's face
into the face of E. Rox, bared his saberlike tusks, and
held them threateningly close, blowing a fetid breath.

"*You* killed Sana?" he roared in disbelief.

E. Rox did not answer.

"I do not believe it!" The squad leader spat, cursing.
He wiped his gaping maw with the back of one huge
hand. "I could kill a score like you!"

"In a pig's ass," Harry muttered.

"What did you say?" the leader roared. "You speak?"

"I said nothing," E. Rox said.

"I heard!"

Outwardly, E. Rox remained silent. Inwardly, he said,
"Harry, for Osmos' sake! There are ten of them!"

"Okay, okay."

Still shaken from a bone-rattling ride, stiff and
cramped from the long hours in the shipping tube, they
were dragged across the eight-sided square and made to
stand against the wall of an eight-sided, cell-like building
that was made of a strange substance more like plastic
than wood or metal or stone. And they were even further
abused. It seemed every one of the squad of Ancans had

to have vengeance of some kind for the killing of Sana—
a swinging, cuffing blow to the side of E. Rox's head, a
blob of foul phlegm spat into his face, or simply a filthy
curse.

E. Rox and Harry endured it all.

E. Rox had insisted that he have control of his body,
and Harry was willing that he should have it—at least,
until a final need required that he take command.

Now he was proud of E. Rox.

The Orcan stood defiantly erect, a fine soldier. Ten
feet tall, as thin as sticks, battered but defiant, his antennae folded tightly down his back, his disklike, china-blue
eyes unflinching—Harry had known a few heroes in his
time, but none he had ever known had stood taller than
E. Rox was standing now.

"Good lad," he said. "Hang in."

"Where can O. Rani be?" E. Rox asked, his voice
thin, strained.

"We'll find her," Harry promised. "If we have to tear
this joint apart brick by brick, we'll find her!"

"They are waiting for someone now."

"Give you odds it's the grand monster himself."

"Tanta?"

"Be my guess."

"Your guess is right," E. Rox whispered in sudden
fear.

Tanta ut Krill, the king of the Ancans, had appeared.

He had come out of the eight-sided building across the
square, pushing a wave of underlings before him and
dragging more in his wake. He was by far the largest
Ancan they had yet seen, a lumbering hulk of a beast.
His white mane was stiffly arrayed above the hairy cape
of his wide, sloping shoulders. His huge, red eyes were
ablaze. The great, gold-encased tusks, curving out of his
upper jaw, reached almost to his chest. His thickly

corded arms hung wide of his body. The bent fingers of his pawlike hands brushed the ground as he walked.

In spite of himself, E. Rox began to tremble.

With reason, Harry had to admit. "Ugliest bastard I ever laid eyes on," he growled. "Meaner-lookin' than a pack of junkyard dogs."

E. Rox could hardly breathe. "Ixxi protect us . . ."

"Want me to take over?"

"No! This is my responsibility."

"Bull! . . . But I'm right here."

The king of the Ancans came to a halt immediately before E. Rox, fury showing in every line of his great, hairy body. His retinue of underlings formed a semicircle at a safe distance, all manes erect, all red eyes glaring. Tanta stared at E. Rox, measuring the tall, very slender, and badly abused Orcan with his belligerent, glowering red eyes, and his anger gradually gave way to disbelief.

"*This* creature killed my son?"

"So it was reported," an underling said.

The squad leader, measuring Tanta's reaction accurately, said, "I do not believe it, sire!"

Tanta swung his red eyes. "Why?" he demanded.

"Sana could have beheaded this Orcan with a stroke of his bare hand," the squad leader said nervously.

"I was told he killed Sana and three others."

"Lies!" the squad leader said, gaining courage.

Tanta turned his eyes back to stare again, measuring again the stiff and sweating E. Rox. "Yes, lies!" he growled.

"Lies," the squad leader echoed.

"Lies," the members of the retinue murmured.

Tanta stared at E. Rox a moment longer. His anger now diminished to disgust. The certainty that he had been lied to became clear in his eyes, and with that certainty came a decision. He swung a big hand up to grasp

E. Rox by the antenna, to lift E. Rox's head high, stretching his neck, and with the other hand he reached for the big, hook-bladed knife that hung at his belt.

He was going to behead E. Rox.

Later, he would have the Ancan who had lied to him brought before him for a disembowelment. Something slow and painful enough to discourage others who in the future might consider lying to him. Since he was in no hurry, and since this beheading was of so little importance, Tanta took his time, enjoying again one of his favorite diversions. He relished beheading Orcans, however unimportant they might be.

"You stinking bastard," Harry said.

And he went into action.

Against just such an emergency, he had had a plan of action formed and ready. He left the mind and body of E. Rox with a sudden explosion of malevolence of his own, bent on doing Tanta ut Krill great bodily harm. But, like so many plans of men, this plan went awry.

"Son of a bitch!" he yelled in frustration.

He had laid hold of Tanta's right arm, the one lifting the hook-bladed knife, intent on twisting it around and up Tanta's back in a hammerlock that would either break his arm or dislocate his shoulder—but he found he could do none of these. He had not yet achieved the power or the skill to accomplish that much as a wraith.

Tanta roared, startled.

He had felt the grip of Harry's once powerful hands on the wrist of his sword arm as he had tried to raise the blade, a grip of hands unseen yet as real as any. Harry could not twist the arm behind Tanta, but neither could Tanta raise the sword.

Tanta roared in fury now.

Who dared? What dared?

Tanta loosed E. Rox's antennae, the frail Orcan forgotten. Tanta ut Krill had been attacked by a demon! An unseen demon! Tanta was not frightened. Nothing seen or unseen could frighten the king of the Anca. He was savagely infuriated. He fought the grip that held fast to his right arm, lunging, surging, roaring. And Harry, the unseen wraith, clung to the massive right arm with both hands now, as savagely determined as the monster he fought to control, and he was dragged and flung about like a dog that might have fastened teeth in a gorilla.

"Help him!"

"Stand back!"

"What is it?"

Excited, helpless cries, frightened cries, came from the retinue, the squad of heavily armed Anca soldiers, and even the squad leader. They were all gape-mouthed. Had Tanta, the king, gone suddenly berserk? He was lunging, fighting, roaring, as if some invisible beast had seized his right arm. Or was it a beast? Was it instead some magical power? Was the same power that had killed Sana, guided by a miserable Orcan, now attacking the king himself?

Tanta stumbled and fell.

"Gods be cursed!" He rolled, screaming in rage, got to his feet, and lashed about with his great right arm. Snapping it here, whipping it there, he tried to free his arm of the painful vise-jawed trap. Harry hung on with grim and fierce enjoyment, cursing and struggling.

"Break, you bastard!"

Tanta's people circled him, wanting to help, too fearful, too mystified to lay on hands, crying out in their anxiety and fear. Harry gauged the effect carefully. When he judged he had done all that could be done, he released his hold on Tanta's arm and stood away. Tanta whipped his arm about twice more before realizing that the mysterious grip was gone. Then he came erect to turn and stare at E. Rox, who had remained against the wall, still erect and defiant.

Tanta stood, rubbing his arm, chest heaving, red eyes smoldering insanity. He crossed back to E. Rox. His voice came from deep in his chest, gargling with barely controlled fury.

"What . . . what did you do to me?"

E. Rox's huge, china-blue eyes did not waver. "I—I did nothing."

"A . . . a force caught my arm," Tanta said. "You sent it!"

"No."

"Who then?"

"The gods," E. Rox said. "For you are evil."

"You—" Tanta lifted his right arm again, to strike E. Rox in the face. And if he had, indeed, struck the Orcan in the face, the strength born of his fury would have crushed bones and turned flesh to bleeding pulp. But he stayed his hand, remembering.

Instead, while staring into the defiant face of E. Rox, he spoke to the squad leader who hovered near. "Keep this Orcan," he said. "Keep him safe."

"Safe, sire?"

"Alive and safe," Tanta said, his great red eyes still fixed on the light blue eyes of E. Rox. "This Orcan has powers I can use." Then, directly to E. Rox, he said, "I will get those powers from you, Orcan! I will tear them out of you."

"Like hell, you will!" Harry said.

Harry had returned to E. Rox. And because E. Rox had not spoken, Harry had used E. Rox's voice. Though Tanta may not have understood the meaning, the tone of quiet defiance was clear enough. Again, Tanta had to control an urge to mangle.

He turned suddenly and lumbered away.

The squad leader watched Tanta disappear into the building across the square and saw his retinue sucked in after him. Then he turned to glare at E. Rox, angered, puzzled, and wary.

"Arrrrack!" the squad leader cursed, and scratched his belly. "You live, filth!" he growled.

Harry used E. Rox's voice again. "Up yours, muck-head."

The squad leader's eyes sharpened menacingly. "What is muckhead?"

"A word of praise." That was E. Rox, who had pushed back into control, trying to avoid a needless smashup. Inwardly, he said, "Harry, for Osmos sake!"

"Yeah, yeah," Harry answered him.

Harry's attention had gone past the squad leader now to a group of Ancans who had just emerged from a building and were crossing toward the building entrance where Tanta had disappeared. The group was made up of female Ancans. Their gender was obvious, since they all were well-endowed with mammary glands. Several of the females wore manes of various colors, and one wore a mane that was violently purple.

"Good Lord almighty!" Harry whispered.

What had caught Harry's attention and was now holding it in open-mouthed disbelief was the fact that floating and skipping along with the Anca females were two smaller females.

One of the smaller creatures was a human being.

The other was unmistakably Jassan.

And Harry knew them both.

Harry used E. Rox's voice again, this time in a bellowing roar.

"Lori! Is that *you*?"

CHAPTER 20

Lori Borg, on hearing that bellowing, telepathic roar from her beloved Harry—hearing it here, in Ancaria, the capital city of these creatures called Ancans, the most horrible-looking race of monsters this side of a nightmare—was so surprised that she jumped straight up in the air a distance of thirty feet, her eyes wide, almost bugging, her skin tingling like a cat struck by lightning, her arms flailing to keep her balance. She tried to scream back at him vocally, telepathically, any way at all: "Harry? Harry! Oh, my God! Harry! Where are you? Where the hell've you been?"

But nothing came out.

She was too startled, or too excited.

And no wonder. The past day and a half had been the most trying, exciting, scary hours of her life. After she had all but wrecked the combat headquarters of the Ancans by tearing up a table and throwing it halfway across the room as a demonstration of what she could provide in the way of magic, things had begun to happen one right after another!

"You are not a tansy," Kana, the queen, had said.

"I'm not?" Lori had responded, gulping.

227

They were in the queen's chambers, the turmoil that had followed the crash of the table—a feat of magic absolutely unprecedented in Ancan history—fifteen minutes in the past. There were probably electrical connections still sizzling and snapping, still yells of alarm, bellows of rage, and shrieks of dismay going on, but they were several eight-sided buildings away now and could not be heard here in the queen's private quarters.

Kana, the queen, resplendent in her purple mane and many-cupped brassiere, and three of her most trusted aides who were almost as striking had brought Lori and Sissi into these almost soundproof chambers for reasons that were just now becoming clear.

They had not been rough or violent.

They had been firm, but only courteously firm, and once out of the sight and hearing of Tanta and the all-male members of his staff, they had become secretive.

Conspiratorial, Lori thought.

And she had also thought: What the heck is going on?

Something important certainly was happening. She could still sense it. The secretive, excited, and very serious way the queen and her maids were acting couldn't be read in any other terms. They were up to something. Something big.

Continuing the conversation, Kana said, "There are no such things as tansies."

"There aren't?" Lori asked cautiously.

"You know it, and I know it," Kana said. "Tanta also knows it. But since the citizens of Anca tend to be superstitious, and since they *want* to believe in such things, he has decided to let them go on believing you are a tansy. And that you *can* do feats of magic."

"So," Lori said, treading very carefully, "If I am not tansy, what do you suppose we are?"

"You are creatures from another planet."

Bingo! The queen had gotten the answer right the first time. She had known all about them all along and hadn't let on—and that scared Lori and Sissi. They moved a little closer together.

Lori had to swallow hard before she was able to speak. "We are?"

"You must be," Kana said. She took a moment to study them. "I know you are frightened. We must seem very strange to you."

"Strange? Yes, you could say that." Lori looked at Sissi again. "Wouldn't you say they were sort of strange, Sissi?"

"Sort of strange . . . yes," Sissi agreed.

"But don't get the idea we're racist!" Lori said hurriedly, turning back. "Just because you've got a different-colored skin, and tusks, and a lot of those, well, you know, bosoms—that doesn't mean you're not just as human as anybody else. Well . . . maybe not human exactly, but . . . you know what I mean. Your Majesty. Ma'am. Don't you?"

The queen smiled—if something that looked like a good-natured snarl could be called a smile—at Lori's clumsy efforts to avoid offending her. "I know what you mean."

"Glad to hear that! Your Eminence. Ma'am."

"There are records," the queen said, "very ancient records that tell of times when the Orcans had dealings with the inhabitants of worlds very far away. We, the Ancans, were not sure whether these records were true accounts or myths."

"They were true, all right."

"Since you are able to do the things you do—spring into the air, as you do, and lift very heavy things," the queen said, "the gravity on your planet must be much stronger than the gravity on our planet. Isn't that so?"

"Hey! You know about things like *that*?"

"We are *not* without some knowledge," the queen said. She straightened the back of her mane, perhaps a little miffed. "Our civilization is a very old one."

"I'm sorry!" Lori said. "I didn't mean to insult you."

"What planet are you from?"

"We're from Earth," Lori said. "Excuse me, *I'm* from Earth. Sissi, here, she's from—well, a planet next door to Earth. It's called Essa. She's a Jassan. And a very nice lady. She's not my handmaiden or my servant, by the way. She's my friend. And our planets are around a star we call the Sun. It's twenty light-years from here . . . twenty *light*-years? Gosh!" Her eyes got big, thinking about it. "That *is* a long ways, isn't it?"

"Yes, it is."

"And we came all that *distance*?"

"You *are* here."

"Imagine!"

It was still very hard for Lori to believe.

"Your civilization is very advanced," Kana said.

"It is?"

"It must be, since your people were able to transport you through space a distance of twenty light-years."

"Oh, that! Well, it wasn't exactly *our* civilization did the transporting. Not the *human* civilization, anyway. I mean, our human civilization is—" Lori twisted her hands in an a-little-of-this, a-little-of-that kind of expression—"well, we're sort of mixed up. We've got *some* smarts, but the truth is, we don't know what to do with them. We keep getting ourselves in a lot of trouble— that's what we do with them."

"But they *were* able to send you here."

"That was Sissi's people who did that!" Lori put her arm around Sissi's shoulders, drawing her close. "Sissi's people are way ahead of us in a lot of respects. Scientifically, they are, at least."

"*Her* civilization was able to send you, then?"

"You've got it! Your Royal Highness. Ma'am."

"*Why* did they send you?"

Lori looked at Sissi, then back to Queen Kana.

"Well, you see, here, on your planet," Lori said then, "you've got a plant—a sort of a vegetable—growing that can save a lot of lives on *our* planet. It's got a chemical in its leaves, like the willow leaves back home have a chemical that makes aspirin, and it—Well, anyway, my husband...his name is Harry. He's big. Wears this beard. And he's got these great teeth. He's the reason I'm here. I'm lookin' for him. Have you seen him? Or heard anything about somebody like that?"

"No," the queen said. "A male of your species?"

"Mine, not Sissi's."

"There have been no reports of such a male."

"Darn! I wonder what could have happened to him!"

Sissi dug an elbow in Lori's ribs. Lori excused herself and moved away a little to whisper telepathically, anxiously, to Sissi.

"Now what?"

"You're talking goofy!" Sissi said.

"I know it! I'm *scared*—I can't help it!"

"They aren't going to hurt us."

"*You* talk to them."

"I'm just your handmaiden, remember?"

"Oh, shoot!"

"Lori!"

"All right!"

They turned and moved back to face the queen, who had been waiting patiently. "Excuse us, Your Majesty. My friend, here, wanted to scold me a little was all. Sir. I mean, ma'am."

"I understand," Queen Kana said patiently.

"*That's* a relief."

"You are not going to be harmed," the queen said. "We are going to ask you to help us."

"You are?" Lori winced at another elbow dig. "I mean, we would be happy to do anything we can to help you in any way we can. Wouldn't we, Sissi?"

"Yes, we would," Sissi said.

Kana studied them both for a moment, her enormous red eyes sharp and measuring. Then, apparently reaching a final decision, she leaned forward to speak conspiratorally.

"You must not repeat what I am about to say."

"Oh, we won't, Your Royalty!"

The queen winced. "Just plain Kana, please."

"Yes, ma'am. Kana. Your Highness."

The queen sighed and then went on. "If your civilization—or your handmaiden's, excuse me, your *friend's* civilization—is so advanced they are able to transport you twenty light-years through space," the queen said, "then they must be knowledgeable in many other things."

"Oh, they are! They are!"

"We have a problem," the queen said. She went on then to explain what that problem was, and she was more than greatly relieved to learn, after a lengthy, highly classified discussion, in which Sissi played a more important role than Lori, that the problem was perhaps no problem at all.

"We had the same one," Sissi said. "And we solved it."

"Can this material be transported?" the queen asked.

"I would think so. Wouldn't you, Lori?"

"They transported us, didn't they?"

It was at that moment that they were all summoned to the chamber of Ra, the creature Lori thought of as the "queen ant," for what proved to be further discussion—most of which was, again, very confidential.

Lori was once again all but overwhelmed at the sight of Ra.

"She's so big!"

At least fifty feet long and twenty feet high, a pulsating, segmented tube, changing color from violet to purple and back again, with the head of a giant ant, mandibles and antennae and all at one end, and an egg-laying orifice, going *pfuuuuut!* and laying an egg every few minutes, at the other, and with pony-size ants scurrying about carrying the eggs away, cleaning her and feeding her—well, in Lori's eyes, Ra was horrendous.

Horrendous and big.

But perhaps what awed Lori most was Ra's *presence.* When one came into this gigantic eight-sided chamber, the first thing one felt was that one was visiting a super-being, a great *mother* of some kind. A mother who gave life, who cared for, who guided. And you couldn't really, not *really,* be afraid of her.

"She's sort of *everybody's* mother," she whispered to Sissi.

"She's a big ant," Sissi said. Sissi was pragmatist of the first order.

She did listen, however, as Ra told them that it was indeed fortunate that Sissi and Lori had come to the planet Orca at this particular time, a time when Queen Kana and all others of her kind were in great need.

"Glad to help if we can," Lori said.

"Our pleasure," Sissi said.

Ra, the mother, was in on the conspiracy with Kana, as it turned out. Lori and Sissi would not have been sur-

prised to learn that it had been her idea in the beginning
—she seemed to be that much in charge of things.

"About my husband, Harry," Lori said. "I was wondering—"

"Yes," Ra said. "I have word of him."

"You have?" Lori's voice was a startled squeak.

"He is here," Ra said. "On this planet."

"Oh, my gosh! Where? Where is he?"

"In the ancient city of Atoxia. He lies waiting."

"He does? Lies waiting? Good heavens? Are you
sure?"

"Certain. My minions brought me this information."

"Sissi, you hear what she said?"

"I heard."

"We've got to go there!" Lori shrieked. She was all
but jumping up and down.

Kana, the queen of the Ancans, intervened quietly
and firmly and took the overexcited Lori out of the
chamber of Ra before she, in her overwrought state,
could do something that might bring harm to herself or
to Ra.

"But I've *got* to go to Harry . . . to Atoxia!"

"That," Kana said, "will not be easy."

"Why not?"

"We are now at war with the Orcans—"

"War or no war, I—"

"—and Atoxia is behind enemy lines."

"Oh, futz!" Lori said.

There had followed a very heated discussion in which
Lori forgot to be as courteous as she ought toward a
queen, but which lack was forgiven, since the queen
wanted so much from Lori; and the queen had finally
said that they would go to Tanta and ask that a special
expeditionary force be organized and sent to take pos-

session of the ancient city so that Lori could then go to Harry.

And it had been while they were on their way to Tanta's combat headquarters to persuade him to begin the battle for Atoxia that Lori had heard Harry's telepathic roar.

"Lori, is that *you*?"

CHAPTER 21

The roar that had sent Lori shooting straight up in the air held her there, it seemed, a long, long while. "Harry? Where are you?" she was yelling.

She could not see Harry anywhere.

There was a group of Ancan soldiers, huge, burly beasts, gathered around a tall, skinny, badly battered Orcan on the far side of the eight-sided square. The Orcan was looking in her direction, his huge blue eyes bulging, his antennae standing straight up like giant jackrabbit ears, quivering. He was waving his skinny arms at her as if he knew her, but there was no Harry anywhere in sight.

She got her feet on the ground finally. "*Harry*! Where *are* you?"

"Here, honey. I'm *here*!"

Lori looked everywhere with desperate excitement. She looked all around the eight-sided square, at all the eight-sided buildings, at all the octagon-shaped windows. She looked in among all the Anca soldiers who had fallen to their hands and knees, facing away, in a gesture of absolute obeisance. It had occurred to them, all at once, that in her excited state the tansy might inadvertently point a wand at them and thus end their existence. But there was no Harry.

"Sissi! Do you see him anyplace?"

"No, Lori!"

"Did you *hear* him?"

"I heard him."

"He's got to be here someplace! *Harry*, damn it! Where *are* you? Show yourself! Do *something!*"

"Easy, now, honey," Harry's telepathic voice said. "Take it *easy!*"

Lori saw the skinny, beat-up Orcan coming toward her, patting the air in a calming gesture, but still no Harry. She was a moment looking frantically in other places, and then a sudden realization scared her so badly that her scalp crawled and her own eyes bugged.

The skinny Orcan was using Harry's voice!

"Harry?" she shrieked. "Is that you?"

The Orcan said, "It's me, honey. Don't panic."

Lori didn't panic.

She went, "Yeeeeeek!" grabbed Sissi, and got behind Queen Kana and her ladies-in-waiting. An *Orcan*? Ten feet tall, skinny as a stick, big blue eyes and *antennae*? Talking like *Harry*? And coming after her . . .

"Damn it, Lori! Listen to me!"

And *swearing* like Harry?

"Get away from me!" Lori shrieked.

Queen Kana and her ladies-in-waiting were less frightened. They formed a barricade between Lori and the Orcan. The queen scolded the Ancan soldiers.

"Stop him, you cowards!"

The Ancan soldiers lunged into action.

The Orcan—E. Rox and Harry, with Harry very much in charge and getting desperate—was already across the square. He had reached the group of female Ancans who had formed up like a herd of musk-oxen protecting their young from wolves, and he was dodging back and forth trying find Lori and Sissi among the Anca females.

"Lori! It's me, Harry! Come out of there!"

Sissi, less frightened, called, "Harry? Harry Borg?"

"Yes, Sissi!" Harry's telepathic voice was pleading. "It's me! Harry Borg. Tell Lori I'm—I'm inside this... this Orcan."

The Anca soldiers got hold of E. Rox, then, and started beating on him. The soldiers had been ordered by Tanta to keep this Orcan safe, but keeping him safe allowed them to use whatever force they deemed necessary to effectively control the Orcan. And they had deemed a lot was necessary.

E. Rox and Harry fought back, cursing.

"Lemme go, you—"

The Orcan, powered by a now infuriated Harry Borg, knocked one of the Ancans down, kicked another in the belly, and all but broke the arm off a third. Lori, peeking through her defensive wall of Ancan females, hearing raging, purple curses peculiar to the man she loved, slowly became convinced that her Harry had to be out there somewhere.

"Hold it! Hold it!" she yelled.

The yell brought the conflict to a halt.

The Ancan soldiers held fast to E. Rox but, on orders from the queen, stopped beating on him. The queen and her ladies allowed Lori and Sissi to edge carefully through their protective cordon. Keeping a safe distance, Lori peered up at the big, blue, and now slightly agonized eyes of the Orcan.

"Harry?" Her voice was tentative. "Are you there?"

"I'm here, honey."

E. Rox was panting heavily, wearily. While Harry Borg, the Earthman, his guest, was using his body, he was still the one who had to provide the strength and the air necessary to make the body function, and he was running short of both strength and air. Very short.

"I—I don't believe it," Lori said.

"It's true, damn it!" Harry said.

"Don't swear, Harry."

"Lori, for—listen. I'm here. Honest!"

"Where?" Lori could see nothing but a big, tall, funny-looking Orcan.

"I'm inside him," Harry said.

"You're . . . wearing an *Orcan* suit, Harry?"

"I'm not wearing a damn suit! I'm *inside* him!"

"Oh, hey!"

"I *am*, Lori!"

"Come on, now, Harry. Cut it out!"

"It's true!"

"I'll bet!"

"Lori!" Sissi said. "I think he's telling the truth!"

"You *believe* that?" Lori was incredulous. "You believe that, you'll believe anything. The Tooth Fairy . . . the Easter Bunny . . . Santa Claus . . . Come *on*!"

She had been staring up at the Orcan's expressive eyes as she talked . . . and now something there, something familiar, began to make an impression, and her conviction began to weaken. "Harry . . ."

"Yes, hon."

"Honest?"

"Honest, honey."

"Well . . . Come out, then."

"I can't."

"You got in there, didn't you?"

"Yes, but—"

"If you got in there, you can get out."

"No, I can't. I mean, you couldn't see me."

"Couldn't see you, Harry? What're you talking about?"

"I'd be invisible. A wraith."

"A wraith?" Lori's voice went a little shrill. Out of the side of her mouth she said, "Sissi, what's a wraith?"

"I don't know."

"It's like a spirit," Harry said.

"A spirit? You're a ghost, Harry?"

"Something like that."

"You're dead!"

"No, I'm not dead!"

"Help!" Lori exclaimed. "I'm going nuts! I'm... I'm..."

"Lori! Stop it!" Sissi said. She added emphasis by punching Lori in the back. Lori stopped her babbling to stand bug-eyed, staring at E. Rox. Sissi spoke urgently to the queen. "Your Majesty, we've got a problem."

Her Majesty, even more bewildered than Lori, was staring at the Orcan, who seemed to be possessed, and then at the little tansylike creature from a distant planet, who seemed about to collapse into idiocy.

"Yes," she said faintly, "you *do* have a problem."

"It has something to do with space transporting."

"Space transporting?" the queen said.

"Something went amiss."

"It sure did!" Harry said, through E. Rox.

Sissi said, "If they could be together . . . talk it out . . ."

"Just a darn minute—" Lori began.

"Hush," Sissi said. She turned her attention back to the queen. "It will be all right."

"The three of us," Harry said.

"The three of us," Sissi said.

"You're not afraid of this Orcan?" the queen asked doubtfully.

"No," Sissi said. "He's somebody we know . . . kind of."

The queen looked at E. Rox. "And you?"

Harry, inside E. Rox, said, "Lady, this little female is my wife. I mean, if I could get her alone, I could explain to her how I got to be in this body."

The queen looked doubtful. "Really?"

"What do you mean?"

"If you could explain something like that to a mate, and make her believe it . . ."

"Give me a chance, that's all I ask!"

The queen looked at Lori. "Are you willing?"

Lori was looking at E. Rox. That great, tall, skinny creature with blue eyes and antennae like a bug—her Harry was in *there*? How could it be? It was impossible. Forget it! Talk to him? No way! It was too dangerous.

Oh, sassafras! What next?

"Okay," she said finally. "For a few minutes . . ."

"Guards," the queen said. "Take them to the tansy's quarters."

CHAPTER 22

In the receiving station in the ancient city of Atoxia, the little quiss had long ago passed the stage of simply being ravenous. The last insect had been found, captured, and devoured. A few decayed and desiccated remnants of old military equipment had been able to sustain the little beast this long after the last insect was gone. Now it needed to eat or die within hours.

There *was* food.

The searching forked tongue of the quiss had located the newly arrived body of Harry Borg. The body was alive, the heart beating, the blood flowing, the chest rising and falling with quiet breathing. To the quiss, the body was a veritable mountain of warm flesh, and it was lying just there, on a plateau out of reach. The quiss could not climb the smooth surfaces that supported the plateau. It could not jump high enough to reach the plateau, though it had tried many, many times.

Now, the quiss lay panting, its forked tongue flickering, its vertically slitted eyes roaming the room, searching.

There were tubes against one wall that led to the ceiling, and outer tubes in brackets that crossed the ceiling to service the apparatus beneath which the warm flesh was lying.

The prehensile feet of the quiss were capable of climbing the vertical tubes, and there was enough space between the horizontal tubes that crossed the ceiling and the ceiling itself to permit the quiss to cross over to a position above the warm flesh. Once there, the quiss could drop and feast on a supply of food that would last for many, many days.

The roaming eyes of the quiss had fixed on the vertical tubes. The quiss was no more capable of thought than an ant or a cockroach. But a lack of an ability to think has never prevented an ant from finding its way with a devastating infallibility to a supply of sugar, or a cockroach to a supply of fat. Nor would the same lack prevent the quiss finding the pathway to the warm flesh.

All the quiss needed was a little time.

Very little . . .

Cutting deeply into the Rota Desert, the vast expanse of red rock and hot sand that had for all memory separated the Ancans from Orcia, was a great gorge, steep-walled, a thousand miles in length. At the bottom of the gorge, a raging stream steamed and roared, finding a tortuous way to the hot sea known as the Ocean of Macomal.

The gorge was known as the Cada.

While Ancan military aircraft could, and did, pass over the Cada, and while ground vehicles could, and did, travel around the Cada, there could be no military victory won against Orca until the infantry, the foot soldiers of Anca, had crossed the Cada in massive numbers.

In order to cross the Cada, bridges had to be built across the raging stream and access paths blasted into the cliffs. Tanta had established this crossing as his first goal in his earliest plans. All the necessary equipment had been designed, and much of it was now being brought into place.

The Orcans, knowing the plans, had developed the best possible defense against such an assault. Heavy weaponry emplaced on the heights could slaughter the invading Ancans as they came to the river and began building their crossings.

And slaughter they did.

For Orcans, whose love of live, all life, was deep and prevailing, this was a most tormenting ordeal.

They killed and killed and killed.

Still the Ancans came in hordes.

Machinery, metal, and stone were needed. And they were used. But the final success depended, as it always has in war, upon living, breathing flesh, on living creatures either brave enough to die or uncaring.

File after file, rank after rank, the Ancans came on.

Lumbering, bobbing, shuffling, their huge mouths agape to show their glistening fangs, their fingers trailing the ground, they were mindless. They had no need of minds or thinking. They were motivated by the single most powerful will on the entire planet: the will of Ran Tanta ut Krill.

They were driven.

They were driven by Tanta's will to walk blindly into that gorge of death, to fall before the scything rays of the cannon on the heights above them, to be trod upon by those who followed, to form a bridge of newly dead that would soon span the river, soon provide a ramp that would be the first step in a stairway that would take them up the far cliff. Beyond the cliff lay the open, almost defenseless belly of the Orcan nation. All that was needed to reach that belly, where they could feast to their heart's content on the entrails of freedom, was enough bodies . . .

And enough time.

Very little time . . .

For Guss Rassan, the moments were racing away like leaves before a gale-force wind, each leaf a fragment chipped away from the life he had left. And when the last was gone, and he was bare of life and empty, they would come for him and carry him, silently screaming, to the instrument of his demise.

Just there, beyond that doorway: the Converter with whizzing many-bladed knives.

He waited, his eight-fingered hands that had so often enthralled audiences numbering in the many thousands with symphonies of the most exquisite fragrances clasped in anxiety, twisting. His golden eyes were sheltered by gray veils. The tips of his tongue lay still, and his lean body sagged almost strengthless in the gray prison garb. He was the hostage, held to assure the safe return of Harry Borg. And if Harry Borg was not brought back before time ran out, Guss would be taken to his death.

Guss whispered a soft litany of prayers.

To the god Sarsis.

For a little more time . . .

The gaudily uniformed officer of the Peacekeeping Force on station in the laboratory had grown smug, Los Ross thought. He had grown smug with the now almost certain knowledge that very soon he would be allowed to send his lunatic force on a mission of punishment. The punishment would be the destruction of this laboratory

and with it every last remnant of the knowledge of the
Ancients, which Harry Borg had rescued from the now
lost island of Tassar, knowledge that he, Los Ross, had
just begun to translate and to bring back into use. The
punishment, which would be wrought because of one
mistake made by scientists long ago, would extinguish
perhaps for all time the last remaining patch of light that
still gleamed before the dark wall of eternal ignorance.

One mistake.

A giant mistake, certainly, one that had almost caused
the extermination of all life as it had then been known.
The scientists had turned the giant force of nuclear fis-
sion from peaceful use to weaponry. But it had been *only*
a mistake and not a deliberate, willful act. It had been
only another of the many mistakes upon which the success of all scientific inquiry is always built.

Mistakes and failures: the building blocks of achievement.

Los Ross watched the clock and saw the hands
sweeping away the time there was left. If the Earthman,
Harry Borg, was not returned, the Peacekeepers would
be loosed, blades and cudgels swinging, and the Earthman, his mate, and Sissi, Guss's mate, would be lost in
the crashing of broken glass and the flashing of torn circuits. With them would die the last hope of relearning
the knowledge of the Ancients, and after them would
come once more an age of dark ignorance.

Just a few hours.

So little time . . .

CHAPTER 23

The guards took E. Rox and Harry, Lori, and Sissi to the eight-sided cell-like apartment that the Ancans had provided Lori and Sissi when they had first arrived.

Thinking that they were providing for a tansy, a magical creature come out of ancient mythology to bring them good fortune, they had provided extremely well. The quarters were not only extremely comfortable, they were extremely secure. No outside force could gain admittance once all entries were locked, which meant, of course, that once inside, with all entries locked, no inside force could get out.

The Ancan soldiers had been told to keep the Orcan safe, and they had considered this to mean that they were to keep the Orcan locked in. Thus, all entries to the living quarters were not only locked, they were barred and guarded.

Guests of the queen they might be—but they were also prisoners of Ran Tanta ut Krill.

In the beginning, the fact that they were prisoners was of little consequence. In the beginning, on being locked into the quarters, they were more concerned with the difficulty, on the one hand, of explaining a very peculiar set of circumstances, and on the other hand, in believing those explanations.

"Now, just sit down here," Harry said, speaking telepathically from within the body and mind of another. "Sit here on this sofa...and I'll sit down—excuse me, my friend E. Rox will sit down—here near you..."

"Sissi," Lori said, "you sit here."

"Between you?"

"If you don't mind," Lori said. "He keeps grabbing at me, not you, and with you there, I'll be harder to reach."

"Oh, for Christ's sake!" Harry said.

"Harry! You're swearing again!"

To Sissi, Harry said, "I'm sorry. I don't want to hurt your feelings, but I can't get through to this scatter-wit if you sit between us!"

"Well, pardon me for living!"

"Don't mind him, Sissi. He's like that—rude!"

"So now you're beginning to recognize me!"

"Hey! He's right! I mean, *you're* right, Mr. Rox... Harry...whatever. If somebody's rude, chances are it's Mister Bigmouth Harry Borg, if *he's* anywhere around."

But it couldn't be so...

All she could see was this Orcan, this long and tall and tired-out character with absolutely enormous blue eyes and those funny antennae whatchumacallems sticking up on his head, or hanging down like broken promises around his cheeks, who kept saying with Harry's voice that he was Harry.

"I *am* Harry," he said.

E. Rox wondered how long his patience was going to hold out. And his strength. The little female earthling he was seeing was a warm and delightful creature. He was sure that, given better circumstances, he would like to know her better. Much better. But the way it was, with the mentally hard-muscled male earthling forcing his way into every thought and situation, he had hardly been able to say two words to her or get to know her at all.

"Here," Harry said to Lori. "Hold my hand."

Wide eyed and very tentative, Lori allowed the Orcan to take her hand, which all but disappeared in those long, long fingers with their gentle but firm grip.

Wow! It was wonderful.

A soft warm glow came from that hand and spread all through her, and she looked up at those saucer-size china-blue eyes, which were sort of agonized now, sort of pleading, and she thought that maybe this was going to be a little bit of all right . . .

"Harry?"

"No, Mrs. Borg," E. Rox said gently. "I'm the Orcan—"

Harry's rough voice cut in. "Get out of the way, will you? She's my wife, after all."

"I was only trying to—"

"Please! All right? Let me talk to her?"

When the voices had changed, the warmth of the hand had changed. It was still pleasant, a good, strong feeling, more the kind of a feeling she would get from Harry's hand, but not the warm, electrical feeling she had had before, when it had been the Orcan doing the holding and the talking.

"Lori, are you paying attention?" Sissi asked.

"Huh? What? Oh. *Sure* I'm paying attention!"

"You'd better!"

"What were you saying, Harry?"

"Oh, boy," Harry said. Lori had always been a trifle fey, but, *goodlordawmighty*! At a time like this? "Anyway," he said, "you're beginning to believe I'm here, a second personality, inside my friend? Isn't that right?"

"Beginning to, maybe," Lori admitted. "There's two

people, that's sure. Hey, and I kind of like the other one. What did you say your name was, mister?"

"E. Rox, Mrs. Borg," E. Rox said, pushing in. "I'm from up around Orcia. My family is very well known in the area—"

"Cut it out!" Harry said rudely. He was getting a little desperate. "All right, Lori. Watch this."

He forced himself out of the body of E. Rox and picked up a box from the table. The box seem to float in the air before Lori's eyes, to open and shut its own lid, to tumble gently, and finally to cross the room and settle on a table against the far wall. Harry came back and got inside E. Rox again.

"What d' you think of that?" he asked.

"Lord have mercy!" Lori said.

"That was me did that, Lori. I left the body of my friend, here, and I carried the box over there. Then I got back in this body, where I am now. Okay?"

"Weird," Sissi said.

"You can say that again!" Lori said.

"Weird," Sissi said.

"*Now* do you believe me?"

"I don't know—"

"All right, honey. Let me kiss you. Try that."

The tall, spindly Orcan reached, puckering his mouth, and Lori's shriek could have been heard clear back home, had anybody there been listening. "Don't touch me!"

"Lori—"

"Mrs. Borg—"

Both Harry and E. Rox wanted to calm her, to reassure her, but Lori was already across the room, her back to the wall, her hands up in a karate defensive set.

"Lori!" Sissi said. "For Osis sakes! What now?"

"I just remembered!"

Wearily, Harry said, "What did you just remember?"

"What that queen ant told me. She said you were lying in that . . . that what'd youcallit?—receiving station. And you couldn't be *there* and *here* too!"

"She told you *what*?" Harry yelled.

"That you were in that receiving station—" Lori broke it off, staring. "What am I talking? This is crazy! I can't be talking to you *here*, if you're *there*!"

"I'm here! My body must be—"

"See? I'm crazy!"

"How did she know my body was there?"

"Queen ants have ways—"

"The insects are known to communicate—" E. Rox tried to say.

"When did she tell you this?" Harry demanded.

"Just a little while ago . . . before we came here."

"Balls of fire!"

A sudden burst of energy drove E. Rox to his feet and to the door. The door was, of course, locked. E. Rox and Harry pounded on it, shouting.

"Open up! Open up, damn it!"

"Harry!" E. Rox pleaded. "What are you *doing*?"

"We've got to get to that station!" Harry said. "I can't leave my body lying around!"

The door was suddenly jerked open by the squad leader of the Ancan soldiers, the biggest and ugliest, and no doubt the toughest, of the lot.

"Lemme out of here!" Harry yelled.

The squad leader swung a club immediately, hitting E. Rox on the side of the head and knocking him down. E. Rox moaned with the pain. Harry only cursed.

The squad leader spat. "You stay!"

The door was slammed and locked.

Lori, who had followed the action wide-eyed, was

now very nearly convinced. Who else could swear like
that but her Harry? He *had* to be in that Orcan.

"Oh, Harry, you poor dear..."

She went to the Orcan, who was sitting now holding a
head that was booming with pain. But she was cuddling
only the Orcan. Harry was out of the Orcan now, raging
around the room... silently, because he couldn't speak
without the body and mind of E. Rox to power the process of communication. But he could break things.

And he did.

Vases, chairs, tables—

When he had exhausted himself and run out of fragile
objects, he regained control and reentered E. Rox to
grapple with the situation on a more sensible basis.

"How am I going to get to Atoxia?" he asked.

It was a question for everybody.

The Ancans were not going to let E. Rox take him
there—that, they all agreed, was fairly certain. Look at
the lump on his head. Could he go by himself? As a
wraith?

"You don't even know the way," Sissi said. "Do
you?"

"It's south of here," Harry said. "Generally speaking."

"See?" Lori said. "You'd get lost."

"How long could you last as a wraith?" E. Rox asked.

"Without a body? I don't know. When I left you at
your girlfriend's apartment and sat out what was left of
the night in the atrium—how long was that? Three?
Maybe four hours? I couldn't have lasted much longer.
Say five hours and that's about it."

"How do you travel when you're a wraith?" Lori
asked. "Do you go *whoosh* and you're there? Or what?"

"I don't go *whoosh*! I go like anybody else."

"You would never get there," E. Rox said.

"*Damnation!*" Harry said, by way of agreement.

Sissi said, "Let me see what I can do . . ." She got up and went to the door.

The other three—Harry, Lori, and E. Rox—were so caught up in trying to find a solution to what was rapidly appearing to be an insoluble problem that they were scarcely aware that she was going.

"I want to talk to the queen," Sissi told the guard.

The leader of the Ancan guard, who had opened the door with his club raised, lowered his club when he saw who it was and heard her demand. She was, after all, if not a tansy herself, at least a friend of a tansy, and he was one of those who thought that when dealing with tansies and their friends it couldn't hurt to be careful.

He let her out and locked the door again.

The others sat together on the sofa, holding hands. They were looking into each other's eyes, trying to give each other comfort—three individuals, who in fact appeared to be only *two* individuals.

"Lori . . ."

Seeing her through E. Rox's eyes, whose vision was perhaps more acute than human vision, his eyes being so enormous, Harry thought his wife had never looked lovelier. Those wide gray eyes, those fresh warm lips, that ample figure—he was filled with a surging affection.

"Yes, Harry?"

"Just a minute, hon." Harry then spoke inwardly to his host. "Roxie, please! All right? Will you take a hike?"

"A what?"

"Go someplace else, y' know? I'd like to be alone with my wife for a few minutes. We haven't seen each other . . . talked for a long time. I mean, d' you mind?"

"Not at all, not at all . . ."

If E. Rox was offended or hurt, he concealed it. He

withdrew into distant recesses, the most remote compartments of his id.

"It's all right," Harry said to Lori. "He's gone."

"Who's gone?"

"Roxie. E. Rox," Harry said. "The guy who owns this body."

"He is?"

"He is what?"

"Gone?"

"Yes."

"Where did he go?"

"I don't know exactly. Somewhere in his psyche. Anyway, he's not watching. Or listening."

"There's just you and me, sitting here, talking, holding hands?"

"That's right."

"I've got news for you, buster!"

"What news?"

"You're full of it. Clear up to here!"

"Lori!"

"Okay, look at it my way. You're telling me you're my Harry, and the other guy's gone away someplace. You know what I'm seeing? I'm seeing a great, lanky—" her eyes roved, dwelling searchingly on each feature as she described it "—Orcan type individual with blue eyes as big as saucers . . . kinda nice blue eyes, when you stop to think about it. And he's got a little ski-jump nose—Bob Hope, eat your heart out—and a nice mouth. He's got antennae instead of ears, but you know I kind of like his antennae—" she reached up to stroke the antennae gently—"they're sort of feathery. Hey, you know I think I like your friend Mr. Rox—"

"It's E. Rox, Mrs. Borg," E. Rox said, "and I like you, too."

"Roxie, damn it!" Harry said. "Will you *please* leave us alone for a *little* while?"

"Oh, Sorry..." E. Rox retired again.

"See?" Lori said. "You said he was gone and he wasn't!"

"He is now."

"Harry! I don't know who I'm talking to!"

"You're talking to *me*, Lori!"

"How do I know?"

"Look, you remember when I told everybody at that Air Force reunion that you used to play third base for the Cardinals? And I said you batted .380 and had twenty-three home runs and 98 RBIs? Remember that? And everybody *believed* me?"

"They did not!"

"They laughed, anyway."

"Okay, but they didn't believe you!"

"How would I know I had said that, if it wasn't me saying this to you now? Tell me. How?"

"You could have heard it from Harry. He's always talking."

Harry was growing very frustrated. He wanted so much to take her in his arms, to hold her, to kiss those soft, yielding lips. With so much else gone haywire for him, he *needed* her, *needed* the warmth of her person, the solace of her love...

"Hold still...please!"

She held still, skin tingling with weird excitement as the Orcan put his two extremely long-fingered hands on her shoulders and bent his head, drawing her close.

"Harry?"

"Yes, hon?"

"You sure...this is all right?"

"Yes."

"But you don't look like you. I mean, you look like

that Orcan fella! And you might get sore if I—I . . . let him . . ."

"It's *me,* sweetheart."

"He's not there? Anywhere around?"

"It's just me, honey," Harry said. "Just Harry."

"Gee . . . I don't know . . ."

His lips touched hers . . .

And, *whooooeee!*

What a *kiss!*

It sent shivers running all through her. It made her skin prickle from head to toe. It took her breath away.

"Harry?" She stared into those enormous blue eyes, searching. "Was that you? *Really* you?"

"It was me, honey."

"You're not just putting me on?" Lori asked shakily. "I mean, Harry, you never kissed like that *before!*"

Harry knew what she meant.

It had been some kind of a kiss for him, too. Coming to him through E. Rox's system, it had been a real barn burner of a kiss. E. Rox's system seemed to be much more sensitive than the human system—all sensations were multiplied a dozen times over. Maybe it was the antennae, maybe it was the climate, maybe it was something else he didn't even know about . . .

And E. Rox also knew what she meant.

He had tried. Being a decent sort, he had tried very, very hard to withdraw, to turn away, to keep his eyes averted, to *not* participate in any way at all. Not being able to leave his body, however, as Harry Borg had left it, he had necessarily remained connected to all his senses, and in being connected, he had experienced all the feelings *they* had experienced. Joining lips with a human lady, he had discovered, could produce some very strange sensations.

Wonderful was what they were.

But he saw no reason to say anything.

"We've been apart so long," Harry said. "That's what it was."

"A week, Harry?" Lori asked. "A week could do *that*?"

"So much has happened," Harry said. "The trip through space and all." He reached out to draw her close once more. "But I'm here with you now. You trust me, don't you?"

Lori's eyes were big, staring into his as he drew close. "Not a whole lot. It's ... it's all so goofy..."

His lips touched her lips, and she immediately began to feel the tingling and the prickling again. All over. Kissing an Orcan who was really Harry *was* goofy...

But there *were* compensations.

She kept going back for more.

When Sissi returned, a little while later, she had good news. As a matter of fact, she had the solution to the most immediate problem. The difficulty now was persuading the Orcan who said he was half Harry Borg—or was it the other way around?—to stop pressing mouths with Lori long enough to listen to her.

"What *are* you *doing*?" she asked.

They broke apart and looked at her. Anyway, the Orcan looked at her. Sissi was not sure where Lori was looking—her eyes seemed to be out of focus.

"Kissing," Lori said dreamily.

"Is that something nice to do?"

"Oh, very."

"It looks yukky."

"But it's nice," Lori sighed. "So very nice ..."

Harry, from inside E. Rox, said, "It's something humans do, Sissi. Don't worry about it."

"I'll try not to."

"Where've you been?"

"Getting you a ride to Atoxia," Sissi said.

The Orcan leaped to his feet so suddenly that Lori was dumped to the floor. "A ride? How? Where? In what?"

"Not *in* anything," Sissi said. "*On* a leta. The queen said you could use hers. It's a racing leta. Very big and fast. Only royalty can own them. E. Rox can't go. But she said you could—"

"Wait a minute!"

"Yes?"

"Sissi! You can't be serious!"

"I am! I talked to the queen. She was very concerned, very helpful. She can't take the risk of letting E. Rox go—Tanta would have her killed. But if you went as a wraith, no one could see you and no one would know. You can take her leta if you'll do something for her."

"Do what?"

"Have Los Ross send her a compound. We have plenty of it in Jassa. It's called PC-Y. Then you can get your body."

"Hell's fire!" Harry was driving E. Rox up and down the room, his old eagerness coming to the fore. E. Rox, the more cautious of the two, was trying to restrain him.

"Sheer madness," E. Rox said.

"It's a chance, pal! It's a chance!"

"You've never ridden one of those letas!"

"I can ride a bolt of lightning if I have to!"

"And you don't know the way!"

"I'll find it!" Harry said. "Somehow or other!"

CHAPTER 24

It was night again. Three of the four Orcan moons had risen, and the red light they shed seemed to turn the sands into a sea of red blood. The air was warm, and the only wind was the wind of swift passage.

The leta ran smoothly.

As a wraith, Harry Borg accompanied, rather than rode, the giant ant, using the creature as a guide rather than a vehicle, though he had positioned himself astride the short neck just behind the huge triangular head as though astride a horse. He could see the mandibles projecting out before the head, the trembling antennae, the many-faceted eyes. The six long legs, working in a curious rhythm, tirelessly and with an effortless speed, smoothed the broken terrain until even the roughest reaches of the desert floor became like glass. It was as if the insect were gyroscopically controlled, the body remaining level while the ground tilted this way and that, flowing swiftly beneath those six swift-moving legs. The exoskeleton of the insect, black armor, smooth and gleaming, clicked steadily with the movement of the joints, a monotone not unlike the clicking of railroad wheels on the joints of steel rails before welding silenced them.

Harry could not communicate with the leta. He could not guide it. He could only trust that Kana, the queen of the Ancans, had somehow been able to program the creature with all the necessary courses and distances. He had only a vague idea how that might have been done—a telepathic line, he imagined, to which he had no access, established when the symbiotic relationship had begun between the insects and the Ancans at the dawn of their evolution.

That did not matter now.

What mattered was the going.

He remembered wondering at the way the tiny ants of Earth found their way across terrain which, while only a relatively well-raked garden path to him, must have seemed to creatures so small to be enormously mountainous, across distances that for him were measured in yards, but in many miles for them, at speeds that were for him slow, but for them swift racing. The proportions had been changed enormously now, but they had been changed equally in all dimensions—size and speed and time each expanded correctly with regard to one another and expanded manyfold.

He was once again reminded that man was perhaps not the most ingenious of God's creations.

Now, marveling, he rode as if riding the wind across the stony desert floor under a black sky filled with a billion stars, the red moons huge, glowing disks lighting the way. The leta carried him, gliding up into and through rugged mountainous terrain, then down again across desert floor, on a straight course he could monitor with the stars, toward what he could only hope would be the ancient city of Atoxia, where he had been given reason to believe his body lay waiting for him.

Effortlessly, tirelessly, the leta ran on and on.

So much was still uncertain, still in doubt.

Those he had left behind waited.

If they were to live or die depended not upon the resourcefulness of Lori, Sissi, and E. Rox now, not upon their physical ability, not upon their bravery or cowardice. Their lives depended now upon forces beyond their control. A single word described their condition best:

Helpless.

The word took on new meaning, Lori found, when one was brought to that extremity. It was like a fall through space, a sea without shores. It was total emptiness. It was something that had to be endured, somehow, for an uncertain period of time—a few hours, a day, a few days—they had no way of knowing.

"One at a time," Lori said. "As best we can."

She and Sissi and E. Rox were alone in the apartment that the Ancans had provided them. They wanted for nothing. There was ambrosialike food if they became hungry. There were comfortable, softly cushioned beds if they wanted to sleep. There was even drink.

"What is this stuff?"

"Ruduso, I believe it is called."

The liquid came in a crystal flask, a golden fluid, sparkling. Sissi had dipped her long, forked tongue into a glass of it and found it not to her liking. E. Rox had taken a cautionary sip and found it pleasant. Now Lori tasted it and found it interesting.

"Robust," she said. "Bold."

She thought she would have a glass of it. E. Rox found her thinking good and agreed to share a glass with her. Sissi wanted none of it and retired to her bed in search of sleep.

"You and me, Roxie," Lori said. "We'll hold the fort, guard the flame, keep a candle in the window... whatever."

"Yes," E. Rox agreed. "As you say, whatever..."

Loneliness and fear—the two evil sisters. They were with Lori and E. Rox as they sat side by side, sharing the glasses of ruduso, the intoxicant of the Ancans. Neither Lori nor E. Rox knew that they were not alone—the evil sisters are insidious. They work quietly in the subconscious, silent corrosion eating away fortress walls.

"Harry's gonna make it," Lori said. "I guarantee it."

"I know he will."

E. Rox was scrubbed clean again. Hardly a trace of the abuse he had suffered at the hands of the Ancans was anywhere to be seen. At rest, his long and feathery antennae lay down his back. His disklike, china-blue eyes were wells of quiet concern, and his mouth moved in quiet smiles. A person of refinement, this Orcan, a gentle-natured person, warm and understanding.

"You're okay," Lori said.

"Thank you," E. Rox said. "Would you care for another?"

"Well, maybe just a teensy..."

Lori had combed, brushed, and braided her wheat-colored hair anew. Drawn away, the hair had revealed the strong beauty of her clear forehead, her straight brows, the long-lashed gray eyes, the firm chin, and the wide and generous mouth. She had a glowing look, only slightly marred by the worry that tugged at her lips and tried to darken her eyes.

"Y'know?" she said to E. Rox. "You're something else."

"Why do you say that?"

They had touched glasses and sipped again.

"I mean, look what you've been through. And what's still ahead of you."

"Is it so much?"

"Come off it!" Lori scoffed. "How many d' you know ever got invaded by a—what'dyoucallit?...spirit? wraith? personality?—from outer space?"

"None."

"There y' go!"

"I feel I have been honored."

"Glad you think so." Lori eyed the glass of ruduso. "Say, this stuff's got a zing to it!"

"Very pleasant," E. Rox agreed.

"But that's not all you've got ahead of you," Lori went on. "Your country is now at war with the Ancans, a war that might mean the end of your race. And you, personally, are on Tanta's hit list. He's going to murder you by inches as soon as he can get around to it."

"That *is* his intention," E. Rox admitted.

"See what I mean? You're some kind of brave, if you ask me."

"Good of you to say so."

"S'true..."

"Not really."

"Hey...y' know something else?"

"No..."

"You're handsome. No, really! I mean it." Lori had another sip of ruduso. "You're different, okay? You're from a different race, okay? But in your own way, there's not a darn thing wrong with you that I can see. You're not *that* much different."

"You are being kind."

"I'm being sincere, Roxie. Believe me. From the bottom of my heart, I'm being sincere." She had another sip. "You're okay."

E. Rox had another sip. "May I say I feel the same about you?" he asked. His tone, like Lori's, had become solemn and sincere. "It does not seem to me now that you are very different from us."

"That's what I mean! Y' stop to think about it, we're not that much different from each other."

"I do see what you mean."

Lori frowned. "I wonder if it's just us. You and me."

"I don't think so," E. Rox said. "When Harry met Rani, my mate, he was very attracted to her. At least, he was kind enough to say that he was."

"He did?"

There was a sharpness in Lori's tone that caused E. Rox some concern. He felt obliged to make some sort of explanation. Speaking hurriedly, he said, "He assured me that his interest was only friendly, and I, as a matter of fact, when I awakened, after having taken too much to drink, found that he had left me alone with Rani and that he had not taken advantage—" and then, realizing that the water was getting very deep, E. Rox attempted to flounder back to shore with: "Which is to say he was gentleman enough to wait in the atrium."

"Harry? A gentleman?"

"Of the first order," E. Rox affirmed stoutly.

"News to me." Lori sipped. "Oh, don't get me wrong. I love the guy. He's kind, brave, handsome, and virile. Very virile. But a gentleman? Well...maybe there's room for argument."

"There are more important things than polished manners," E. Rox observed somewhat ponderously.

"I couldn't agree more!"

Lori sat a moment, thinking about these more important things. The cutting edge of her worries and fears had been blunted by the glowing warmth of the ruduso. More, the warmth had begun to glow exceedingly. She found herself looking at the gentle lines of E. Rox's lips and remembering.

"Y' know something?" she said. "When Harry was in there—in there with you, I mean—and he kissed me . . . using your lips, of course . . . well, now! That was something else! I don't know where you were, but I sure got a bang out of that kiss. Uh . . . those kisses."

"I have a confession to make," E. Rox said, looking away.

"What's that?"

"I was there, too."

"You mean you—"

He looked at her, deep apology in his wide blue eyes. "I tried to leave . . . to *not* participate in any way. But I was not able to disassociate myself . . . and I—I shared . . ."

"You *did*?"

"I am sorry."

"Okay! Okay! I accept your apology."

"Shameful of me . . ."

Lori took two more sips, thinking. "How was it?" she asked him.

"How was what?"

"The kiss. The kissing, I should say."

"Wonderful," he breathed softly. "Like nothing I had ever experienced before."

"For me, too," she said.

"We Orcans entwine our antennae."

"I don't have any . . . antennae."

"I know. But your lips . . ."

"Gave you the same feeling?"

"Yes. Very much so. And you?"

"Biggest buzz of my life," she said.

"Very strange."

"Harry said it was because the trip through space heightened our sensations—something like that."

"I suppose that could be true."

"I wonder..." She was looking at E. Rox's lips again, her eyes gone a little distant. "Roxie...I was wondering...you know...what if we checked it out. I mean, you wouldn't think me forward or anything...if we...sort of...to see what would happen..."

He was looking at her, his eyes just as distant. "Not at all..."

"As a matter of...scientific interest," she said.

"That, too," he agreed.

Their lips met gently, then pressed.

It had *not* been the trip through space, Lori discovered. At least, not the trip alone. No way. Wow! Kissing an Orcan, whether Harry was inside him or not, started everything zinging. It made her eyes water. Her ears ring.

And it wouldn't stop.

With every kiss it got better and better.

Some time later, perhaps as much as an hour later, the sleepy, telepathic voice of Sissi called, "Lori!"

"Yes?"

"It's late. Come to bed."

"I *am* in bed."

"Oh..."

The quiss fell with a soft plop, landing on the chest that was slowly rising and falling with measured breathing. The small, ravenously hungry little reptile remained motionless for a moment, forked tongue flicking out to lick up the scent of fresh meat, vertically slitted eyes searching for the most promising place to start. The eyes fastened, finally, on a projection that stood out above what seemed a dark forest, a projection that held two tunnels from which soft draughts of air blew at regular intervals.

The quiss moved up across the chin, across the lips, and settled down before the nose. The long, forked tongue shot out to lick the nose, testing—and then a hand caught the quiss by the neck.

The hand lifted the quiss and snapped it down into a far corner, where it squeaked and squealed, broken and dying.

"Sorry, pal. That nose belongs to me."

Harry Borg, still a wraith, stood looking down at his sleeping body—big, warm, breathing quietly, no worse for having been missent to some distant planet, no worse for the wait, no worse for the wear...

Or was it?

There was only one way to find out if the answer was going to be yes or, for all eternity, no. He had to get inside. Now. He moved up, swung himself over the body, and slowly lowered himself into the body... gently... gently... imprinting himself, a wraith, into the flesh and blood of a human being.

There were a frightening few moments.

A terrifying few.

Nothing worked.

Then, suddenly, it all worked.

It had taken a bit of doing, a few moments' time, for the circuits to reestablish themselves—whatever the circuits were that connected the corporeal to the spectral— but once connected, the circuits worked fine. A deep inhalation swelled the chest, the mouth opened and closed, and the eyes snapped open, dark blue, glowing.

Harry Borg was home again.

"Harry..." a distant voice was calling. The voice of Los Ross. "Harry, are you there?"

Harry Borg pushed himself up a sitting position. He looked around at the empty laboratory for several moments before he realized that the voice was coming from within his head.

"I'm here," he rumbled in answer.

"Are you well? Do you function correctly?"

Harry extended his big hands, opened them flat, then closed them in to rocklike fists. He got off the table, planted his feet on the floor, and flexed his knees. "Everything's fine," he said.

"Oh, thank Osis!"

Moving about the receiving station, Harry found the telepathic voice of Los Ross fading, becoming very distant, scratchy. As he moved back to a position under a glowing tube, the voice became clear again. Harry controlled his position carefully.

"You thought something could go wrong?" he asked.

"Harry . . . with these things, one can never be absolutely sure . . ."

"You sent me, though. You sent Lori and Sissi—"

"They are there? Safely?"

"They're here!"

"It works!" There was pure joy in Los Ross's voice. "It works!"

Disgustedly, Harry growled, "Works, he says. Now he tells me he didn't know if it would work or not. Los, I'm going to unscrew your head when I get back there—"

"Did you get the ursis seeds, Harry?"

"I got them. They're here."

"Put them under the transmitter."

Harry lifted the sack of ursis seeds down from the hook where he had hung them out of reach of the quiss, put them under the transmitter tubes, and watched as the tubes glowed and a ray of strange blue light seemed to dissolve the sack of seeds into nothingness.

"They're gone," he said.

"Good. Now Sissi, Lori, and you . . . in that order."

"Can't do it."

"But you *must*, Harry. At once!"

"They're not here, damn it! They're many, many miles away. I don't know how many. A lot."

"You must get them! You must come back to Essa. It's imperative! A matter of life or death!"

"Whose life or death?"

"Yours! Theirs!"

"Los! What the hell's goin' on?"

Harry was a few moments learning what the hell was going on. In his hysteria—and there could be no doubt that it was real—the little Jassan scientist had difficulty in speaking coherently. The hell that was going on was that time had almost run out. The Peacekeepers were about to feed Guss, who was being held hostage, into the Converter—

"Being held *what*?"

"Hostage, Harry. So that the Peacekeepers would not destroy my laboratory and leave you and Lori and Sissi stranded, Guss gave himself as a hostage. If I have not brought you home by this time tomorrow, he will be executed!"

"Christ! What else?"

"Can you get Lori and Sissi, Harry?"

"Not in less than two days!"

"That will be too late!"

"It's the best I can do!"

"The Peacekeepers will not wait, Harry!"

"Hell!" Harry Borg's dark blue eyes were almost black. "Can you get in touch with my lads, Los? Chad? Homer? Any—"

"Sir!" It was Chad's voice, sharp and clear. "I'm right here, sir."

Harry hit himself on the forehead and tipped his head

back to breathe a deep sigh of relief. "The rest of the squad, Chad?"

Chad said, immediately, "Sound off!"

"Ho!"

"Here!"

"Yo!"

"Hyah!"

Four other voices, almost as one—Homer, Eddie, Sam, Arnie—strong, cold, sharp. Damn! He had heard nothing in his life that sounded better. Five young men of Earth. Five young Americans. Five of the very best.

"Do you have weapons?"

"Yes, sir!"

"Secure your area," Harry said. "Hold it at all costs!"

"Sir!"

"And get Guss loose, y' hear? I don't care how many asses you have to kick. Kick and kick hard until he's safe inside your perimeter! Take it to the very top if you have to, but get it done! Is that clear?"

"Clear, sir!"

Remembering his promise to Sissi and Queen Kana, Harry said, "And Los! Here's something for you."

"Me?" Los Ross's voice was weak.

Harry then asked Los Ross if he knew of a compound Sissi had described as PC-Y, and Los Ross replied that of course he did. Could he get and send a large amount of it? How large? A ton. Great Essnia! That much? That much. When? Immediately.

"I—I can try."

"I don't want to hear 'try,'" Harry said. He yelled: "*Do* it!"

The connection was broken just then. Whether because Los Ross had fainted again or because some sort of violent action had begun at that moment he could not tell. Of one thing he was certain, however: If it were possible, the five lads and the little scientist would get their appointed tasks completed on schedule. Even if it were slightly impossible, Harry was sure they would somehow find a way.

Totally impossible?

He was not so sure . . .

Chapter 25

E. Rox had spent a lot of time in recent days—had it been only seven?—wondering what his guest looked like. *Really* looked like. In the flesh. He'd been given a rather detailed description of Harry Borg, Earthman, to be sure; but since the description had come from Harry Borg himself, a personality given to exaggeration, he rather doubted that the description was accurate.

That well formed? That handsome? That powerful?

An Orcan such as himself could possibly meet all the specifications as Harry had described them. But a species from a distant planet?

Not likely.

The Earthman, by his own admission, did not have antennae, for example, if such a deformity could be imagined. He was also diminutive by any reasonable standards—the top of his head, by his own account, reached no higher than midchest to an average Orcan. While such a body might be suited to certain forms of vigorous physical activity—sturdy was perhaps the accurate description—it surely lacked the refined slenderness so important to the well-proportioned Orcan. And the Earthman's eyes! By his own admission, they were not a fifth the size of an Orcan's eyes, and how better to describe eyes that small than to call them birdy? Bright little beads looking out of a rather small head, cunning, if not intelligent, is what they must surely be. And though the Earthman had described his eyes as being blue, they were described as a much darker blue than a Orcan's eyes and therefore could not possibly be anywhere near as appealing and expressive.

The Earthwoman, Lori, whom he had come to know quite well, was very beautiful by any standards, he was willing to warrant. And he was more than willing to admit she had a warmth, a vitality, and an inner glow that he had never experienced before. But then, she *was* female—oh, indeed! very female—and could not be judged by the same standards one would use when judging a male.

Particularly not a male who had become an alter ego of himself, a male to whom he could not help but *compare* himself—his own body, his own strength, his own ability, his own *person*—a male whom self-respect would not allow him to concede was superior to himself in any way. And that self-respect, he had assured himself many times over, was not the product of false pride, or vanity, or conceit. It was simply the product of a fair and unbiased assessment of all features and qualities that together comprise the male of any species—the plain truth, to put it bluntly.

He had prepared himself to be neither condescending nor patronizing when he should finally meet Harry Borg for the first time after the Earthman had regained the use of his own body. He had vowed to treat him as an *equal*, however difficult that might prove to be. Now, since certain events had transpired, he could see that any kind of treatment was going to be very difficult.

Very difficult, indeed.

Now, he was pacing up and down in the quarters he shared with Lori and Sissi—and, since early that morning, with O. Rani, whom Queen Kana had caused to be brought here—pacing, because he had just learned that Harry Borg had returned from Atoxia and was presently going to walk in through that entrance.

While pacing, E. Rox was consumed with a variety of anxieties, remorse and guilt being not the least among them, even though Lori had assured him everything was going to be all right.

"I can handle it, Roxie! Don't *worry*!"

Remorse and guilt, he had found, are not so easily dispelled.

Add to the remorse and guilt a head that felt swollen and ached boomingly—that Ancan drink was absolute poison—

A stomach that quivered as if full of beetles, and a vivid memory of how violent Harry Borg could become when sufficiently aroused, and it was all so enormous that he could scarcely keep from running to a window and shouting for help.

"Rosho!" he moaned silently. "Will I *never* learn?"

And then Harry Borg came striding in.

"Oh, my Ixxi!" E. Rox breathed.

The others, at that moment, were not in the room, and E. Rox found himself facing this moment of truth by himself.

"This?" he asked himself, staring in wonder at Harry Borg. "*This* creature resided in *me*?"

True, the creature was shorter and more sturdily built than an Orcan male. But that smaller body fairly exuded power—his feet, as a matter of truth, seemed to scarcely touch the ground. The eyes, while a darker blue and smaller than an Orcan's as promised, gleamed with a light one could only describe as fierce. The short dark fur on his jaws did nothing to hide the strength of them. And, exactly as described, a row of white teeth were revealed in his broad smile. And the voice was good-natured thunder.

"Roxie, baby!" Harry said. "What d' you think?"

He displayed himself before E. Rox—chest swelled, hands in fists, biceps bulging—in the manner of a body builder, shamelessly perhaps, because he had not gotten over his joy in having his own body once more.

More likely because he was vain as hell.

"Remarkable," E. Rox breathed.

"See what I meant?" Harry said. "Some kind of a bod, right?"

"Harry, I've got something to tell you—"

That was as far as he got before a shriek cut him short.

"Harry!"

Lori had come rushing into the room to throw her arms around Harry Borg's neck, to kiss him with total and vigorous enthusiasm.

The enthusiasm was fully shared by Harry.

Harry had, to be sure, kissed his wife while in the body of E. Rox, but that kissing, while strangely exciting and gratifying, had not been quite like the real thing.

Humans kissing humans was best, he decided.

Godfrey mighty! It was *good* to see her with his own eyes, to hold her with his own arms, to kiss her with his own lips. And for several minutes he couldn't get enough of it. Then, however, other more serious, and certainly more desperate, exigencies demanded that they be given full attention.

"No time for this," he said.

He told them then that he, Lori, and Sissi had to return to Atoxia and be transported back to Essa at once. He could not hope, he said, that Chad and the lads could hold off the forces of the Peacekeepers, and very likely the Jassan police, very much longer. Once they were overrun, he said, all hope of a safe return home would be lost forever.

The resulting shock and dismay were considerable.

"What about E. Rox?"

"What about O. Rani?"

Harry found O. Rani, the lovely Orcan mate of E. Rox, staring at him with a wide-eyed amazement and interest verging on awe, and—somewhat diffidently, to be sure—he took time now to cross to her, to take her hand, to tell her how glad he was that she had been unharmed. She, in her turn, was finding it difficult to believe that any part of *him* had been able to live, however briefly, in E. Rox, and she required a lot of explanation be given her.

"It's true," Harry assured her. "Y' see, my body— this body—got missent to some other planet, and all that came through was me ... or I guess you'd say my spirit ... wraith? ... and I needed a someplace where I could wait, see? And Roxie was handy."

"I can't believe it!" she said.

"Look. Say, for instance ..."

While he plunged on with this vague explanation, Harry was aware that E. Rox was trying to get past Lori to speak to him, an enormous anguish of some sort in his eyes, and that Lori had, with a sharp kick to the ankle, hissed, "Don't be a damn fool, y' dummy!" Or something like that. But it didn't make any real impression on him. Not right at that moment, anyway.

He was too busy with O. Rani.

When he finally convinced her that he had shared E. Rox's body for almost a week's time, she said, "I *thought* he seemed different. He was more ... more ... well, capable ..."

"That was me, honey," he said before he realized and damn near bit his tongue off for saying it.

Lori broke in then. "Did you send the ursis seeds?"

"They're on their way," he said. "We can leave right away."

"I'm not going," Lori said.

"You're not *what*?" Harry demanded.

"Going back with you," Lori said stubbornly.

"Neither am I," Sissi said.

Harry stared at both, shocked. "You aren't?"

Lori crossed to stand beside E. Rox, to thread her arm through his, gripping him firmly, aligning herself with him, taking his side in all respects. Sissi did the same with O. Rani.

"What's goin' *on*?" Harry asked.

"I'm not going to leave E. Rox," Lori said.

"Or O. Rani," Sissi added.

Harry was staring at Lori and E. Rox, noticing the way she was holding herself tightly, protectively against the tall and skinny Orcan and seeing the look on E. Rox's face that was as guilty as the face of a kid caught with his hands in a cookie jar. Then he remembered the kick he'd seen Lori give E. Rox's ankle . . .

A light was beginning to dawn.

"What's with you two?" Harry began.

Lori said firmly, "After you kissed me, using Roxie's body—and you promised me it was all right, mind you —let's just say I developed a feeling of deep friendship for him, all right?"

"Yeah, sure. But—"

"Leave it alone, Harry!" Lori warned.

Harry glanced over at O. Rani. And maybe somewhere in the back of his mind a voice said, "Fair's fair, Harry," though maybe it didn't. Maybe it was just good sense and sound judgment that made him look back at

Lori and shrug elaborately. "I'm glad you feel that way. He's my friend, too!"

"Atta boy," she said, and gave him a sunny smile.

And so passed a crisis in both their lives . . .

"But we can't take Roxie and O. Rani with us when we leave here. The Ancans would never allow it for a minute. And . . ." His voice dwindled to nothing.

"Shoot!" he said then. The ejaculation had a rougher edge, coming from Harry's mouth, coming as it did as full realization penetrated his thick skull. Leave E. Rox and O. Rani to the mercies of Tanta? Leave *all* of Orca to the mercies of Tanta? Not by the wildest stretch of imagination.

"No goddamn way!"

"It finally sank in," Lori said. "I knew it would."

She gave him a sunny smile.

"Knock it off!" Harry said. "I wasn't thinking straight, okay? Now I am. Now I've got to think what the hell to do. Can't take them with us, can't leave 'em. That's what you would call a rock and a hard place."

"No, Harry," E. Rox said. "We are not your problem—"

"Shaddup!" Harry said, not unkindly. "I'm trying to think."

Sissi said, "Did you get the PC-Y for Queen Kana?"

"Yeah. I told Los Ross to send it. He said he would. It should be in Atoxia now."

"Then," Sissi said, "I suggest we talk to the queen."

"Why? The queen and I made a deal—I could go to Atoxia and get my body if I would get her the PC-Y. Mission accomplished. Deal's closed. What's to talk about now?"

"I think you'll be surprised," Sissi said.

"I know he will," Lori agreed.

Harry stared at them. "Is there anybody dumber," he asked, "than a couple of smart-ass females?"

"Yes," Lori said.

"What, for God's sake?"

"A *smart* smart-ass male."

"Boy!" Harry said, slapping his head. "I asked for that one!"

"See?"

These were the last few moments of his life . . .

Guss Rassan knew that with absolute certainty.

They were coming after him!

A lifetime of selfless devotion to giving pleasure to his fellow Jassans would end very soon. Endless hours totaling years spent at sissal keyboards practicing the skills that would make him by almost unanimous acclaim the greatest composer of symphonic fragrances of the past one hundred years—wasted. An artist who had given unstintingly of his wealth, his time, his energies, who had never asked more in return but quiet appreciation, would presently be put into the Converter—into those whizzing knives.

Headfirst, he prayed, so that it would end quickly.

How long had he waited here in this stark, windowless room, dressed in these miserable garments of coarse weave, shivering with bone-deep fear, unable to eat or sleep? Seven days? Impossible! Seven centuries was more the truth, the way it seemed. Only centuries could have held so much torment. And those centuries had somehow, by some evil magic, been suddenly compressed into short minutes, minutes that were swiftly flowing away.

He could feel the vibrations of their booted feet.

He kept the gray inner lids across his golden eyes, concealing the vertically slitted pupils, his faintly scaled, usually blushed gray skin now gone the color of wet ashes. His eight-fingered hands, the fluid masters of the sissal keyboard, were gripped together in an aching strain, as if they, alone, were all that was left to keep him from screaming insanity.

Perhaps they were all that held him.

He had gambled and lost.

He had never, when he had offered to stand as hostage—he knew this now—never, never believed that there had been even a remote chance that Harry Borg could fail in his mission, that he would not be returned in the allotted time, or that he, Guss Rassan, would be called upon to pay for that failure with his life.

His offer had been only a dramatic gesture.

Heroism was not for him.

He was an artist, a composer, a person of gentle leanings, given to introspection, to pondering the meaning of life in all its various aspects, to study, to quiet conversation with friends. Violence was to be avoided at all costs.

Death was an abyss . . .

But they had accepted him as a hostage. Seven days of life had been granted him—seven, and only seven, if Harry Borg failed to return. Those seven had passed now, and Harry Borg, if he were even still alive, was still in some distant part of the universe. Guss's jailers were coming for him . . . the insatiable, cutting, shredding blades were ready, only a short distance down the hall, only short moments away.

They were at the door!

He must not scream . . .

He stared unbreathing, golden eyes wide, forked tongue hanging limply from the side of a mouth gone slack with fear. He expected the sound of a key in the ancient lock. None came. Instead, he heard a quiet telepathic voice.

"Stand clear of the door, Guss."

Guss had time to leap away and press himself against a far wall before the area of the door around the lock was vaporized by the beam of a ray-gun and the door was kicked open. Striding in, then, came the most magnificent sight his eyes had ever beheld—a six-foot-tall human being with a deeply tanned skin, white hair, and cold, cold gray eyes.

"Chad!" Guss shrieked mentally. "Oh, zat! It can't be!"

"Can be and is!" Chad answered. "Let's go!"

Behind Chad, the dark-skinned, wide-smiling human called Eddie Cole motioned at the shock-frozen Guss Rassan. "What's keepin' you, baby?"

"We haven't much time," Chad added.

They left the prison building, running. An aircraft waited in the prison courtyard, with the human called Arnie at the controls and the wide-shouldered human whom Guss knew as Homer Benson standing over the remaining guards who were lying face down in shivering fear on the ground.

The aircraft took them to the ancient stone, castlelike fortress that Los Ross had converted into a secret laboratory. The laboratory was secret no longer, but it was, Gus soon learned, a fortress again. It was a fortress being held by the humans against the forces of the Peacekeepers, who were determined now to destroy this last bastion of scientific inquiry in the name of peace—peace at any cost.

"So far fifteen dead on our side," Sam Barnstable reported to Chad Harrison. "And maybe thirty of theirs."

"How many do we have left?"

"Like ten of our old Red Flames, besides us." He lifted a meaty hand. "Hey, Guss! How y' doin'?"

"This is unbelievable!" Guss said.

"Think so?"

"Just *you*? Against the Peacekeepers *and* the police?"

"It ain't an even shake, that's sure."

"How long can you hold out?"

"Not long."

"Why would you even *attempt* such madness?"

Sam Barnstable gave the agonized Guss a sudden grin. "Old Iron Balls says do it, we *do it*!—and that's for double-*damned* sure!"

CHAPTER 26

He was the main event. Those now in the amphitheater were the prelims. They were like Christians about to be fed to the lions, only they weren't Christians, they were Orcans, and they were about to be fed not to lions but to beasts the Ancans called grolls.

The Orcans were a forlorn group of perhaps twenty. They were mostly males, though there were a few females, one of whom held a child in her arms. Angular sticklike creatures, all of them, scantily clothed and held by short ankle chains to stakes driven into the red sand floor of the arena.

Harry Borg didn't know why he had been brought to see this.

They were hoping to terrify him, maybe? Or was it the Anca idea of a treat, a last favor for a visiting tansy who was soon to be honored with a glorious death of his own at the hands of their exalted leader, Tanta Ut Krill?

Some treat.

Three grolls were let into the arena now. They came charging out of a barred gate, spraying sand in their eagerness, their black, oily hides glistening over powerful muscles, tails held high, six legs with paws that were

283

heavily clawed digging, heads like skinned wolves. Nasty creatures. Bloodthirsty. The Orcans had been given machetelike blades, supposedly to defend themselves, but actually, Harry knew, to prolong the spectacle, to make it more bloody. The blades could wound and infuriate the grolls but could not kill them.

Harry Borg watched three Orcans die bravely.

Then he turned his eyes to the spectators. They were packed solidly into seats that ringed the octagon-shaped arena floor in tiers holding several thousand. The spectators all were high-ranking members of the military, lion faced and fanged. Their manes were dyed many colors, their eyes red, glowing disks. Their mouths were agape as their lower jaws sagged, and their roaring was a storm of sound, a steady booming.

There were no female Ancans here.

Harry looked carefully and saw not one. Perhaps, then, what he had learned from Queen Kana was true. The Ancan females did not share the pleasures of slaughter with the males.

Perhaps the females *were* united in secret rebellion.

Before taking him to see the queen, Lori and Sissi had provided an explanation. "They have been kept barefoot and pregnant," Lori had said, putting the plight of the Ancan female in human terms, "for thousands of years. That way the Ancan males have been able to keep the females practically in chains, no better than slaves."

"They're tired of it?"

"Fed up to here, Harry," Lori said. "When the Ancan ladies have kids, they have *litters*!"

"Like Labrador retrievers?"

"Those boobs, Harry? Y' know? They need them *all*!"

"The young are ninety percent male," Sissi said.

"Even a mother couldn't love those ugly suckers," Lori said. "Now do you see why the PC–Y?"

Harry said he surely did. "With that kind of fertility," he said, "I don't think a ton of PC-Y is gonna be enough."

"It's just for openers," Lori said. "That's all. They'll need a lot more later. This first lot will let the Ancan ladies know that they *can* get out of bondage—that they *can* stop having litters of male kids, one right after another."

"Stupid male kids," Sissi put in.

"Which is the very worst kind," Lori said.

"Hey, now!" Harry said.

"*These* male kids anyway," Lori amended. "All these male kids want to do is grow up and be warriors. Fight and kill. It's all they live for! All they know."

"And the Anca ladies don't like it?"

"Harry! After all they've gone through? All that trouble? Birthing them? Diapering them? Nursing them? They get teeth early, Harry! You think a mama's going to like suffering all that just so her kids can grow up to play soldier and get shot to death?"

"Not likely," Harry agreed.

"Queen Kana has a way she can solve the problem— that's what she wants to talk to you about," Sissi said.

"Me? Where do *I* fit in?"

"You're the solution," Lori said. And then she added hurriedly, "Now, Harry. Don't fly off the handle. I didn't say you *would*! I just said she should talk to you. That's all! Just talk!"

"Talk about what?"

"Like . . . well, fighting Tanta, for instance—"

When Lori had seen the sudden, startled fury turning Harry's blue eyes almost black, she had moved quickly behind her Jassan friend. "You tell him, Sissi."

"Thanks a lot!"

"Bloody hell!" Harry had begun to rage, but on seeing the frightened but steadfastly determined way the two females were confronting him, he managed to control himself, to force himself to listen.

Taking turns, Lori and Sissi gave the explanation.

The Ancan males, all born with scarcely sense enough to know which boot went on which foot, all came out warrior-types. Like warrior ants, it was what they were born to do. Given time, they could be trained to do other things, like plowing fields, working in factories, and washing windows. But fighting and dying is what they did naturally and did most.

"When they have a leader," Sissi said.

"Without a leader, they're zilch," Lori said.

"A leader like Tanta," Harry said on cue.

"You've got it!"

In all of Ancan history, Kana had told Lori and Sissi, there had never been another like Tanta ut Krill. A maniacal, power-mad, bloodthirsty tyrant. He also hated Orcans with a passion. He, Tanta ut Krill, he alone, Kana had said, was responsible for the present war with Orca. Without Tanta, there would be no war.

"You beginning to get the picture?" Lori asked.

"If Tanta is dead," Harry said, "the war ends?"

"That's right."

"And she wants *me* to fight—to *kill* Tanta?"

"That's about it," Lori said.

"No one else would," Sissi added.

No Anca, male or female, that was sure. It would be like slaying God—unthinkable! But if someone from another planet, someone who had already killed his son—and both the queen and Tanta knew that it wasn't any skinny Orcan named E. Rox who had *really* killed Sana—well, that would be called destiny.

"Okay?"

"No. But go on, I'm listening."

Lori and Sissi went on to say that Kana was sure Tanta would go for it. A public fight to the finish between the king of the Ancans and the tansy who, while inhabiting the body of an Orcan, had slain his son, Sana —given the right kind of PR, a fight like that, one he would certainly win, would surely make him immortal.

"Only *you'll* win," Lori said.

"I will?"

"Of course."

Sissi said, "And then, with their leader gone, the Ancan males will just start marching around in circles and the war will end."

"At which time," Lori said, "the Ancan females will take over! With the PC-Y, a birth-control pill, they can keep from getting pregnant. And if they don't have to have litters of kids every few months, they can take over from the stupid males and run this country the way it ought to be run."

"*Negotiate* settlements—things like that," Sissi said.

Harry had looked at both the ladies for several long moments. Remembering what had happened to him the last time he had made a clever remark, he was careful this time to sum up their thinking with exactly the right word.

"Hogwash!" he said.

Now, as his eyes were drawn back to watch the last of the Orcans die before the ravenous grolls, he remembered how Lori and Sissi had again made him eat his clever summation. They had simply pointed out the consequences of *not* agreeing to fight—and kill—the leader of the Ancans:

E. Rox and O. Rani would die.

The Orcan nation would die.

He and Lori and Sissi would die.

With a bunch of alternatives like those, he had to admit, almost any way of going became worthy of sober consideration—even mortal combat with a monster like Tanta ut Krill.

And no hogwash about it.

Tanta had gone for the deal. Harry was never going to forget the way the big beast had skinned his lips back off his long tusks, the way his big, red eyes had gleamed crazily, when the queen had told him that Harry—and not any skinny Orcan—was the one who had killed Sana, and that Harry wanted now to test his skills against the greatest warrior of them all.

To the death.

In front of everybody.

Never mind that Harry was so small that his head hardly reached to the armpit of a *short* Ancan. As long as the Ancan troops thought Harry was a tansy, with magical powers, he would be an acceptable opponent. So if the king had to carry Harry for a few rounds to make it look like a fight, who was going to know?

Harry could almost see Tanta's mind working.

Tanta had set up the fight as a high-budget production. Marching squads, dancing females, Orcans fed to the grolls—the whole bit. A gala event. And now, with all the rest of it out of the way, it was time for the featured main event.

King Tanta ut Krill versus Tansy Harry Borg.

The satiated grolls were driven back behind bars. What was left of the mangled bodies of the Orcans was hauled away. The stakes were pulled up. The arena floor was raked and swept, and fresh red sand was scattered over the bloody stains.

Hushed silence came, then a blare of trumpets.

And Tanta ut Krill made his entrance.

Harry, standing in the opening to a tunnel, the way

out blocked by massed Ancan soldiers, watched Tanta make his entrance. The king was a performer—give him that. He knew how to play the crowd. Maybe not with affection, but with appreciation of what he gave them: fighting, bloodletting, dying. Gore, that was what they liked. The gore of others, their own gore—it didn't matter. Just so there was lots of gore.

Tanta strutted around the perimeter of the arena floor.

Watching the king of the Ancans, the hair on the back of Harry's neck suddenly erected. What the hell were those things on Tanta's hands, dragging in the sand one minute, glittering in the pale red light as he lifted his hands to the crowd? Strapped-on *claws*? They sure as hell were! And his fangs? Christ! He had fitted his fangs with long, curving, glittering blades!

Hand to hand, your ass!

His hands and the king's cutlery.

Well, you fought a king, you had to expect the king to stack the deck, give himself a little leverage. Royal prerogative, was what it was. Cheating! The dirty bastard. It was too late now to do anything about it. There wasn't even time, Harry thought, for a man to get his TS ticket punched.

"Rowwrrrrr!"

Every so often on his strut around the arena, Tanta would drop his lower jaw, tip his white-maned head back, and let go with a roar that seemed likely to bring the roof down. The crowd loved it. They roared back. Then they chanted his name.

"Tanta! Tanta! Tanta!"

It made Harry Borg feel like an outsider. There was nobody yelling for him. Nobody cheering for the human, for the visitor from another planet. The underdog. The tansy, the Harry Borg—whatever a Harry Borg was. He was nothing but the sacrificial offering. The victim.

The goat.

Harry roared in sudden rage. He lunged out of the tunnel entrance before the startled Ancan soldiers could lay paws on him. Tanta, in the center of the arena now, hands and claws uplifted, was facing away, bathing himself in the flood of adulation that streamed down from the roaring crowd. He didn't see Harry coming. Harry only touched ground once before leveling himself out like a thrown javelin and driving his heels into Tanta's back.

"Yahhhh!" It was a roar of Harry's own kind.

The kick in the back sent the king of the Ancans on a long slide, face down, leaving a furrow in the sand on the arena floor. It bloodied his nose and shocked the crowd into a stunned silence.

Harry came down to where the king had been standing. And he remained there, straddle-legged, arms akimbo. He was, undeniably, a fine figure of a man.

Since this fight had been sold as a bare-handed fight to the finish, Harry had been allowed only a breechclout; and, though the Ancans had no way of knowing it, they were seeing a superb specimen of the human male— beautifully muscled, broad of shoulder, lean of hip, long of leg. A powerful neck supported a strong-jawed head. Dark blue eyes blazed under a bar of dark brows. Short-curled brown hair and beard, small ears lying tight, a gleam of gold in one lobe—he was magnificent.

He was also, he knew, on the short end.

Tanta came at Harry in a rush, roaring. His arms were wide, the knife blades on his hands ready to tear Harry's entrails loose with sweeping blows, his saber tusks reaching to hook into neck or shoulders.

Harry had only one weapon: a body tuned to a much

stronger gravity. He used it now, leaping high into the air.

Tanta swiped air where Harry had been.

Harry, high above, gloried in his ability to leap.

He could stare down at the upraised face of the king and, safely out of reach, laugh into those furious red eyes. But it was a triumph of only a moment. He had to come down. Nothing he could do could keep him suspended long, and his slow descent gave Tanta time to prepare, like a batter waiting for a slow, hanging curve.

Harry thought he had lost it all.

He ridged his belly muscles, sure that they were about to feel the slice of those strapped-on knives. And Tanta could have killed him then. But he wanted more than a quick decision. Sure of himself, certain of winning, he wanted to prolong this moment of glory by toying, catlike, with this excrescence from some distant planet.

He swung a backhanded blow.

Harry was struck while still in the air. He felt an explosion of pain, saw the arena floor suddenly above his head, felt himself flying...and then he collided with the arena wall with shattering force. The pain was extreme, his vision was fogged, and his mind was numbed. He had never been hit that hard before. He knew he couldn't be hit that hard again and live through it.

He lay crumpled against the arena wall.

The roar of the crowd pounded on him. They were loving it. And, seeing Tanta through a haze, he saw that Tanta was loving it. The king of the Ancans was strutting again, chest beating, playing to the crowd like a heavyweight professional wrestler, ignoring his opponent, disdainfully turning his back—telling his people that the Earthman was crap. He could kill him any time.

"Crap, am I?" Harry growled.

Crap or not, he had something Tanta did not have. Tanta was enormously strong. He was quite possibly the strongest Ancan alive, but his strength was strength measured against Orcan gravity. The strength of Harry Borg, conditioned to the gravity of earth, was far, far greater. It was greater than anything Tanta dreamed possible.

Harry got himself together, got his vision cleared.

Another long leap carried him across the arena. The gasp of the crowd warned Tanta—but not in time. Harry reached him just as he was turning. Before he could raise a blade-tipped hand, Harry had caught the arm in a hard grip that all but crushed the bones. He dug in his heels, heaved.

"Bastard!"

Tanta's feet left the sand. He tried to claw Harry's face, to slice Harry's belly. But his free hand could not beat the force of the whirl. Harry spun, spun again, and spun a third time, then released the whirling body of the king like a hammer thrower letting go a hammer in an Olympic field event. Tanta crashed into the arena wall and lay stunned.

The arena fell silent.

Harry did not roar or strut.

He drove straight at Tanta, caught him, lifted him, and slammed him down so hard that red sand lifted in a cloud. The force would have killed most Ancans. Tanta was not most Ancans. He was Tanta ut Krill, the greatest of them all. Though badly stunned, he struggled to his feet, his clawed hands sweeping, his bladed tusks reaching.

"Arrrraawh." The roar held pain now, as well as anger.

Those claws and tusks were still lethal. No more than

a touch would disembowel Harry Borg, and he knew that well. Now he let a clawed hand sweep past his sucked-in belly, caught it, and twisted, driving Tanta into the red sand, face down ... now he planted a foot on Tanta's shoulder and heaved ... now he tore Tanta's arm out of its socket, ripped it, twisted, and pulled the arm free.

"Arreeeeee." Tanta's roar was a scream of agony.

Still, he was not finished.

Harry Borg stood away as Tanta lunged up and charged, savagely swinging the remaining clawed fist. Again the fist was caught. Again Tanta was driven down. Again his shoulder was pinned, the arm was twisted, the joint broken, the arm torn free.

But Tanta was not done, not yet.

He still had bladed fangs.

He drove those fangs at Harry, red eyes blazing, blood streaming from armless shoulders, and they were twin javelins, those fangs, sure and agonizing death if they found flesh. Harry caught them, a fang in either hand, his strength more than enough to hold the armless king helpless now.

"You're gonna die!" Harry told him.

Harry's furious dark blue eyes stared into the burning red disks that were the eyes of Tanta. Tanta was the leader of the Ancans, the slayer of the Orcans, certainly the cruelest tyrant the planet had ever known.

But he was no coward.

He knew how to die.

Harry forced Tanta to his knees, then to a prostrate position on the red sand. Then, holding those tusks in the iron grip of either hand, using the strength that the gravity of Earth had given him, he twisted the head of Tanta ut Krill until the neck snapped—he twisted it more, his feet holding the body down, until the head was torn free from the body.

Then he held the bloody head high for all to see.

And he yelled defiance. "On your knees, you bloody bastards!"

"Ahhhhhhh . . ."

They moaned.

And they obeyed.

CHAPTER 27

The face of Lori, his beloved wife—he could not have asked for anything better as the first thing he would see when his vision cleared, when the high, keening whine of swift, disassembled transport passed, when solidness returned and he was once more whole.

"What took you so long, Harry?"

It was Lori, all right.

"Sissi," he asked. "Did she make it okay?"

"Hours ago!"

"I am here, Harry." It was Sissi's telepathic voice. "I came through perfectly. Are you all . . . in one piece?"

"In one piece," Harry reassured her. "No wraith this time."

He got up from the chair, stretched, and grinned at those who had been standing around anxiously waiting for him to arrive—or not arrive—here, in Los Ross's laboratory at the end of his long journey through the stars.

"Hey! Quit worrying! I'm fine!"

Sissi and then Lori had come through before him.

As predicted, once Tanta ut Krill had been removed, Queen Kana and the female Ancans, liberated from bondage by the Pill, had been able to take control. A cease-fire with the Orcans had come about immediately. Lasting peace was sure to follow.

A reciprocal trade agreement between Orca and Essa had been established. The value of Los Ross's laboratory—the value of scientific experimentation—having been proved once more, Los Ross had been given permission to go on with his inquiry into the knowledge of the Ancients. As long as he didn't blow up anything.

Harry had been the last to leave Orca.

Because of his track record, his record of being accident-prone—he had proved himself to be one of those Murphy's Law-types, then, hadn't he?—he had given those who waited cause for a certain amount of concern.

They were all present when he arrived.

Guss Rassan, that fine, close friend, was here. Los Ross, the little Jassan scientist, his golden vertically slitted eyes gleaming proudly behind spectacles canted crookedly, as always, on his muzzle, his smock buttoned crookedly, as always, was here. Chad, Homer, Sam, Eddie, Arnie—they were here. His lads, who had rescued Guss and who had guarded this place against destruction by the Peacekeepers, had been given citations for bravery by the President of Jassa.

And the president himself had become a convert, finally, to the cause of science and learning. He had even ordered that this ancient castle be made a national shrine and that Los Ross, instead of being burned as a devil, be made a hero and privileged to wear a medal that had been struck in memory of the occasion.

A medal they had named Torch of Fear, as a reminder that controlled scientific exploration could lead to one hell of a lot of misfortune.

All these—and this—were waiting.

Lori, Sissi, and Tippi, too.

"Where's Charlie?" Harry asked Tippi after she had almost broken his neck with a most fierce hug of welcome.

"Home, packing." The young daughter of Lori was kidding, of course, because Charlie, the infant son of Harry and Lori, wasn't a year old yet.

It was her way of saying that they all—Harry, Lori, Tippi, Charlie, Chad, Homer, Sam, Eddie and Arnie— were going to be given their reward: a rather substantial sum, with priority rights to any trade that might be forthcoming between the Jassans and the humans, certain patents, free tickets to sporting events, less certain commissions and taxes, to be sure. They were to be given a reward for all the things they had done for Jassa and Jassans, for all the inhabitants of the planet Essa, actually, and allowed to go home.

Home . . . to Earth.

And so it came about.

Nobody said anything about good riddance as they left.

"Thanks," they said.

"Been nice knowing you," they said.

"Walk in comfortable shoes . . ."

ABOUT THE AUTHOR

Ward Hawkins, born and raised in the Northwest, began his adult life with a high school education and a wife, and his professional career with the hammer and spikes of a heavy-construction worker. He took to writing as an "easier way," sold to pulp science-fiction magazines, *Thrilling Wonder*, etc., went on to the *Saturday Evening Post, Colliers*, the *American*, etc. When they went bust, he moved to L.A., joined the Writers Guild of America, and began writing for the motion-picture and television market—*Rawhide, Bonanza, High Chapparal, Little House on the Prairie, Voyage to the Bottom of the Sea*, etc.

He lives now in the L.A. area with Adeline, the only wife he has ever had, near his children and grandchildren, plays golf to a five handicap, and writes only what he enjoys most.

Introducing...

The Science Fiction Collection

Del Rey has gathered the forces of four of its greatest authors into a thrilling, mind-boggling series that no Science Fiction fan will want to do without!!